CHILDWALL MANSION

Edgar Waldgrave

CHILDWALL MANSION

The Witch Chronicles

Rise of the Dark Witch High King

Book Three

Hometown Publishers

Hometown Publishers
www.hometownpublishers.com

© Copyright 2021
Edgar Waldgrave

First Published by Hometown Publishers September, 2021.

ISBN: 978-1-7777725-0-5 (Paperback)
ISBN: 978-1-7777725-1-2 (E-book)

Library and Archives Canada (LAC) national library collection.

Cover Design by Edgar Waldgrave.

Dedication

To B, D,

J, & M

To my dad and mom,

C & M

Acknowledgements

Thank you for reading my fictional account

of The Witch Chronicles as they pertain to

the White, Gray, Black, and Dark Witches

of the Northeast Region of the United States.

Please note that the towns of

Amare, Seneca County, and Charlotte, Cayuga County,

even though described and geographically

portrayed as being in the State of New York,

are fictitious.

Thank you to all the people and establishments,

in the eleven Northeast States in the USA.

Enjoy...

Chapter One

September 7, 1980

2 p.m. News Conference

Amare Townhall, Seneca County

"Good afternoon and thank you for coming. For those of you that don't know me, my name is Sheriff Baker," he said picking up a piece of paper and reading from it. "I want to confirm that the body of twenty-nine-year-old Jason Campbell was found last night at his place of residence in Amare, Seneca County. Deputies arrived at his home at 10 p.m. to arrest him for the abduction and murder of Amanda Peterson, aged 11, and Heather Downs, aged 12. After entering his home, they found the deceased, and next to his body, a suicide note, in which he admitted to taking and killing Amanda Peterson and Heather Downs, two and six months earlier." The sheriff paused briefly then continued. "After a thorough search of his residence and the surrounding area, inside his camper, which was located next to his home, we found articles of clothing belonging to the two young girls. Clothing that they had been wearing on the day of their disappearance," he said looking up momentarily. "At this time, I can confirm that the investigation into finding Amanda and Heather's abductor and murderer is closed, and we will now concentrate our efforts on locating the missing girls' bodies," he declared before putting down his statement and looking up at the group of reporters. "I will be glad to answer any questions you may have." Then pointed to one with her hand raised.

"Is it true that the suspect had carved himself with a knife from pubic mound to chin, and from ear to ear?"

"Mr. Campbell died severing his carotid arteries with a knife. Next question?"

"Is it true that he practiced witchcraft and black magic?"

"No. Next question?" he asked swiftly signaling to another.

"A reliable source has revealed that Jason Campbell wrote in his wordy suicide note that he was, and I quote, a 'Servant of Satan' and that he was 'called to sacrifice innocence in His name.' Can you confirm this?"

"Mr. Campbell was a very sick man on medication, which, if not administered regularly left him confused and hallucinatory. Yes?" he asked motioning to another.

"Can you tell us what type of knife was found at the scene, and was it his?"

"It was a steel-bladed Bowie knife, and yes, it was his. Final question?"

"Many people in this town have stated that they were not only shocked to learn Mr. Campbell was being charged with these murders, but to his admission of guilt, that he actively practiced witchcraft and black magic, and had offered these young girls to Satan. They say, and I quote, 'Jason was a nice, respectable young man,' that, 'he was very well-liked in the community,' and, 'I think they have the wrong person; Jason wouldn't do such a thing.' Can you comment on these?"

"For the record, we have no evidence of him practicing the occult or sacrificing these young girls to Satan," confirmed Sheriff Baker. "In regard to the charges against him, here in Seneca County, our Sheriff's Department sticks with the facts, not local gossip. And the facts are as follows: first, the accused, Jason Campbell, committed suicide; second, in his hand was the knife that he used to take his own life; third, a suicide note was written by the accused confessing to the abduction and murders of Amanda Peterson and Heather Downs; and lastly, we recovered several articles of the girls' clothing from his residence…Thank you."

Chapter Two

Present Day - Friday, July 10

"It's a beautiful home."

"It is," replied Liam turning around to face the young woman approaching.

"Mr. Wilson?"

"Yes," he answered reaching out to shake her outstretched hand. "And please, call me Liam."

"I'm Vanessa, Vanessa Moore. It's a pleasure to meet you," she said with a friendly smile. "I hope I haven't kept you waiting too long, I was delayed showing a home to a young family."

"No, not at all, I just arrived moments ago and only made it as far as the front lawn."

"Mr. Childwall's lawyer, Mr. MacDonald, contacted me a few weeks ago asking me to show you around, and to be honest with you, I was just shown around the house myself yesterday, but I'm sure you won't be disappointed. It's quite spectacular."

"So, this is a rental listing?"

"No, I've been paid a fee to show you around," she answered with a perplexed look.

"The reason I ask, is that I was told I would be staying at a hotel but that a house had been rented for me instead."

"Oh, I see the confusion," she said nodding her head. "Originally the Amare Historical Society was going to put you up at the hotel but when Mr. Childwall heard about you coming, he insisted that you stay here instead. They offered to pay him rent, but he refused, and stated that you would be his guest" she explained. "And as an extended courtesy to him, I was asked and paid to show you around."

"Oh, okay," replied Liam satisfied with the clarification and looking up at the mansion.

"It's a classic Greek Revival structure, early 19th century, and was designed to replicate a temple," revealed Venessa. "It's been repaired and repainted over the years but hasn't lost its elegance."

"No, it hasn't" agreed Liam. "It's extraordinary."

"I would say even more so, with the newer, modern houses lining the street," she added.

"I believe you're right," he confirmed looking up and down the street. "It's as if time stood still while everything around it grew."

"And moved on."

Liam smiled to himself at her words, she was spot-on.

"I think Mr. Childwall is somewhat excited to meet you, as are the members of the Historical Society," she suggested searchingly, before deciding just to ask. "You're him?"

Liam glanced over at her thoughtfully for a moment.

"I'm so sorry," she said quickly realizing she was being very inappropriate. "Would you like to see inside?"

"I would," he said following her.

"As you can see, the home has a large front porch and a terrace above. Its design is rectangular in shape, and has a main floor, second floor, attic, as well as a basement. The electricity and heating have been updated throughout the years and are up to modern-day standards. Most of the wood fireplaces have been replaced with electrical ones, and all the appliances are brand new," she said unlocking the door.

Liam looked around the majestic foyer, then admired the magnificent staircase as it curved up to the second floor.

"Incredible, isn't it?"

"That it is," he said amazed.

"Most of the originally wood flooring is throughout the house, with the exception of the kitchen and bathrooms, which have been updated with ceramics and modern amenities," she explained. "Please, this way to the parlor...As you can see it has contemporary furnishings consisting of a large coffee table nestled between to sofas and armchairs, to entertain guests with drinks and sandwiches. A gas fireplace, and these charming drapes have been pulled back to reveal a picturesque view of the street…please, follow me" They left the room and went through the foyer to the adjacent room. "They call this the Main Room, today, we would refer to it as the family room…It's much longer that the parlor, has similar furnishings, as well as a gas fireplace. The difference, is that it has a large sixty-inch flat screen TV, with surround sound, and an entertainment center that has a satellite receiver, DVD player, and PlayStation." She watched him as he walked over to the window and looked out. "Do you play?"

"Not very well," he replied walking over to her. "My niece and nephew like me to play Star Wars and Call of Duty games with them and take great pleasure in sneaking up on me and taking me out. In fact, sometimes they sign up for the other teams, just to hunt me down, and find it very amusing."

Vanessa smiled at him; she could see him being a fun uncle.

"Do you have children?"

"Two, a boy in elementary school, and a girl starting middle school." She didn't need to ask him if he had any.

"And do you live in Amare?"

"I have, all my life," she replied. "It's a great place to grow up in and raise a family."

"Is that the reason why you became a real estate agent?"

"One of them," she admitted. "I sell properties throughout Seneca County, but mostly in towns along Seneca Lake, like Amare." She wondered why he was asking.

"You said Mr. Childwall hired you to show me around?"

"I did. He came across one of my advertisements and asked his lawyer to contact me."

Liam strolled up to her, stopped, and thought momentarily before giving her a smile. "Shall we continue."

"This is the Great Dining Room," she said opening the doors and walking in.

"No furniture," noticed Liam.

"Mr. MacDonald mentioned that you probably wouldn't be having dinner parties, and to let me know if that wasn't the case."

"He's right, I won't."

"Those two doors over there open to the parlor, and these open to the library," she explained, following her through. "This is the only room that had a wood burning fireplace. I'm guessing back in the day the men would retire here after dinner to smoke cigars, drink brandy, and talk business."

"I can see that," agreed Liam walking around the room and surveying the books on the shelf.

"Mr. MacDonald said to feel free to help yourself to any of the books, the brandy in the liquor cabinet, and the cigars on the table."

"It's very charming," he said pleasantly.

"It's my third favorite room."

"Third?" he asked curiously.

"Please, this way," she instructed, then took him out into the hallway towards the back of the house where she opened a door to her left and they went inside. "This is the den. It has a large desk, soft leather chairs, a side window, and a majestic mantle over the fireplace," she said favorably. "Isn't it wonderfully warm and cozy?"

"Yes," he sighed, "it's enchanting."

"Enchanting," repeated Vanessa. "I never really thought it about it that way, but now that you mention it, it does have a captivating element about it."

"Captivating," whispered Liam to himself.

It is him! she thought. "These French doors open up to let the morning sunlight in and give you access onto the desk."

They walked through them, down the steps to the garden, and stopped at the gazebo.

"The sun shines on the backyard early in the morning. To enjoy it, your best bet are the chairs on the deck, but if you prefer shade, then I would recommend, here, on the swing in the gazebo. At noon, as the sun slowly continues heading west, you can enjoy its afternoon rays back there on the picturesque stone patio, and if it gets too warm, you can seek the comfort of an umbrella until it moves on to the front of the house."

"Okay," he replied then headed toward the back of the garden.

Vanessa trailed behind, till he stopped at the patio, then followed his eyes as they looked up at the tall hedges that surrounded the perimeter of the backyard.

"I guess he liked his privacy," she suggested.

"I guess so," he conceded before looking down at the old patio stones."

"That reminds me, Mr. MacDonald asked that you be very careful on these old stones, and also asked that you don't do any gardening."

Liam looked over at her.

"Apparently, he has a gardener that's very particular about the grounds."

"It's okay, I don't garden."

She wanted to laugh but gave him a quick smile instead. "The garage is locked and off limits," she revealed. "But you can pull your car up the driveway as far as you like to the garage."

Liam nodded his head, then followed her down the garden path onto the deck and went inside the doors close to the kitchen.

"This is the breakfast solarium, with your basic kitchen table and six chairs, California blinds," she said walking on, "and over here, a large kitchen with a magnificent island…You will find all the utensils in these drawers, and the pots and pans in the cupboards below."

"You said the den is your third favorite, I'm assuming the kitchen is your second favorite?"

"You're right about the den, and the kitchen, but I was thinking more about your choices. Am I right to say this kitchen would not be in your top three?"

Liam laughed. "That would be a safe assumption."

"Call it an agent's intuition," she said laughing with him. "Looking at you, I'm thinking library will be number three, but the den and one more room, will be one and two, although I'm not sure in which order yet."

"Let's find out," he said, following her.

"Before we go upstairs, let me quickly show you the basement," she said leading him down the stairs. "There are three rooms down here, and a winterized back door that opens out to several steps that lead up to the left side of the garden, close to the driveway. The first room is the laundry room," she said as they quickly looked in before closing the door. "The next room is locked and can only be entered by entering a code on the keypad."

"It must be a big room," suggested Liam, "it takes up half of the basement."

"You're right it does, and the windows are blacked out and have iron bars on them, so I'm thinking artifacts, family heirlooms, that sort of thing."

"Hmm, must be quite the collection," he said following her to the last door.

"Now, this door is locked, and you don't have a key for it, but it's the wine cellar," she said glancing over at him. "Mr. MacDonald opened it and showed me inside. There are a lot of old dusty bottles of wine in there."

"Too bad, I would have liked to have seen that."

"I wouldn't have minded sampling a bottle or two!" she said with a nervous laugh.

"Me too," he replied with a kind smile.

"Seems such a waste to lock something up and let it age, rather than be enjoyed in the moment."

"You have a way with words," he said, complimenting her.

"English and history major," she revealed. "I only do this during the summer and on weekends during the school year, I'm actually a teacher at the Geneva Middle School. Some people paint or bake as a hobby, I sell and rent real estate."

"That's interesting, can I ask why you do both?"

"Teaching kids is my first love, and I would never give that up. But I'm out going, I know a lot about the area, and I like meeting new families...and interesting individuals," she explained. "Plus, you can make a lot of money selling real estate. Especially with the prices of the houses and estates around here, and along the lakefront. So," she said with a smile, "if you find yourself not being able to leave here, and are interested in finding a place, please let me know."

"You will be the only person I call," he promised.

"Well, thank you, and enough about me and my sales pitch, let me show you the upstairs."

Liam followed her out of the basement towards the front door, where she stopped and showed him the powder room, before turning and walking up the staircase to the top.

"There are eight bedrooms, four bathrooms, and a walk-in linen closet. So along here, the north side of the house, are three bedrooms, a full bathroom, and a walk-in closet that has towels, lines, blankets, and extra pillows," she explained before showing him them. "Over there, on the south side, we have the same setup: three bedrooms and a full bathroom. The only difference is that the door that leads into the closet on this side, on that side, it opens up to the stairs to the attic," she said pointing to it as they headed towards the master bedroom. "None of these six bedrooms are furnished because it was felt that you wouldn't be needing them. This room, the West Room, on the other hand has been fully furnished, and I must say, very tastefully."

They walked in, and Liam looked around at the magnificent four poster bed, sofa, armchairs, lounge chair, and coffee table. The elegant mantle had a fireplace below it, and a fifty-inch TV above.

"This room is the entire width of the house. Down here at the south end, is a full bathroom with a separate tub and shower, and through these doors is a walk-in closet. These doors over here, lead out to south hallway" she explained. "There are several windows across the length of room, and they are only interrupted in the middle by two French patio doors that lead out to this," she said opening them out, and walking him outside to a large terrace containing tables, cushioned chairs, and loungers. "It's the same size as the porch below, except this has a spectacular view of Seneca Lake."

"Breathtaking," sighed Liam as he walked over to the spindle railings, leaned on the column, and looked out at the rows of houses and roads leading down towards the lake. "This is your number one?"

"It is," she replied. "For you, the den or this?"

He glanced over at her. "Would I be bailing out if I go with a tie for all three?"

"Probably," she said lightheartedly, "but I guess I can let you get away with it if you tell me the reason why."

"To me, each room has its own purpose and set of emotions."

"I can't argue with you there," said Vanessa standing next to him and looking out at the lake. "For me, it's this view."

"It is spectacular."

"Along the lakefront," she said pointing, "there is a boardwalk with restaurants, bars, boat rentals, fishing tours, sunset tours, arcades, and a fishing pier. As well as several family-oriented hotels and quaint B&B's. And from this vantage point, I'm sure you will witness incredible sunsets."

"I believe so," he concurred.

"Let me show you the rest of the house, so I can go, and let you get settled in."

He followed her out the south doors to the end of the hall and into the East Room.

"This room is the exact same set up as the West Room, except it is smaller in length, because the staircase going up to the attic takes up the space. It has two queen beds, and the view is of the garden," she described as they went outside. "The terrace is the same size and has a pretty view of the garden and gazebo. The large hedges and surrounding trees limit its view of the surrounding area, giving it more privacy."

They left the room, went through the doorway, and climbed the stairs to the attic.

"There's nothing in here," Vanessa stated as they reached the top and entered. "The room is the width and length of the house, so it's excessively big. The floor is carpeted, and it has several large windows, with the most scenic being the large rectangular one at the front of the house overlooking the terrace." She watched him walk over to it, briefly look out, then around the room before making eye contact with her suggesting he was done. Then led him down the stairs to the front door and outside onto the porch. "I almost forgot. Two of the women from the Historical Society, Mrs. Stewart, and Mrs. Jones, will be coming by at one to welcome you. I believe they have been in contact with you regarding your stay in Amare?"

"Yes, a few times over the phone."

"I believe that's it. Let me give you my business card in case you have any questions or concerns," she said walking over to her SUV, opening the door, and grabbing one. "It has my cell and Gmail."

"Thank you, and thanks for the tour," he said taking it from her, "I would have been lost trying to find everything on my own."

"Oh, my pleasure," she replied with a smile. "Do you have any questions before I go?"

He studied her briefly. "You asked me earlier, if I was him?"

"I'm so sorry, that was so unprofessional of me, but I'd heard—"

"Please, don't apologize. I was just wondering who you thought I was?"

Vanessa gathered her thoughts before she spoke. "I heard you are a consultant, and that you help historical societies by reviewing their exhibits and giving them advice prior to public viewing. Your main area of expertise is in the research, locating, and interpretation of local history and artifacts. Although, you have also helped historical societies locate objects, remains, and places, that are spiritual or supernatural in nature, which has raised questions about how you were able to locate them, and your…gift," she said tentatively, and decided it was best not to say anymore.

Liam could sense her hesitation, and realized she was worried about him saying something to someone that would potentially get her, or her source, into trouble, and decided to put her at ease. "You want to know if I'm the person who sees ghosts, finds their hangouts, and unearths the tools of their trades?" he asked mischievously.

Vanessa was silent but her eyes gave her away.

"You're him," repeated Liam chuckling. "You asked it as a question, but you already knew who I was and wanted to see my reaction, very clever. How did you even know I was coming?"

"It's a small town and people talk," she lied unpersuasively.

He gave her an unconvinced look. Liam had already been informed only a handful of key people knew of his arrival and that it wasn't public knowledge.

"Okay, okay, a few weeks ago one of my best friends told me you were coming this summer, but not when," she divulged. "I promised her I wouldn't tell anyone, not even my husband, but when I saw you…at this house…and you're meeting later on. I put it all together and realized who you were."

"You're a regular detective," he said teasing her.

"You're not far off, my dad's the sheriff, and I guess he rubbed off on me a little. But my best friend, she's brilliant at accurately deducing a situation."

"Your best friend?"

"Well, I know you've heard of her, it's Rebecca Anderson."

Chapter Three

"Good afternoon, Mrs. Stewart, Mrs. Jones. Please, come in," offered Liam opening the door and watching the seniors come in.

"Oh please, call us Edith and Agnes."

"Nice to meet you, Edith, Agnes, and please, call me Liam."

"Liam, this is for you, it's fresh fruit and vegetables," said Edith lifting up the bags of groceries. "I'll take them into the kitchen."

"And I have some homemade sandwiches and pastries," said Agnes holding a picnic basket.

They walked into the kitchen and Liam watched as Edith placed the vegetables in the fridge and the fruit in a bowl then placed the empty bags into the garbage. While Agnes put on the kettle, pulled out a tray from the cupboard, and placed the sandwiches and pastries on plates.

"Tea will take a few minutes," said Agnes looking over at Edith, then Liam. "Oh, we came in yesterday and dropped off your groceries. In your freezer there are several meals prepared by members of the Historical Society as well as steaks and chicken," she explained opening the door and pointing them out. "Each are labelled with their contents, and before you run out, please let us know. Down here you have luncheon meat, eggs, bacon, sausages, deserts, milk, juices, beers, and so on."

"The cupboards are fully stocked, too," added Edith. "If you need anything else, please contact us, our numbers are on the fridge."

"Thank you, ladies, and please extend my thanks to all of the members that contributes, that's extremely nice of you all."

"It's just Amare's way of welcoming new families, couples, and guests to our community."

"I think it's a lovely tradition," complimented Liam.

Once the teapot was filled and placed on the tray, Liam picked it up and walked with the ladies into the parlor. He placed it on the coffee table, waited for them to pour it and offer him a sandwich, before speaking.

"So, you ladies are members of the Historical Society?"

"We are," replied Agnes.

"We're both part-time and our roles are more administrative in nature," acknowledged Edith. "All the members, with the exception of Rebecca and her assistant director, Brittany, are volunteers."

"So, how many members in total?"

"Fifteen. Five of those, including myself and Edith have designated roles and responsibilities, and the other eight are on an 'as needed' basis. Rebecca and Brittany round out the fifteen and are salaried," she explained. "We also offer subscriptions at a very nominal rate, and most of the town's people are subscribers. This not only helps with some of our costs but supports preserving our history, strengthening our community, and enticing tourists to our town."

"Well, I think that's wonderful, and I hope other historical societies, along with their communities, consider your avant-garde model and adapt it into their framework," said Liam impressed. "And the fact that Rebecca has all of your help and support, I'm somewhat envious of her."

"You have no one?" asked Agnes somewhat surprised.

"No one, just me."

"Not even an assistant?" queried Edith.

"Not even an assistant, but to be fair it's more my personal choice rather than an unviable option," confirmed Liam. "You see, I'm always on the road travelling to different cities, town, and villages, and I can be away from home for months on end, living out of a suitcase. Then there's the late nights of research, early morning excavations, hotel rooms, motel beds, and eating lots of take-out. So, it can be very demanding. And it would be unfair of me to ask, or expect someone, to partake in that lifestyle. They would need to be extremely strong-willed and devoted."

"Sounds like our Rebecca," suggested Agnes glancing over at Edith, who was nodding in agreement, before returning to Liam. "Where do you call home?"

"I have a place in Boston but was born and raised in Worcester."

"Both beautiful places," admitted Agnes.

"With wonderful people," added Edith.

"Yes, they are," agreed Liam. "I just spent the Fourth of July weekend with family and friends at both places. It was busy going back and forth, but enjoyable, and much needed."

"Did you come here straight after seeing your family?" asked Edith.

"I took a few days to myself in Boston," he replied sipping his tea, "but this already feels like a home away from home, thanks to you, and I want you both to know how much I appreciate everything you have done for me."

"It's our pleasure," said Agnes cheerfully.

"From what we understand, your role here is that of a consultant?" probed Edith.

"With the brief conversations I've had with Rebecca, I believe it is, and I'm looking forward to helping her out in any way I can."

"Your reputation of helping communities set up their exhibits, not only in museums but in historical homes proceeds you, and she's very excited to have your input."

"We all are," added Agnes. "At our last meeting, Rebecca went over several of your major accomplishments, and we feel very honored to have you here."

"Thank you, that's very kind of you, and I will do my part to help Rebecca and the Amare Historic Society put together a top, national-ranked exhibit."

"I'm sure you will," said Agnes placing her cup on the tray. "Rebecca had requested that we keep a lid on your coming to Amare, which we have, but eventually the locals will hear whispers sooner rather than latter—"

"It's a very small town," interrupted Edith.

"And the cat will eventually have to be let out of the bag," continued Agnes quickly glancing over at Edith who was eying her to ask. "What we were thinking, was rather than waiting for the gossip to circulate and mount, we could have a local reporter do a small piece on you and nip it in the bud. Perhaps, tomorrow," she suggested. "The interview would make the Sunday edition, be on their website, and be posted on social media."

"I think that's a great idea," said Liam. "This is your community, and it's important they are aware of what's going on, and why I am here. Plus, any input they may have, is just as valuable to the success of the project as is mine."

"That's wonderful," said Agnes delightedly, then glanced over at Edith's. "Sounds like we will need to talk to the paper soon."

"The interview would have to be tomorrow morning so that the piece would make the Saturday cutoff," suggested Edith looking at Agnes then over Liam.

"That's fine with me, but I believe Rebecca should lead the interview, choose the location, and prescreen the questions," advised Liam.

"Of course, we will speak to her after we leave, and she can get back to you with the details."

"That's perfect."

"Rebecca was planning on dropping by this afternoon to introduce herself and meet you," said Edith with a concerned look. "She hasn't contacted you yet?"

"No, but my phone has been charging," he replied. "Give me a second and let me go check it." Moments later he came back. "Yes, she had texted and asked if five was okay, and I have just replied it was."

"Oh, good," said Edith.

"Edith, we should get going and drop by and see Rebecca, then my Arthur."

"Arthur?" asked Liam.

The two ladies looked at one another and giggled.

"Arthur is the owner and editor of the Amare Banner newspaper," revealed Agnes, "and also my husband."

"And you never let on about me coming?"

"No," confessed Agnes, "but I'm sure me handing him this interview will appease him somewhat."

Liam grinned and nodded his head. "Well, I'm glad to help out."

They both stood and Edith who was reaching to pick up the tray.

"Don't worry, I'll take care of that," he said taking it to the kitchen and coming back with her picnic basket. "Here you go."

"Thank you, you're a lovely young man," expressed Edith.

"Indeed, you are," Agnes concurred.

"It was a pleasure meeting you both, and thanks again for the groceries and the warm welcome."

"You're most welcome," replied Agnes.

"Have a wonderful afternoon," said Edith.

"You too," he replied opening the door, watching them walk down the path and out of view before closing it.

Chapter Four

"Rebecca, please come in," offered Liam.

"Hello, Liam, nice to finally meet you," she said shaking his hand.

"You too."

"How do you like the place?" she asked looking around.

"It's beautiful," he replied as he watched her walk over and glance into the parlor. "Would you like a quick tour?"

"I was in here a couple of times about a month ago," she admitted, "but I wouldn't mind a third."

Okay," he replied curiously and swiftly walked with her through the house, ending at the front terrace.

"You would never get tired of this view," she said looking out at the lake, "it's breathtaking."

"It is," he agreed as he briefly studied the attractive brunette.

She picked up on it. "You're wondering why I wanted to look around?"

"It crossed my mind," he confessed.

"When I had my last tour, the house contained all the antique furnishings, even the spare bedrooms," she stated looking at him. "Mr. Childwall said he was going to change some of the furniture before your arrival, and do cosmetic upgrades to the bathrooms and kitchen, which he did. I was just surprised how much, but it looks nice, modern."

Liam thought momentarily. "He did all this, just for me?"

"Yeah," she said nodding her head, "and all within a month."

"You seem upset, are you?"

"Oh sorry, no, not at all. I was just thinking about something," she said with a pretty smile, and decided not to worry about where the antique furniture had gone at this time. "The upgrades aren't an issue, we are probably going to remove the bathrooms in the bedroom anyway to create more exhibition space…but wait, I'm getting ahead of myself. Is there anything else you needed?"

"No, not at all."

"Edith and Agnes were here earlier dropping off groceries and told you about the prepared meals?"

"Yes, they were, and made me feel very welcome."

"And Vanessa spoke to you about the house, gave you the keys, and the WIFI password?" she asked nervously.

"She did," he replied noting her uneasiness and changing the subject. "How was lunch with your best friend? And your conversation with her about the Ghost Whisperer arriving in town?"

Rebecca's face went red. "Please, tell me she didn't call you that?" she asked horrified.

Liam laughed. "No, she didn't, but she did politely point out that I have also helped historical societies locate objects, remains, and places, which are spiritual or supernatural in nature, which has raised questions about how I was able to locate them, and my…gift."

"She said that and used the word gift?" asked Rebecca wanting to jump over the railing and run.

"Yes, she did," he reconfirmed then joked, "better than calling me a Ghost Whisperer."

Rebecca giggled and shook her head. "What am I going to do with her?"

Liam laughed along. "Vanessa figured out who I was, and I must admit, she did choose her words carefully."

"She did tell me that, but not what she said."

"I wonder if your face could get any redder?"

Rebecca looked at him wide eyed, and pondered what it was he was about to say next.

"I asked Vanessa how she even knew I was coming? She tried, unconvincingly, to tell me it was a small town and people talk. But from my expression she could tell I wasn't buying it. So, she threw you under the bus, and told me her best friend had said I was coming this summer—"

"And that I also told her who you were," she said despairingly.

Liam chuckled.

Rebecca looked on wondering what was so funny and waited politely for him to tell her.

"Vanessa never said who told her, and I didn't know."

Rebecca turned towards the lake, closed her eyes in disbelief, and whispered, "Vanessa throwing me under the bus is one thing, me throwing myself, is another."

"Don't beat yourself up," he said reassuringly. "I'd figured it had to be you, and to be honest, you've done a great job bringing me in under the radar."

"Thank you for that," she replied, realizing that she had, and feeling better. "Do you know Vanessa is convinced you must have a special power? In fact, I think she called it a superpower. I guess I should be grateful she used gift instead," revealed Rebecca, making them laugh.

"I don't think I would call it a superpower or a gift," suggested Liam.

"One day you will have to tell me what it is," she suggested, not wanting to push him and make him feel uncomfortable.

"Maybe one day I will, but you may be disappointed," he replied aware of the embellished stories surrounding him. "From our previous conversations, what you are asking me to do here is rather straightforward. Which begs the questions, why the secrecy in me coming?"

Rebecca slowly smiled at him, hoping it would buy her some time to come up with at least an answer that would satisfy him for now. "Well, I wanted to meet with you in person, go over the details, and then make a formal statement."

"The interview for the paper?"

"Yes, the interview," she said thankfully, having forgotten about that. "I had promised Agnes that if she kept a lid on you coming, Arthur would have the exclusive for his newspaper and could post it on social media."

"And Edith, what did you promise her?"

"Hmm?" she asked confused, before realizing what he was asking. "Oh, for keeping the lid on?" she said stalling for time.

Liam nodded.

"That we would conduct the interview in her goddaughter and husband's new restaurant," she lied, but convinced herself it was only a white lie and would have to call Edith and Agnes and tell them it had been moved from the mansion.

"Not here or at the museum?" he asked feeling something was up.

"I told her we would mention their restaurant in the piece, and it would be a good photo op for them," she said on the fly. "What can I say, we are a tight community, and we look out for one another."

"I can see that," agreed Liam, "and it's wonderful that you do."

Rebecca swiftly changed the subject. "Well, I promised you dinner, and I thought we could walk there, and on the way, I could give you some background on the town, the Childwall's, and this house."

"I would like that."

"Are you ready to go or…?"

"No, I'm good to go," he confirmed and followed her off the terrace, through the bedroom, and down the stairs. "I told Vanessa that she was quite the detective for figuring me out."

"She is, and gets that from her father," replied Rebecca glancing back over her shoulder.

"So, she said. She also mentioned that her best friend was brilliant at accurately deducing a situation."

"Maybe I have a superpower, too," she suggested, giving him a playful look before facing forward and smiling to herself.

Chapter Five

Outside, they walked to the sidewalk and headed east. "William was the son of a predominate architect and builder in Boston, and Victoria, was the highly educated middle-class daughter of a banker. They met through mutual friends of the family and married in 1815. Around 1818, they surveyed this land and purchased a rectangular plot that stretched three miles east from the lake, and four miles north and south. Upon seeing the land and lake for the first time, Victoria immediately fell in love with it and called it 'Amare,' which is Latin for 'love.' A couple of years later, the land was cleared down by the lake, and a temporary log cabin was built for them to live in during the summer months. Several years later, in 1823, with the land cleared and the mansion completed, they moved into their summer retreat."

"Did they clear all their land?"

"No, they cleared…" she said stopping, turning towards the mansion, and pointing, "about the length of twelve houses on either side, and from the lake past their home and another quarter of a mile east…The main road came into the back of their property on the left, which is where they had parking. The rest of the land at the back and in the front to the lake was landscaped. The surrounding land was left untouched and was mostly forests."

"Why did they have the front of their house facing the lake?" asked Liam wondering why not the back.

"In the morning, the couple wanted to feel the peaceful morning sun in their backyard while they were having breakfast and their cup of tea. In the afternoon, they wanted to sit on their front porch or terrace and enjoy the lake view and evening sunsets."

"Feel the peaceful morning sun?" questioned Liam giving her an odd look."

"Victoria's words, not mine," she said with a smile. "I found her diaries very descriptive and her quite romantic."

"You admire her?"

"I do," replied Rebecca without hesitation. "She was strong, independent, kind, and passionate."

"And William?"

"He was the perfect husband, and did whatever she told him to do," she said matter-of-fact and began walking. "During this time—"

"Hold on a second," said Liam catching up.

She tried her best to keep a straight face but broke out into a laugher. "I couldn't help myself," she blurted out, "and the look on your face was priceless."

"Ha, ha," he said sarcastically and grinned at her playfulness. "Are you always this much fun?"

"I have my moments," she replied, liking his smile. "Where was I? Oh yeah, during this time, they also started to build several guest houses on either side of the property, and they were completed over the next few years. A say guest houses, but they were far from it and very impressive, two of them they still stand today."

"And the log cabin?"

"They gave that to the workers to live in, but overtime with wear and tear, it was eventually torn down and replaced as the last guest house."

They crossed over on to Park Street and headed west towards the lake.

"Over there is our Town Park. It has a splash pad and playground for the children, outdoor concerts every Wednesday night in the summer, and a skating rink in the winter. We also hold all our festivals and holiday celebrations there."

"A hub of activity," said Liam.

"Without a doubt," she replied. "Now, getting back to William and Victoria, they spent their summers here with family and friends, but lived in Boston, where William had his business. His company was rapidly growing, and offices were sprouting up in Albany, Syracuse, Rochester, Buffalo, and Pittsburg, and with Amare being central to all of them, Boston was requiring less of his attention. They decided that over the next few years they would move here permanently, and it was at this same time that

Victoria came up with the idea of making Amare a town. So, they drew up the plans, which had four simple key points: first, a street for businesses to set up shop, a Main Street, and it would be located behind their home and run north and south; second, that their property be cut up into affordable plots and sold to families and businesses alike; Third, to attract hardworking tradespeople, farmers, and professionals; and finally, to have a community consisting of roads, schools, libraries, churches, a townhall, town park, movie theatre, and so on. All this, they believed, would help put the town of Amare on the map…and voilà," she said outstretching her arms and motioning to the town proudly. "They were right, and here it is."

"It's very impressive," said Liam. "The town's structure we see today - it's streets leading down to the lake, the houses facing east and west, Main Street, the community building's, the farmlands on the exterior, the lake front – these were all part of that initial vision."

"Yes, and it's referred to locally as 'Victoria's Vision.' The townspeople even use the term fondly to describe someone with imagination, insight, or wisdom."

"Victoria's Vision," whispered Liam. "I like it."

"I thought you would," said Rebecca favorably. "Shall we continue?"

On the way, she pointed out one of the original guest houses, the area where the forest had been cut down to expand for the growing town, and the background on the lakefront's planning and construction up to its current completed state. "So, the boardwalk is not only a draw for people to live in Amare, but to visit, and invest in," she said as they walked along it.

"It really is a well thought out beautiful design."

"It is, and we have had a lot of interest from other towns around the Finger Lakes who have reviewed what we have done here, and looking to use it as a foundation for the construction or refurbishment of their lakefront, one that comes to mind is Charlotte," she said as they continued along the boardwalk, before entering The Westview and being seated on the patio.

"I noticed the mansion is on Victoria Street and the road along the lakefront is William Street," stated Liam.

"Thanks for pointing that out, I meant to mention that earlier, but got distracted talking about the beach. Apparently, the Childwall's didn't want any buildings named after them, but during planning it was discussed that, at the very least, they should have a street named after them. They accepted only because it was going to be their first names, which they both agreed were quite common, and would help give the town an authentic charm. One more thing, Victoria loved Latin, Greek, and British literature, although she may have been resolute in not using their names, she definitely had no problems using one of these three languages in naming or engraving quotes on noteworthy structures around the town."

"Which would explain her choice of the Greek Revival architecture for her home?"

"Precisely. Which is a nice segue into the home's history," she said, and waited for the server to place the drinks on the table and take their order before continuing. "When the house was completed, the next thing Vitoria did was decorate it from top to bottom. When she had finished, she said that 'Amore was her love and her home was 'cor eius' or 'her heart,' which is what she fondly referred to it, from that point on."

"I didn't see that on a plaque by the front door or on any of the columns?" queried Liam.

"No, she never put one up. As far as she was concerned, it was her name for it. Over time, the townspeople referred to it as the Childwall Mansion, and still do to this day."

"That's interesting," said Liam now understanding why the Childwall name had never been put on the house.

"As I mentioned earlier, during the planning stage, the Childwall's agreed to sell plots of land. With many of the initial ones going on either side of Victoria Street, Main Street, and Market Street, which was the next street east and parallel to Main," she explained. "This also meant that the Childwall's backyard would end on Main Street, which had been purposely planned by them, because Victoria was going to build and run the first town's store on the back of their property and have its entrance on Main Street."

"What kind of store?"

"A general store," replied Rebecca, and she called it just that, "General Store."

"For her love of the three languages, she kept that quite simple," suggested Liam with a chuckle.

"Yes, she did," agreed Rebecca laughing with him.

"So, people started moving in?"

"They did. Houses were constructed on Victoria and Market Streets, stores and establishments were built on Main Street, farms were erected on the outskirts, then public buildings, municipal buildings along Main, and so on," she described. "I will show you Main Street tomorrow and let you see for yourself."

"I would like that," he said approvingly. "I do have a question about the Childwall home."

"Sure, what is it?"

"I noticed where the backyard ends that there are hedges with a wooden fence behind it separating it from the store's property?"

"There is," she confirmed. "When Victoria had the store, that area was one long manicured backyard, that way she could walk back and forth freely. Over the years, the store has changed into a soda shop, a fifties diner, and an American restaurant. Today it's a trendy upscale Italian ristorante. But back when they were renovating it to a soda shop, they decided that they wanted to put picnic tables out back for customers to eat their food and enjoy the sun. So for privacy, a fence was erected, and hedges placed on either side. There used to be a wooden gate off to the side to allow the family access to both properties, but that's long gone now."

"The Childwall's owned all the businesses?"

"Throughout the years the next generation would take over the shop and adapt it to what they thought the current town needs would be, and all of them were met with remarkable success. James Childwall, the current owner of the home today, eventually renovated it into a restaurant. For him it was just an investment, he never worked there, instead, he had the cook and his wife run it. Several years later, in the late-eighties, he sold them the business and property at a great price. About a year ago the couple retired, their daughter and her husband took ownership of the property and made drastic refurbishments to the restaurant that seem to be paying off for them," she concluded, then took a sip of her drink before glancing up at him. "That's the Childwall mansion and their Main Street ventures in a nutshell."

The meals came, and as they ate, she talked to him about the newspaper interview, the questions Arthur would be asking them, and their responses.

"So, you want me to start on Monday?"

"I do," she replied, "and I'll have more information in regard to the logistics then, if that's okay?"

"That's fine, you figure out what best, and let me know" he said finishing his meal and taking a sip of his drink. "This is a fantastic view of the sun setting,"

"The Westview has one of the best patios to watch it: no obstructions and a perfect view of the west," she said, picking up her wine, leaning back in her seat, and thinking. "How about we pick up the town's history tomorrow, relax, and enjoy the rest of the night?"

"Ah, I'm glad you said that I was just thinking the same thing."

"Oh, no! I forgot you've had a long day today. I should have stopped earlier."

"No, I'm glad we did what we did, it's been very informative, and it'll help me get through the interview tomorrow," he said with a smile.

"All right, then there's no need for me to feel bad about it, but I do feel I do need to make it up to you," said Rebecca leaning towards him. "After we watch this amazing sunset, there's a cozy pub we can go to and unwind, I really think you will appreciate its ambiance." Then gave him an impish grin before leaning back and enjoying the sun's fading rays on her face.

Chapter Six

"Shakespeare's," read Liam glanced curiously over at Rebecca.

"What till you see the inside," she said as he followed her through the front door, down the stairs into a quaint room, and sat opposite her in a cozy booth. "Beer?"

"Yeah."

"Two pints of your best ale, wench," said Rebecca looking up at the server wearing a period costume dress.

"Ay, my lady," she replied pleasantly then left.

"What do you think?" she asked looking over at Liam's stunned face and chuckling. "Relax, and look around, this room is called Shakespeare's Cellar, or simply The Cellar. It's designed like a late 16th century tavern, and you are encouraged to talk to them in Early Modern English. And look at the walls," she said pointing at them, "they have famous Shakespearian lines, sonnets, and soliloquies written directly on them and in frames. They also have pictures over there of the great man himself, Stratford-upon-Avon, and London," she said motioning around the room before making eye contact and giving him a cute smile.

"I just wasn't expecting it and you took me by surprise," he said laughing then realizing something. "You set me up?"

"Who me?" she replied giving him an innocent look.

"So that's how this is going to play out, Gertrude?"

"I'll take that name as a compliment, Hamlet!"

Liam gave her a smile. "I must admit. This place is awesome."

"Do you know, if you can recite one of Shakespeare's sonnets or soliloquies to the customers, you get a free ale. And, if you do one without an error, and with conviction, you get your ale plus your picture put on the wall along with all the other honorary Lord Chamberlain's Men…Tis quite the honor," she suggested playfully.

"Have you ever done it?"

"Me, no, but you should try."

"Maybe after a couple of ales."

"Speaking of which…it's about time, wench!" she snapped looking up at her.

"Really," retorted the server unamused. "Do you want me to poor these over your pretty head, Flower-seller?"

Liam broke into a laughter making the girls look at him then each other.

"Hey, Becky, how are you doing?" asked the server putting down the pints. "And who's your educated date?"

Rebecca stood and hugged her. "Crystal, this is Liam, a fellow curator. Liam, Crystal, one of my best friends, and a brilliant English teacher at Geneva High, and also head of the Drama Department."

"Pleased to meet you," said Liam.

"You too," replied Crystal. "I see you liked my jab at my dear friend."

"Immensely. I loved the wit, the timing," he said charmingly.

"Thank you, kind sir, for thy compliment," she said liking him. "I was wondering how long Becky was going to keep it going, but apparently her banter pales in comparison to mine, poor sweet Flower-seller."

"Am I missing something here?" asked Rebecca. "How's calling me pretty and referring to me as a flower, a jab and witty?"

This made Crystal laugh, and realized it was time she swiftly exited stage left. "I'll see you later, Flower-seller, nice meeting you, Liam."

Rebecca watched her leave then looked over at Liam, her eyes desperately asking him what she had missed.

"Flower-seller?" he asked her.

"Like I said, it means pretty like a flower and I'm selling it, you know, the whole package…a compliment."

"You're partly right, you are selling it," said Liam trying not to laugh. "Unfortunately, the way she meant it was slang, as in, a prostitute…Covent Garden…London…16th century."

"Oh, it does, does it," whispered Rebecca slowly as it sunk in, "and it means me selling my flower…Well, well." She tried frantically to think of a clever comeback but failed miserably, and instead, noticed the look on his face. "Oh, go ahead, have a good chuckle at the Flower-seller's expense!"

Liam started laughing, and she joined him.

"I guess she got me."

"Yes, she did."

"You know, I'll have to come up with some brilliant curator humor to get back at her."

"Good luck with that!" stated Liam.

Which made them laugh again.

"Yeah, we aren't exactly known for our bellyaching jokes or creative pranks," she confessed before taking a long sip of her beer.

"So, why did you become one?"

"I'm pretty, my body's not too bad," she said admiring herself.

Liam gave her a nice smile. "I can't argue with you there."

Rebecca blushed and quickly changed the subject. "Oh, you meant a curator?"

Liam nodded, picked up his drink, and sat back.

"Well, my great-grandmother started collecting antiques as a hobby, some of them she sold, others that she thought of as 'special' she kept. My grandmother followed in her footsteps, as did my mother."

"And you?"

"No, I didn't collect or sell," she replied. "Over time they had accumulated so many items, so as a teenager, I decided to research them, categorize them, clean, and preserve them. I soon began to realize their historical significance and decided to study it in university. So I went to Syracuse University, took their Museum Studies program, got my M.A, and my master's degree in history. Obviously, not Covent Garden history!" she said with a giggle. "I worked as an assistant curator in Syracuse, Buffalo, and New York, before going on my own to help smaller communities set up either their town museums or historical houses. About tenth months ago, I was hired on a year's contract as the curator for the Amare Museum."

"A year?"

"Once it's up and running, my assistant Brittany will take over on a more permanent basis."

"And you?"

"Let's just say, I'm keeping my options open for now," she replied with a shrug of her shoulders. "And what about you?"

Liam chuckled. "I'm sure you researched me before asking me to come here."

"Okay, okay, of course I did," she said with a laugh. "You did the college thing too, similar to me, except at a younger age and throughout your teenage life, and you have an extensive background in archeology. Thanks to your father, who is very well-known and highly respected in the field, and also a professor. And your mother, his gifted assistant, also highly respected and a professor too…How did I do?"

"Very thorough and complimentary."

"Good," said Rebecca, wondering if she should just ask him, then remembered she'd said to him that one day he would have to tell her about it, and today wasn't that day. Although, if he didn't tell her soon, she would have no option but to ask him about it.

"You suddenly have a serious look on your face. Is everything okay?"

"Sorry, yes, I was just thinking that after this drink we should go upstairs, and I can show you The Pub and The Deck."

"Leaving me, are you?" asked Crystal overhearing her.

"We are," replied Rebecca, "I'm going to take him upstairs before we leave, we have an early start in the morning."

"Oookay," said Crystal slowly, and giving Rebecca a look as if to say, 'it was none of her business.'

"No, not like that!" countered Rebecca realizing what her friend was implying, and playfully pushing her.

"Well, not yet like that, yet," added Liam nonchalantly, "we still haven't agreed on a price."

Making the girls laugh.

"Becky, I think you've got a keeper here," suggested Crystal leaning towards him.

"No, it's only a professional transaction, no strings attached."

"Really," she cooed moving closer. "How long are you in town for?"

"A few weeks."

"Where are you staying?"

"The Childwall Mansion."

"Very nice, are you a relative?"

"No, just a guest."

"Oh," she said with a smile. "Any free time?"

Rebecca knew what her friend was trying to do, and it wasn't going to work.

"Actually, Rebecca and I have a lot of work to do," he replied, "so I'm not sure how much free time I'll have."

"And that free time we do have, will be spent with me showing him around town, and entertaining him," stated Rebecca unsuccessfully trying to stop the words before they came out, and now wanting to hide under the table.

"And as her guest, I would expect nothing less," said Liam, saving her.

Crystal stood upright. "Okay, sounds like you're busy," she said with a satisfied grin. "Check?"

"Please," they both replied, then watched her leave, and were silent until she returned.

"Here you go," she said placing the bill on table.

"No, I've got it," insisted Rebecca picking it up first.

"The debit machine's over by the bar," said Crystal. "Why don't you come over there with me and save me the trip back?"

Rebecca followed her, and as she looked on at her friend deliberately taking her time processing the payment, she whispered, "what were you doing back there?"

"Come on Becky, he's cute, funny, charming. Don't you think?"

"Of course I do, but I didn't ask him here for that, and besides, it would be unprofessional. Wouldn't it?"

"Right now, you're acting like you're living in the 16th century," she said making them giggle. "Besides, it's not like you're working in the same office."

"I guess not," she said thinking about it. "By the way, you trying to get me jealous didn't work."

"I've seen the way you were looking at him."

"Oh, that was more admiration."

"Sure," replied Crystal quickly glancing at her. "My Flower-seller worked, too."

"Yeah, thanks for that, I didn't even know what it meant!"

"But he did," she said with a sly smile, "and he was willing to pay for it, so to speak, and he also wants to spend his free time with you."

"As my guest," she said discouraged.

"Come on, I know you don't believe that's his only reason."

"Do you think he likes me?"

Crystal squeezed her best friend's hand. "Rebecca, what's there not to like? It's time to get your beautiful face out of those books and that killer body out of that museum. Trust me."

Rebecca knew she was right, too often had she used her work to ward off the advances of men, but then again, none of them were ever quite like Liam. "Thanks, Crystal," she said squeezing it back before taking the receipt.

"You two have a fun night," she said with a wink.

"Oh, please," she replied, and started to walk away, before suddenly turning around. "Crystal, how did you know, he would know what a Flower-seller meant?"

"You brought him here, didn't you," she asked.

"Yeah, so?

"Why?"

"Because he enjoys English literature, and likes to quote Shakespeare," answered Rebecca and staring at her friend peculiarly. "Did I tell you that?"

"Maybe once or twice," she lied, it was more like a dozen.

"At least a dozen," corrected Rebecca.

Crystal nodded her confirmation and mouthed, "Love you!"

Rebecca mouthed the same back, smiled, then went back to the table. After they finished their drinks, she took him upstairs to The Pub, then outside.

"What did you think about The Pub?" she asked as they walked onto the wooden deck.

"It was livelier and a lot of fun. Although I must admit, I really liked the banter and period costumes downstairs."

"The Cellar is more suited for quiet conversations, first dates, privacy, that sort of thing…And it allows you to call one of your best friends a wench!" she added with a laugh. "While, well, as you've witnessed, The Pub is catered more towards loud music, lots of drinking, and tomfoolery."

"It definitely lives up to that," he said as they stopped at the deck's railing and looked at her. "Downstairs Crystal asked if we were on a date?"

Rebecca shook her head and smiled. "That's just her way of trying to bait me."

"I noticed you didn't take it."

"No, she has to be sharper than that," confessed Rebecca. "Like Flower-seller."

"I hate to say it, but that was good."

"It was," she conceded with a sly grin, "although, I get her back by calling her a wench every time I come her, and I always encourage people to talk to her that way, it drives her mad when I do it."

"Oh, so you're not supposed to?"

"The rule in The Cellar is that if someone talks to you in Early Modern English you have to answer back in that language."

"All night."

"Yep," she said taking a drink of her beer. "If you hadn't had told me what a Flower-seller was, she would have kept on calling me that all night and let me believe it was a compliment. So, thank you for that, kind sir."

"My pleasure, milady," he cheerfully replied then followed her gaze.

"Look at the bright moon shimmering on the lake, and the couples and families walking along the shoreline. It's beautiful,"

"It is."

"I walk along it sometimes in the morning and the evenings," she revealed looking at him. "I find it, relaxing."

"I'm sure it is. Do you live nearby?"

Rebecca moved very close to him and motioned toward William Street. "Do you see the fourth house from the end?"

"I do."

"That's where I live.

"Wow, right across the street from the beach, you must have a great view from your place."

"It's unbelievable," she sighed, "and is totally unobstructed."

"Do you swim in the lake a lot?"

"Not as much as I should but as often as I can," she explained and pointed to the side of the deck. "Those stairs get you to and from the beach. So, you can come up here for a drink and something to eat then go for a walk in the sand afterwards."

"Now, I'm just jealous," he admitted with a grin.

She smiled back. "You have several weeks to enjoy it here, so I'll make sure we make time, okay?"

"Deal," he cheerfully responded.

They had a couple more drinks, talked about music, then left and walked silently along the beach before crossing the street to her home.

"Now I know why you walked up to meet me today," said Liam.

"Because of this," she said motioning to her house, "and the beers."

"Thanks for showing me around and taking me out, it was a lot of fun. I haven't had a night like this for a long time."

"Me too, and thanks for walking me all the way home," she joked and started up her walkway before turning around. "I'll see you in the morning, goodnight."

"Goodnight," he replied, and watched her walk to her front door, open it, and give him a smile before going inside.

Chapter Seven

"Mom, where are you?"

"In the kitchen."

"Good morning," said Rebecca giving her a hug.

"Morning, dear, have a seat. Do you want something to eat? I'm making poached eggs and toast."

"Sure, I have time," she replied, pouring herself a coffee, and sitting.

"So?"

"So, what?"

"How's Liam settling in?"

"Fine, I guess."

"You guess?" questioned her mother.

"He's doing fine," she confirmed. "I met him at the house around five...Did you know that most of the original furniture, artwork, pictures, and artifacts have been taken out, and that the parlor, family room, and two bedrooms have been updated with new furnishing and big flat screen TVs? And that the bathrooms have been upgraded?" she asked looking up at her. "There's even a PlayStation."

"I had heard that," she replied, placing the eggs on toast, and bringing the plates to the table before taking a seat.

"Really, when?"

"Once we heard Liam was coming, James Childwall called and asked me what I thought about fixing it up."

"And?"

"Obviously, I told him it was a good idea," her mom stated.

"Why?"

"He was expecting to be stay in an upscale hotel, not a mausoleum."

"Nice choice of word, Mom."

"That more was for dramatic effect," she explained giving her a half-smile. "Plus, Agnes and Edith dropped off cooked meals, groceries, and beer for him. So, I'm sure he's more than happy staying there."

"Mom, he loves the place, and we both know the real reason why we want him to stay there," said Rebecca. "When I asked you why, I didn't mean, why he's staying there. I meant, why didn't you tell me about him removing the furnishings and the upgrades?"

"I didn't think it was a big deal, and I was going to tell you today," she confessed. "Besides, I wasn't expecting you to go barging in there, I thought you were picking him up," she said, then noticed her daughter was attentively eating her eggs and avoiding eye contact. "Rebecca, you didn't invite yourself in and ask him for a tour, did you?"

"Good eggs, Mom."

"You did."

"No, he invited me in, I saw the parlor, and he asked me if I wanted a quick tour," she said in her defense. "He asked me why I wanted to look around. I lied and told him I was curious to see what changes had been made, changes that I had no idea about, and that I was surprised about how many and how modern it looked. Then I said the upgrades aren't an issue, and we are probably going to remove the bathrooms in the bedroom anyway to create more exhibition space."

"Did you talk about anything else except the mansion and its contents?"

"Yes, we did," replied Rebecca curiously, then glanced up at her mother who was silent. "Mother, don't tell me the reason you didn't tell me was because you wanted me to be invited in, see the changes, and walk around the mansion with him."

"I thought it would be a nice icebreaker," she confessed. "Was it?"

Rebecca shook her head. "Am I that predictable to you?"

"No, dear, you're just like me," she confessed, "because I would have acted the exact same way if I had seen the parlor."

"I'm not so sure whether that's a compliment or not?" she queried.

Her mother smiled at her knowing that her daughter would soon find out how similar they really were. "Tell me what you did after the tour."

Rebecca told her about their conversation in the mansion, what they talked about walking down to the boardwalk, dinner, and Shakespeare's, leaving out the Flower-seller part and her private discussion with Crystal about him.

"He sounds very charming."

"He really is."

"You seem somewhat surprised."

"No, not with that, we just clicked. It was like we had grown up together and we'd known each other our whole lives. Does that sound odd?"

"I don't think so," she said matter-of-fact. "You both have the same backgrounds, interests, schooling, and professions."

"Yeah, that makes sense," said Rebecca finishing her eggs, sipping her coffee, and thinking. "I don't think he's going to believe much longer that we only brought him here to give his input on my exhibit."

"I know," she agreed looking at her. "It's all your fault, you know."

"What? My fault, how?" she asked taken aback.

"If you weren't such a brilliant curator, we could have convinced him quite easily that you needed his help, and why he was here."

"Liam's not going to know my work."

"I disagree. Without a doubt he would have researched you, just as you did him, and yet, here he is."

Rebecca thought about what her mom had just said, and wondered if that were the case, why did he still come.

"You will just have to go along with this charade for as long as you can, at least till you either tell him or he starts asking the right questions."

"I would prefer to tell him before it got to that."

"It will probably have to be sooner rather than later if we want him to figure this out before he leaves."

Rebecca nodded her agreement, then drank her coffee in silence for a few minutes before her mother broke it.

"What's on the agenda today?"

"I'm going to drive over to the house, walk with him to the interview, then show him around Main Street and the museum."

"The interview was an exquisite touch," complimented her mom.

"Spare of the moment," confessed Rebecca, "and he was behind it a hundred percent. He felt the town shouldn't been in the dark about why he was there and should be a part of the process."

"He's right," said her mom, "but it also buys us time, and more importantly, gives him a cover for the real reason he's here."

"True," she replied. "Are you coming to the interview?"

"No, I'll meet him when the time is right."

"When will that be?"

"Dear, you'll know."

Chapter Eight

"How did you feel this morning?" he asked as they walked down Victoria Street.

"I little groggy," she revealed. "I went over to my parents early this morning and had breakfast with my mom. Did you eat?"

"I did."

"They're going to have some juice, coffee, tea, and a small buffet," explained Rebecca. "They don't usually open till eleven thirty and thought the lunch crowd would be distraction if we had it later."

"That's okay," said Liam, "it's better this way, just the two of us and Arthur."

Rebecca went quiet and looked away.

"What?" he asked stopping.

She turned around and walked back to him. "There's going to be a few more than three. Agnes is going to be there, Edith and her husband Karl, several other part-time Historical Society members, the owners, their parents, and the photographer-slash-videographer."

"Videographer?"

"They want to post our interview on social media, and it's only him videoing," she explained and moved closer to him. "They're all so excited to meet you."

Liam chuckled. "You should really think about becoming a salesperson, you're a natural."

"I have another superpower," she joked, then went serious. "Are you oaky with this?"

"It's all good," he replied pleasantly.

"Great, let's go!" she said grabbing his arm and pulling him. "Now, the restaurant we are going to is called Essentia, which is Latin for 'substance, being, actuality, essence, essential things," she explained.

"That's a cool name, and I like the meaning behind it."

"Thank you," she said proudly. "It's only been up and running for about seven months and the owners took six months prior to renovate the interior. It was a restaurant and the previous owners passed it on to their daughter and her husband, Liz and Marco. Their background it Italian, as is their cuisine, and their fine dining establishment is classy and chic, with a warm, friendly, soothing ambiance."

"Sounds beautiful."

"It is," she confirmed. "This is Park Street, yesterday we walked west past the town park towards the lake. Today, we are heading east toward the next major road which is Main Street. If we had taken a left out of the mansion, we would have arrived at Oak Boulevard, and needed to take a left to get to Main," she said pointing.

"It's a rectangle?"

"Yes, most of the roads create rectangles in this area, so it's easy to find your way around," she revealed and continued their walk. "When you enter Essentia, there's a small, cozy bar where you can wait to be seated. Then off to the left, and down, is the main dining area. And if you continue towards the back, you will eventually walk outside onto a patio and then down steps to a good-sized garden with table and chairs. During the day, the restaurant is casual, and in the evenings it's fine dining. They even put linen on the tables out on the patio and in the garden, so couples can enjoy a romantic evening outside under the stars."

"I can't wait to see it," said Liam enthusiastically. "Seems that you really like it?"

"I do, and they are such a nice couple, and them hosting this interview will help them market and promote their restaurant well beyond Amare and Seneca County," she said as they took a right. "This is Main Street, I would love to stand and point out some of its finer details, but if we don't hurry, we'll be late."

"I understand," said Liam glancing over and giving her a kind smile which she appreciated.

Rebecca suddenly stopped. "Okay, we're here. How do I look?"

Liam hesitated. "You look…amazing."

"Thank you," she replied shyly. "And you look great." She quickly looked over at the restaurant door then back at Liam. "There's one more thing."

"Okay," said Liam and waited for her to tell him.

"This building used to be the Childwall's General Store back in the 1800s," she blurted out.

"What!?"

"Come on, let's go," said Rebecca promptly grabbing his hand and pulling him inside.

"That wasn't too bad," she whispered as their interview came to an end. "Now, just some pictures, coffee, bite to eat, quick chitchat, and were good to go."

Thirty minutes later the crowd had dwindled down to Liz and Marco, their parents, and Agnes and Arthur, who were packing up and about to leave with Edith and Karl.

"Becky, Liam, can we speak with you both for a moment in private?" asked Liz, with Marco standing next to her.

"Sure," replied Rebecca as the four of them moved away from the others.

"We would like to invite you back here tonight, for dinner, on us," said Liz nervously. "We were hoping you would have been here during business hours, but Arthur said he had a deadline to meet and that it would have been a distraction during the interview."

"We'd love too," answered Rebecca without hesitation then realized she hadn't even consulted with Liam. "Is that okay?"

"Of course, it is," he acknowledged. "Besides, Rebecca's the boss."

"I know that feeling," joked Marco.

"Hey, watch it!" said Liz giving him a lighthearted push with her shoulder.

"I'd better, or I'll be sleeping on the sofa tonight," said Marco putting his arm around her. "My father and I are going to cook you a very special, and traditional, Italian four course meal tonight—"

"It's our family's favorite," interjected Liz, "and not on the menu."

"That's very kind of you," expressed Rebecca.

"All I need to know, is if you have any allergies?" asked Marco.

"No," they replied.

"Perfect!"

"And I, along with my amazing niece, will be taking care of you at your table. So, the only thing I need to know is where you would like to sit?" asked Liz. "It's going to be a beautiful evening, and the best tables will be either the ones at the front of the restaurant, where the windows open out to a picturesque view of Main Street, and you can enjoy our live piano music, or outside, in our quiet, intimate garden, under a romantic and enchanted starry sky?"

Rebecca and Liam looked undecidedly at one another before being interrupted by the group of four leaving. After they said their goodbyes, Liz suggested that they have a look around, and take their time before deciding. Rebecca and Liam strolled to the front of the restaurant first, then towards the back and out to the garden.

"On the other side of those hedges and fence, is the Childwall Mansion," said Rebecca pointing.

"And this used to be their store property?"

"It did," she replied, as she watched him walk around, and wondered what he was thinking.

Liam stopped next to her. "To be, inside, or not to be, that is the question?"

Rebecca giggled. "I don't know, you choose Ham-let!"

Liam was caught off guard by her reply and laughed loudly. "That's a great comeback."

"Thank you," she said happily and moved closer to him. "Liam, I think you should decide, you're my guest."

Liam shook his head. "No, you should, because I am the guest."

"Looks like neither of us wants to choose," concluded Rebecca glumly.

"I've got it! How about we stand facing one another, cover each other's eyes, then we count down from three, before we hit zero, we either have to point to the ground or inside?"

"Okay, I like that, it sounds like fun," she said enthusiastically.

"Marco, what are they doing?" asked Liz, who had sent him down to spy on them. "I hope they choose inside," she said turning to their parents then back to her husband. "Marco?"

"They're facing one another… and now they're covering each other's eyes," he replied in as loud as a voice as he dared.

"What?" asked Liz with a blank look.

"Three, two, one, zero," they said.

"Okay, let's slowly remove our hand from each other's eyes," said Liam.

After they did, she quickly looked to where he was pointing. "Inside!" she said animatedly.

Marco noticed them heading towards the door and quickly ran down to his wife and family. "They're coming. They pointed this way."

"What does that mean?" asked Liz to his unsure response.

"We've decided to take a table inside," confirmed Rebecca.

"Oh, that's wonderful!" said Liz who swiftly glanced at Marco motioning him to ask.

"Is there something else?" asked Rebecca.

"I hope you don't mind me asking" he said hesitantly, "and I know we already had pictures taken earlier with you, but we were hoping we could take some tonight?"

"Marco, Liz, it would be our honor," answered Rebecca, "and hopefully we can take some with your parents, and any of your friends that may drop by."

"And please, feel free to let people know we will be here tonight, and to encourage them to stop by our table to say hello," offered Liam, opening the door for Liz and Marco to basically do whatever they wanted.

Liz wanted to kiss them both on the cheek to show her gratitude, instead, she gave them a heartfelt thank you, and waited for them to leave before jumping up and down and screaming ecstatically with Marco. Once they stopped, Liz ran to her phone to post the announcement on their social media pages.

Chapter Nine

"They're such a great couple," said Liam walking out into the sunshine.

"And so cute," replied Rebecca. "Do you know, we all went to school together, and they started dating in their senior year? I was a bridesmaid at their wedding. So was Crystal and Vanessa."

"That most have been some wedding?"

"It was so much fun," she stated, as they started walking south. "That was nice of you to give them an open invite to promote us tonight."

"You said they needed a hand marketing their restaurant beyond Amare and Seneca County, if their lucky, maybe a newspaper from Syracuse, Rochester, or even Buffalo may pick up the story."

"Arthur told me he was going to give them a generous plug in the interview piece, so hopefully that works out for them, and helps get them on the map," she said optimistically and giving him a smile. "Okay, so this is Main Street. Over there is Mapia's Place, a café—"

"Greek for Maria."

"Yes," she said impressed. "Then there's Burt's Diner, Siena's Salon, Main St. Sports Bar, Alfred's Fish & Chips, Brat Haus Brewery…I'm only highlighting a few establishments because I wanted to point out the diverse culture of our town," she explained. "But generally, Main Street is known for its local businesses, and catering to locals and tourists alike. Most of our large grocery-chain stores, banks, and retail businesses are located further east. If we were to continue heading south, we would pass more stores, the bowling alley, arcades, bingo hall, and movie theatre. Actually, you can see them from here."

"Oh, yeah," said Liam following her finger as she pointed them to him.

"On the next street over, Market Street, is the courthouse and town hall, "she said as they waited for the lights to change before crossing. "Oh, this is Oak Boulevard."

"Why was it named Market Street?"

"Back in the day, it used to be the spot where locals would come to sell produce, cattle, furniture. Today we still have the Farmer's Market were local farmers sell produce, but it's held every Saturday morning at the Town Park. You can also buy a coffee, pastry, or breakfast sandwich, and sit on the grass and listen to local musicians performing on the small stage. It's really nice," she said glancing over at him. "I'll take you one weekend."

"I would like that," he replied interestedly.

"From the viewpoint, you can see the stores on the other side of the street."

"One thing I will say, Rebecca, is that Main Street is charming, quaint, lively, and friendly," he said impressed. "It's great to see so many people saying hello and good morning as we walked past them."

"Amare is a fantastic community. We all get to know one another, welcome, and embrace new residents, and treat every tourist as an extended member of our town's family," she admitted proudly. "And it's Victoria and William Childwall that we have to thank for kickstarting that philosophy."

"It must be a wonderful place to grow up in and raise a family."

"It was, well, the first part I can answer," she said laughing, "I can't vouch for raising a family yet, but my parents, my friend's parents, and Vanessa, can."

"I understand," he said laughing with her.

"You're a good listener," she acknowledged, liking him more and more.

"I find it's the best way to learn."

"About a town?"

"Yeah," he said looking at her, "and a person."

Rebecca blushed, looked away, and wondered what he thought of her.

"What's that building there?"

"That is the new library," she confirmed. "It was built a couple of years ago to accommodate the growing need for space, study rooms, meeting rooms, screening room, computers, printers, and a cafeteria. It also offers an area for school kids to put their backpacks and winter coats."

"It's a striking modern structure with lots of windows."

"Originally, it was a struggle to decide what type of design to agree on for the facility. Some townspeople wanted it to reflect the same structure as the old library, which was Victorian, others wanted it to reflect the Greek Revival architecture like the town hall, courthouse, and Childwall mansion."

"Only those three building have that architecture?"

"Victoria didn't want any homes built in the same style as hers but did agree to the government building. So, technically, the new library did fall under that category, although it was quickly pointed out by the opposition, that she had chosen the Victorian design for the old library when she clearly had the option of the Greek Revival."

"Quite a quandary?"

"It was," she agreed with a grin, appreciating his lighthearted tone.

"But you never mentioned anyone wanting a modern design?"

"None of the townspeople did," she revealed mysteriously.

"Okay, I'm hooked," he said wanting to hear more.

"As the townspeople bickered back and forth about which of the two designs to choose, a very intuitive woman stood up and made a suggestion…"

"What?" he asked stopping and looking at her with anticipation.

Rebecca looked into his eyes. "She said, since the facility was being built for the children and teenagers of the town, that she had a very simple solution to our problem, ask them what they wanted."

Liam chuckled. "Eliciting customer input."

"Exactly!" said Rebecca. "Something that is a key cornerstone to me being a success curator."

"I couldn't agree more," he replied, "and you're very intuitive."

"Well, I was proud of my moment," she said timidly, believing he was making fun of her.

"Oh, I wasn't teasing you at all," he said sincerely. "On the contrary, I've read your papers, I Google searched you, your exhibits, and know all about your work ethic. I think you're pretty amazing."

"Thank you, that's a wonderful compliment," said Rebecca beaming. She thought he was too but kept that too herself for now. "So, we identified the kids' needs, built it, and they just love it."

As they continued their stroll, she talked about the shops, how long they had been in business, and their owners. At Culture Street they crossed over, walked past the library, and stopped.

"This is the old library, now the Amare Museum," she said turning toward it. "It's a three story, nine thousand square-foot High Victorian manner built in the 1860s, and its exterior still retains its original elegance and beauty."

"Wow, it sure does. It's incredible!"

"Now, the interior has been altered over the years when it became the museum-slash-cultural center, and even more so when it became just the museum," she explained. "I'll show you around tomorrow afternoon after it closes to the public."

Chapter Ten

"Come in," said Liam, and watched her enter the foyer.

Rebecca was wearing a burgundy floral print short sleeve wrap dress, which showed off her athletic figure and shapely tanned legs. Her brown hair was off to the side and hung down past her shoulders. She had no make-up on, allowing the cute light freckles on her nose to compliment her hazel eyes. Her lips were full and covered with a sheer liquid nude rose lipstick. And judging by his reaction, she had his undivided attention.

"You're breathtaking," cooed Liam, who had only seen her sporting a shirt, shorts, and ponytail.

Rebecca smiled at his compliment then admired him. "I like what you're wearing," she said looking at his blue cotton shirt, beige pants, and brown leather slip-on shoes.

"Not too casual?"

"No, you look...perfect," she replied, she had wanted to say extremely handsome but was hesitant. "Shall we go?"

He followed her outside and onto the sidewalk. "Where's your car?"

"I left it at home and got dropped off by Crystal," she replied. "Chances are they won't let us out with just one glass of wine, and I didn't want to have to leave it here...It's a small town," she half-joked.

"Come on, that's the best time to do it," he suggested.

"Why's that?"

"When you explain that you innocently left your car here because you had one too many glasses of wine at Essentia, everybody will be wondering whether you're telling them the truth, or just fabricating that story to cover up your indiscretion."

She hadn't thought about it like that, and Vanessa and Crystal would have been bending over backwards to hear the juicy details. "Now I wish I would have," she said regretfully.

"Don't worry, the night's still young."

"Yes, it is," she said mischievously.

When they arrived at the restaurant, they were met by a smiling Liz who swiftly showed them to their table.

"This is amazing, thank you," said Rebecca taking a seat.

"It's the least we could do," replied Liz. "This is my niece, Mia, and she will be taking care of you tonight."

"Hello, Mia," said Rebecca, "Home for the summer?"

"Hey, Becky, I am. Getting ready for my final year."

"Time flies, you still liking it?"

"I love it!"

"Mia, this is my friend and fellow curator, Liam, from Boston."

"Hello, Mia, nice to meet you."

"You too, Liam," she replied anxiously. "I've read all your research papers. I would love to discuss them with you."

"Mia!" cried Liz. "Where are your manners?"

"I'm sorry," she said embarrassed.

"Please, don't worry about it, maybe later on when it dies down you can let me know your thoughts on them?"

"Okay, I'd like that," she said holding back her excitement. "Rebecca, what would you like to drink?"

"I think we will start off with a beer, and look at your wine list," recommended Rebecca glancing over at Liam for his approval, which he gave.

"I'll get those for you, and be back shortly," she said leaving.

"Liz, probably told her she could say something to you, but not so soon."

"You're probably right," agreed Liam. "Although, you have to admire her on seizing the opportunity, she probably realized there wouldn't be a better time."

"You know, I would have done the exact same thing," said Rebecca laughing.

"So would I," said Liam with a grin. "What's she studying at college?"

"Exhibit Designer."

"I can see why she asked me, why didn't she…?" Liam stopped in his tracks because he knew the answer.

"Ask me?" she said putting her hands on her cheeks and giving him a look of dismay. "Oh, I see…you think she only wants to hear from the great, distinguished, talented, illustrious, Liam Wilson! Not that unexceptional, mediocre, middling, second-rate, small-town girl Rebecca Anderson from Amare."

"I couldn't have said it better myself," he joked, then smiled at her. "Are you finished, Ham?"

Rebecca laughed. "I am," she replied and realized she was staring.

"Here are your drinks, and the wine list," said Mia placing the glasses down in front of them and handing the list to Rebecca. "My uncle has said that although there are many fine wines produced locally, he wishes to recommend a 1983 Fattoria Montagliari Chianti Classico Riserva from Tuscany, Italy."

Rebecca handed her the list back. "Thank you, he must have a fine wine cellar?"

"My uncle Marco takes great pride in his wines," she replied. Then leaned over and whispered, "my aunt Liz says that the cellar is his 'bambino piccolo' or 'little baby.'"

Rebecca and Liam laughed as she walked away.

"So, I take it you've already spoke with Mia?"

"Yes, I have. She's visited me several times at the museum throughout the school year, and I've also helped her with some of her assignments."

"Did you hire her last summer?"

"No, she went backpacking through Europe, and spent a lot of time in Italy. She wanted to visit the museums and local attractions. I didn't realize she was going to be home this summer," she said considering it, as she gazed out the window. "Liz is right, this is a picturesque view."

The wine was served, and the courses came out throughout the evening. They talked about the food, wine, Amare, and the people walking by. With the exception of Liz, Marco, and Mia taking a few pictures with them when the main course was served, they were alone, but once they finished dessert and halfway through their second bottle people started dropping by. Some just said hello and welcomed Liam to the town, others asked him work-related questions, and none of them left without getting a picture with the couple. One of the last people to come over was Liam's friend from Boston.

"Johnny! What are you doing here?"

"I was doing a piece on a famous celebrity couple getting hitched, and they had their ceremony and reception yesterday at a local vineyard, not far from her," he disclosed. "Afterwards, the guests were shuttled back to their hotel in Geneva, and the following morning we all had brunch together, before the couple departed for their honeymoon…It was very hush, hush."

"How did you manage that exclusive?"

"Really Liam, I'm the best entertainment journalist in Boston, no Massachusetts, no—"

"Okay, I'm going to stop you there."

He leaned in and whispered, "here's the scoop, the girl this celebrity is marrying is my first cousin, and we were close growing up. I never took pictures, or ran stories of them during family get-togethers, which sucked because I would have made a killing. So, to thank me, they invited me to their small, intimate wedding and gave me the exclusive," he explained and sat back. "The story runs nationwide tomorrow!"

"That's incredible."

"Thank you, I am," he said humorously then noticed Rebecca. "I'm sorry, please forgive me for my rudeness, who is this ravishing beauty?"

"This is Rebecca," replied Liam, "I'm helping her here in Amare with her exhibit. Rebecca," he said looking at her, "this is Johnny Lens, Journalist to the Stars."

"Hey, I like that introduction," he said with a grin. "Nice to meet you Rebecca, and don't listen to this guy, I also do pieces on premiers, events, restaurants, and…exhibits."

"You never miss a beat," declared Liam shaking his head.

"If I did, I wouldn't be any good at my job, would I?"

"Yeah, yeah, okay. You still didn't say what brings you here?"

"You did," replied Johnny. "Ears to the ground, I heard about you working out here, and thought I'd take a detour and pick up your story before heading home," he explained. "Just several questions, maybe a couple of pictures with you two at the table with this scenic background, and over at the bar. What do you say?”

Liam glanced over at Rebecca then back at Johnny. “All right, but on three conditions.”

“Name them.”

“A picture of us outside with the restaurant name in the frame, and make it look as if we were just arriving.”

“Deal, I would have loved to have had that snap anyway. Second?”

“You name the restaurant in your article.”

“Not a problem, I ate here earlier, and the food was impeccable. Plus, this place is beautiful. Third?”

“I’ll tell you after we finish up.”

“Oh, Mr. Secretive,” kidded Johnny.

Johnny conducted his interview, took several pictures inside and a few outside, and on their way back into the restaurant Liam asked Rebecca to continue to the table while he told Johnny his third condition. When he arrived, Rebecca wasn’t there and filled up their glasses, before he finished, she sat down and joined.

“Had to go powder my nose,” she explained picking up her glass, taking a sip, and noticing Johnny talking with Liz and taking pictures. “He’s quite the character. How do you know him?”

“We met in college and became close friends, and any newsworthy events, I always call him first to see if he’s available.”

“He’s definitely got the personality for it.”

“He sure does,” agreed Liam.

“And?” she said asked wanting to know. “What was you third condition?”

“I asked him to do a piece on Liz, Marco, and Essentia.”

“That is so nice of you,” she said moved. “When will they run it?”

“I told him it had to run simultaneously with our piece.”

“Where?”

“My hometown, Boston, Albany, Syracuse, Rochester, and probably Buffalo.”

“Are you kidding me?”

"Johnny Lens may be quirky and funny, but he's honest, and he's the best," divulged Liam.

They took a few more pictures with guests, said goodbye to Marco, and walked with Liz and Mia to the door. They were about to walk out when Rebecca suddenly noticed Mia's face and whispered in Liam's ear.

"Mia?"

"Yes, Becky," she replied then followed her off to the side.

"I'm sorry Liam didn't have time to talk with you tonight, but tomorrow evening we are going to the museum after it's closed to the public, if you're free would—"

"What time?"

"Seven," answered Rebeca with a smile, "meet us at the back entrance."

"I'll be there."

"Okay, see you then."

They left the restaurant, walked down Main, then took a left on Park Street to Rebecca's house, on the way she put her arm through his.

"Here you are home, safe and sound," said Liam stopping in front of it.

"Thank you," she said removing her arm. "Would you like to come in for a nightcap?"

"I would love to."

He followed her inside the house and into her living room. She quickly turned around, walked towards him, and they kissed passionately. Liam put his hands under her dress and lifted her up. She wrapped her legs around him as he carried her on to the sofa.

Chapter Eleven

"Good morning," Rebecca said snuggling into his chest.

"Morning," replied Liam putting his arm around her and pulling her close.

"Just so you know, I'm blaming it on the wine," she whispered.

"Just so you know, I'm blaming it on you," he whispered back.

"Stop it!" she said tapping his stomach, then softly rubbing his abs. She glanced up and kissed him. "Do you want some coffee?"

"I'd love some," he said as he watched her get up and put a pink robe around her naked body.

"What?" she asked, noticing his stare, and joining him back on the bed.

"Just checking you out."

"And?"

"You're perfect."

She smiled happily then kissed him tenderly. "Come on, get up."

Liam got dressed, followed her downstairs into the kitchen, and watched her put on a pot of coffee. Once brewed, she poured two cups.

"Cream and one sugar?"

"Please," he replied.

She passed him his coffee, grabbed his hand, and led him to chairs on the porch.

"You get to wake up to this every morning?" he sighed.

Minus you, she thought, looking at him and following his gaze. "I do, and I love it!"

As they drank their coffees, he reached over and held her hand, and enjoyed the captivating view with her in romantic silence.

Liam finished his coffee and stood. "Another one?"

"Sure," she said, delighted with how comfortable she was with him, and him with her.

"Hey, how about we take our cups of coffees on a walk along the beach?"

She didn't reply but jumped up. "Give me five minutes to get dressed," she said excitedly and took off.

They crossed the sandy beach to the shoreline and strolled along it.

"Do you have any brothers or sisters?"

"I have an older sister, Janice. She's married to Rob, an engineer, and they have two children, Isaac, eleven, and Sophia, nine."

"What does your sister do?"

"She's a stay-at-home mom," he replied, "it's what she always wanted to be. I think it may have something to do with all the traveling we did with my parents when we were younger and her wanting to be at home with her children."

"She was never interested in archeology?"

"No, but she loves history, and has her master's degree," said Liam. "She told me that once the children were old enough, she was planning on teaching, but I don't see that happening. I think she loves being a soccer mom, going to PTA meetings, helping out at the school, and the community work she does too much to give it up."

Rebecca wondered what it was like to be a mom, drive a minivan, and go to PTA meetings.

"And you?"

"One day."

"One day?" queried Liam.

"Yeah, be a mom."

"Oh," said Liam with a kind smile. "I actually meant your family. I don't know anything about them."

Rebecca giggled nervously to hide her embarrassment. "Well, my great-grandparent's moved to Amare in the late 1800s and bought a large parcel of land northeast of the town."

"Farmers?"

"Not really, they both came from money, and had this dream about leaving the city and owning a farm. My great-grandfather hired someone to run it and hire staff, he just managed the farm and helped out as best he could. My great-grandmother did the housework, raised the children, and as told you before, collected antiques. All of their four children went to college, three married and moved away, but my grandmother stayed and inherited the farm. She married a local man, who was raised as a farmer, and he helped her turn it around. They had two children, my mom, Christine, and my aunt Tammy. Now in the seventies, a young Italian farmer and his wife were looking for land to grow grapes on and make wine and approached my grandparents. They agreed to invest in them and give it a trial run. So, my grandparents loaned them a section of their land east of the farm, built them a house on it, and bought them equipment. In return, they would split the profits fifty-fifty. My grandparents hoped for the best but had their reservations. Well, wouldn't you know, it was an enormous success, and my grandparents expanded their plot of land. Now during the eighties, something affected them personally, and by the nineties, they decided to leave the farm and move to Florida. The house, farm, and vineyard were left to my mother and her sister. Neither of them wanted to run a farm. So, they made a deal to keep the vineyard going, and made the Italian family partners, and gave them forty percent of everything. Then sold their farmland to developers and made a fortune. Now, they did keep a healthy portion of land along Main Street, where they built two houses on several acres of land, one for each of them."

"That's an incredible story," said Liam. "So, you own a winery?"

"Actually, my mom, my aunt, and the Russo's do."

"What's it called?"

"Anderson Russo's," she replied, "and the brand name is 'Nettare degli Dei,' which means, 'Nectar of the Gods,' and it produces the best-selling wines in the Finger Lakes region," she explained. "I never started it, I'm not involved in it, so between you and me, I'm not interested in it at all," she said honestly. "My aunt and uncle are involved in the daily operations, while my mom and dad are silent business partners who review the books with them monthly. Me, I just love what I do too much."

"They must be proud of you?"

"They're very proud of me, and my brother, too," she said with a smile. "Oh, I have an older brother, Glen, he'd kill me if he found out I'd forgotten to mention him. He's a doctor, like my dad."

"And your mother?"

"She has her business degree, and takes care of the family businesses, but her passion has always been collecting antiques. So, I'm definitely like her in that way," she explained. "She's the one who taught me the fundamentals of being a curator, but to be a great one she said, was in my hands."

"Well, I think you're well on your way," said Liam encouragingly.

"Thanks," Rebecca replied. She wanted to tell him how someday she would like to uncover secrets and solve mysteries like he had but didn't want to get into the conversation now because it wasn't the right time. "We should head back; you must be hungry?" she said turning around.

"I am, are you?"

"Starving," she admitted, and thought about holding his hand but he grabbed it before she could decide. "I like talking to you."

He stopped and looked into her eyes. "So do I."

"I've never talked this openly before, it's nice."

"I know, me neither," said Liam, and kissed her tenderly. "I think you're beautiful, intelligent, thoughtful, and a lot of fun to be around."

"I like laughing with you," she admitted, "I haven't had this much fun in a long time." She wondered how she was going to say what she wanted to next without pushing him away or hurting his feelings.

"How do we move forward?"

"Oh, what a relief! I was just contemplating that myself and was searching for the right words. What do you think we should do?"

"Did you just turn it back on me?"

Rebecca giggled. "No, I don't think so," she said with a cute look. "So?"

"I think we chalk this up as a mistake, blame it on too much wine, and regain our professionalism," he stated frankly and looked away.

Rebecca wasn't sure if she was hearing him right, and for a moment thought he was serious, until she noticed him trying not to laugh. "You stinker!" she cried and chased after.

Liam suddenly stopped and turned around. Rebecca jumped up, wrapped her arms and legs around him, then kissed him.

"That's some willpower you have there," he teased, "I'm sure you will have no probably keeping it quiet or drawing attention."

"What are you going to do about it, huh?" she asked provokingly.

Liam looked deep into her eyes. "Nothing."

Rebecca just stared back, then closed them as he slowly kissed her, only opening them after he pulled away and gently let her down. "I guess we can talk some more about this back at my place."

"Okay," he whispered then lightened up the conversation as they began to walk. "In the meantime, why don't you tell me what's on the agenda for today or do I have a free afternoon, boss."

"I like the sound of that," she confessed. "As you know I have a shopping date with Crystal and Vanessa this afternoon, which means you do have the afternoon to yourself. Unless you want to go shopping for clothes with us girls?"

"Hmm, let me think long and hard about that."

"Okay, smartass, I'll take that as a no…and since you obviously prefer your own company, I'll meet you at the back entrance of the museum at six."

"All right," he said arriving at her house and following inside to the kitchen.

"Time to cook breakfast," she said glancing at him, "I hope you have a big appetite, because I'm making us a farmer's breakfast."

"Sound good, anything I can do?"

"Just rinse the mugs, fill them up, and watch me work my magic."

As they ate, Rebecca looked up at him. "What do you think?"

"It's delicious. I can't eat it quick enough it's so good, thank you."

After they finished, she picked up the dishes, and put them in the dishwasher. "Come upstairs with me" she asked pulling him up.

Liam followed her into the bedroom, sat on the bed, and watched her get her clothes ready.

"What do you think we should do?"

"Act professional."

"That's it, that's your plan."

"That's our plan."

Rebecca sat next to him. "Just act professional in front of others, that's it."

"That's it. Can you handle that?"

"Me? The question is, can you?"

"I don't know," he admitted pushing her onto the bed and laying on top of her.

"We have fifteen minutes, then I need to get in the shower and get ready," she warned then kissed him. "Maybe twenty."

After they made love, Liam went downstairs and waited while she got ready.

"Liam where are you?" she asked looking in the living room, then the kitchen before noticing him in the backyard. "Here you are."

"You look nice."

"Ah, casual today, but thanks," she replied standing next to him.

"This is a good-sized garden."

"It is, unfortunately, I don't have a green thumb."

"I'm the same, I like admiring gardens, just not creating them."

"You prefer visiting your Flower-seller?" she asked putting her arms around him.

"Oh, I didn't know it was like that he said pulling out bills."

Rebecca shook her head and chuckled. "You keep that up and this Flower-seller's shop is going to be closed."

"I wouldn't want that, now."

"No, you wouldn't," she said kissing him.

"What time are your friends coming?"

"They'll be here any minute."

"I should go before they get here," he said grabbing her hand and heading towards the back door.

"Wait, I thought we'd have some fun with them? Any suggests."

He thought momentarily. "I have an idea!"

Rebecca opened the door, and let her friends in, they immediately noticed the pillow and blanket on the sofa.

"Did you sleep down here last night?" asked Crystal.

"Hmm, what?" said Rebecca playing it aloof. "Oh that, no, I had a friend stay over."

Liam came down the stairs with wet hair and buttoning up his shirt. "Hi, Crystal, Vanessa, nice to see you again."

"Did you find everything okay?" asked Rebecca.

"I did, thanks," he replied as he sat on the stairs and put on his shoes. Crystal and Vanessa looked on dumfounded.

"I'll see you at six?" he asked.

"Yeah, I'll see you then," she replied.

"Enjoy your shopping ladies, bye."

"Bye," they replied, and watched him leave before looking over at Rebecca.

"Is there something wrong?"

"Let's start with the half-naked guy that just walked down your stairs," suggested Vanessa.

"Did he just get out of the shower?" asked Crystal.

"Yeah, he grabbed a quick one."

"I spoke to you ten minutes ago and you just got out of the shower."

"He didn't use mine; he used the bathroom in the hallway."

Crystal glanced over at Vanessa then at Rebecca. "And I suppose he slept on the sofa?"

"Uh-huh," she answered uninterestedly. "Last night, we went out for dinner at Essentia, he walked me home, came in for a drink, he, actually we, drank too much, so he crashed here."

"Becky, he lives ten minutes away, he could have easily walked home."

"I guess," she said shrugging her shoulders, "but then I wouldn't have been able to go for a walk on the beach with him or cook him breakfast."

"Oh, you definitely slept with him!" stated Crystal.

"Yes, yes I did," said Rebecca candidly.

"See," said Crystal, "I knew it!"

"He also left the Flower-seller five hundred bucks upstairs on her end table!" said Rebecca, trying not to laugh.

"Flower-seller? What's that about?" asked Vanessa.

Crystal suddenly realized what Rebecca was doing. "Becky is getting back at me because I called her a Flower-seller at Shakespeare's on Friday night," she said glancing over at her, "that's a 16th century prostitute."

"But that still doesn't explain why he would get a shower here?"

"He asked if he could, what am I going to do, say no," she replied with a chuckle. "Let's go."

Vanessa and Crystal looked at each other as they walked out the door not sure what to believe, while behind them, Rebecca smiled.

As Liam passed his next-door neighbor's house, he heard a voice calling hello and looked around before noticing a woman walking down her driveway towards him.

"Hello, I'm Sandra your neighbor."

"Hello, pleasure to meet you, I'm Liam."

"I heard someone was moving in for a few weeks. You're the curator from Boston?"

"That's me."

"Welcome to the neighborhood, and if there is anything you need, please don't hesitate to let me know.

"Thank you, I won't."

"Who's this, Mom?" asked one of the twin boys joining her.

"Liam, this is Jay and Sam, they're eleven," she said touching the tops of their heads. "Boys, this is Liam, and he'll be staying next door for a few weeks, say hello."

"Hi, Liam," they said in unison.

"Hey, guys."

"I won't keep you any longer, I just wanted to introduce myself," explained Sandra. "My husband's name is Tom, so if you see him around, please come over and say hello."

"I'll make sure I do."

"Have a lovely afternoon."

"Thank you, Sandra, you too. Bye, boys."

"Bye, Liam."

Chapter Twelve

At five thirty Liam strolled into the library and scanned the books on the shelves. He thought he heard children playing by the side of the house, glanced over at the window, and listened. Hearing nothing, he went back to perusing them. The laughter started again, realizing it was the twins next door, he walked over to the window, pulled the drapes aside and gazed out. He could hear them, but couldn't see them through the hedges, and decided to go back to the books. The playing and laughter grew louder prompting a smile on his face and him to leave the room. He went outside onto the deck and followed the laughter to the side of his house. As he walked towards the end of the deck, he tried to spot the kids playing in their backyard but couldn't see them. When he got to the handrail, he realized the laughter seemed to be coming from the side of his house, and as soon as he stuck his head around the corner it stopped. He quickly glanced over at the neighbor's house but couldn't see or hear them, then around his backyard, nobody. Thinking nothing more of it, he headed to the door and suddenly heard the children giggling behind him, and realized they had been hiding and smiled as he went inside. He walked to the front door and left the mansion. As he walked by the neighbor's house, he glanced down the driveway but there was no sign of the boys and continued to the museum.

"Hey, how was your afternoon?" she asked.

"Well, I went through my Gmail. My sister called, then I called my parents. I ate. Looked around the place. Reviewed the books in the library, and listened to the twins playing next door," he replied, then told her about them laughing and hiding.

"Sandra's boys, Jay and Sam?"

"You know her? Of course you do."

"Sandra and Tom are great, the boys are too," she said opening the door.

"How was shopping?"

"It was fun, I bought a couple of dresses," she revealed and told him what happened after he left. "All day they were badgering me about you, and us."

"What did you tell them?"

"That we were professionals, and we would never consider crossing that line," she said in a stern voice and with a straight-face, before breaking into a laughter.

"Did they buy it?"

"Yeah, I think so," she replied optimistically. "They know I take my work seriously, so that's in my favor, but at the same time, they know the type of person I am, so they wouldn't put it past me to hoodwink them."

"Do you feel bad?"

"Kind of, they're my best friends, and we tell each other everything, but…"

"You don't want to break our trust?"

"No, I don't."

"Would they tell anyone?"

"No, not about us," she said confidently, "but don't worry about it, I like watching them trying to figure us out."

"All right," he said with a grin.

Rebecca slowed down, looked at him, and began. "This will just be a high-level tour because I really want to convey to you three things: what we have done, where we are at, and are plans moving forward," she explained. "And hopefully, this will give you an overall idea of our vision and the challenges we have ahead."

"Perfect, lead on."

She took him to the museum's front entrance. "This is our reception area, to the right and through those doors, are our offices. There are three: one is an open concept with three desks; the second is Brittany's, my assistant, and the third, is mine. We also have a small lunchroom with a coffeemaker, microwave, and fridge. These wide stairs in the middle of the structure allow clients to access the three floors, and the basement. The basement is split into two rooms, the biggest is used by the museum for the unwrapping, cleaning, repairing, and temporary storage of our items.

The other room is split into smaller rooms: one is a cloakroom, and the other is a lunchroom with vending machines. We also have women and men's restrooms downstairs with baby changing stations, and a water fountain."

"Is the lunchroom for the school children?"

"Mostly, they eat their snacks and lunches down there. We also get a few seniors who like to sit, have a rest, and chat, so we put a coffeemaker in the room for them," she answered, then continued. "As I mentioned, the stairs are in the middle of the building and divide the floors into five large exhibit rooms that are approximately fifteen hundred square feet each, and for our purposes are named A to E," she described as he followed her to Room A. "Rooms A to D, the 'History of Amare' exhibit, begins with the background of the Finger Lakes region, to the building of the Childwall's mansion and guest homes, then the design, planning, and building of the original Town of Amare, up to present day."

They slowly walked through and out Room A, passed the back doors they entered through, and continued through two large wooden doors. "This is our screen room and replicates a small movie theatre. Throughout the day we put on fifteen to thirty-minute documentaries about the area, out town, and our community. And throughout the winter, we play children's movies and well-known Hollywood family movies, were we sell tickets and popcorn."

"Fundraiser?"

"It is, but we charge such a nominal fee that we don't make too much from it, so we label it as a community event.," she replied as they left the room. "This is our elevator. Patrons use it during the day, and we use it when the museum is closed, to move items between the basement and the floors. We also have a wheelchair ramp out front and an accessible restroom downstairs. This is the corridor we came down," she pointed out as they walked along it, then took a right onto the stairs, and climbed them. At the top, they made a U-turn, followed the hallway to the front of the building and entered Room B on the right. She deliberately walked slowly to allow him to view the items on display, and occasionally stopped on the way to answer his questions. They strolled out of Room B, and leisurely walked through C, then took the stairs up and entered Room D, and continued slowly through that, before entering E.

Rebecca stopped. "This room is designated for the 'History of the Childwalls' exhibit, that's a working title, and as you see we already have the room-slash-exhibit six eighths completed."

"So, this exhibit is purely based on the Childwall family?"

"Yes," she said with a smile. "It begins with Victoria and William's background, and how they met, where they married, and the birth of the first family member, Elizabeth, to the last successor, James. It entwines their family's history from the purchasing of the land, to the building of their wooden home, their mansion, up to and including, the present Town of Amare."

"Hmm," said Liam impressed. "The objects and items for Amare's history, were the ones that your family collected over the years, plus the ones given, donated, or purchased from the community, as well as those given to you by the Childwall's."

"Yes," she said enthusiastically.

"And this exhibit, the objects where all owned and given by the Childwall's?"

"That's correct," she replied. "Over the years, the Childwall's accumulated many personal items and gifts, the overflow, and those that were replaced in their home overtime, were originally stored in the mansion's basement. Overcrowding eventually forced them to move the items to a warehouse, where they continued to add items. Ten months ago, I was asked to come to the museum, and set up the 'History of Amare' exhibit. At that time, I was given access to the warehouse and catalogued the items. Some were incorporated into that exhibit, but most into this one. Today, that warehouse contains mostly furniture."

"And the remaining two eighth?"

"Are for the items that have been removed from the home, and those currently in the library and den."

She followed Liam as he strolled through the 'History of the Childwalls' exhibit, looking at each of the items, and stopping often to ask her very specific questions about them.

"Good," he concluded. "What time is it?"

"What?" she asked taken by surprise and fumbling for her phone. "It's five minutes to seven."

"All right let's go meet Mia," he said as they started for the stairs.

Mia, thought Rebecca, she'd forgotten about her. "Aren't you going to say anything besides good?" she asked.

"Would you prefer me to talk now and rush through what I had to say and keep Mia waiting? Or meet Mia, and talk later when we have more time?"

"Later," she replied knowing he was right, "I'm just anxious."

"The 'History of Amare' exhibit is excellent, in fact, it's perfect," he said with a smile, pulling her close, and kissing her gently on the lips. "And trust me, with the 'History of the Childwalls' exhibit, you have nothing to worry about, I only have few suggestions to make."

Rebecca, somewhat relieved, kissed him vigorously, then grabbed his hand, walked with him down the stairs to the back door and opened it.

Chapter Thirteen

"Hello, Mia."

"Hi, Becky, Liam."

"Shall I come in or…?" asked Mia.

"I wouldn't mind going somewhere and getting a drink?" suggested Rebecca looking at Liam.

"Me too," replied Liam walking out into the warm evening air.

"Okay, Mia," said Rebecca locking the door. "Where do you think we should take this tourist?"

"I was planning on meeting my friends at the Lake House Tavern at eight. We could go there?"

"That's perfect," said Rebecca. "You didn't drive, right?"

"No," she replied.

"All right, let's go."

They headed towards the lake, and on the way, Mia asked him about his research papers, being a curator, and visiting different places.

"You used to set up your own exhibits in museums and historical homes, but over the last few years I noticed you just help other curators with theirs, why?"

"Many of the individuals setting up their exhibits are volunteers and have little or no experience, so I not only help them, but teach them what to do. That way when the exhibit is ready, and I leave, they have the experience and confidence to continue on their own."

"Do they contact you after looking for advice?"

"Sometimes, but not as often as you think, once you go through the process of helping set up an exhibit they quickly catch on. Also, after I leave, I set them up with professionals in the fields of research, cataloguing, and so on, who will help them in the event they acquire new antiques at a later date for their exhibits."

"So, do you help them with their initial research?"

"If they need it, I do," he replied. "It depends on what level of help they require, sometimes it can be as simple as auditing their exhibits before it goes public or starting from scratch."

"I noticed that you only work with smaller communities and historical homes now, not with major cities' museums, why?"

"Setting up a community exhibit or historical home is much easier, and goes much quicker because of its smaller scale," he explained. "It also means I get to travel to more places, meet many interesting people, and see thousands of artifacts."

"I never thought about that way," she revealed. "Two more question, and I've saved the best for last."

"Okay, ask away."

"There are reports that you see apparitions, have intuitions, and dreams that help you locate artifacts, burial sites, and supernatural objects," she said naively. "Is that true?"

Rebecca was just about to interject and tell Liam he didn't have to answer that question.

"That's what the papers say, and if I were you, I wouldn't believe everything you read," he said lightheartedly. "What's your next question?"

Rebecca had wondered how to approach him on this subject, and there was young, innocent Mia, naively asking him. Although, she would have pressed him more on his response.

"Can you tell me how you found Amy's love letters when nobody else could?"

"A romantic, hm?"

"I am, and I love the story," she said gaily, "and I would really like to hear it straight from the horse's mouth, so to speak."

"We're here," said Rebecca stopping and motioning to the bar.

"Why don't I tell you the story inside with a drink, that way when you retell it, it will sound a little more romantic?" suggested Liam.

"Yes, that would be much better," she said keenly, as they climbed the stairs to the tavern's entrance.

"Remember the other day when I said there were two original guests houses still standing, and a pointed out one, and it was a B&B?"

"I do."

"Well, this is the second, and it's a bar with three levels and a large patio."

Inside, they walked across the main floor, and decided to sit outside on the deck. Once the drinks were dropped off, Liam started.

"About nine months ago, I was contacted by a family telling me that the Victorian house that their great-great-grandparents lived in was being turned into a museum, and they wanted my help to locate some letters before it was turned over to the historical society. After I arrived, they tell me the story of their great-grandmother, Amy, and the fisherman she had an affair with, Joseph, and the son they had. Which I will now share with you," he said and began. "In a wealthy Victorian home in Boston, there lived a young eighteen-year-old girl, Amy, who was in love with a young local fisherman, Joseph. Because Joseph was poor and uneducated, and therefore came from different social classes, her family forbade their love. But this didn't stop the young couple from meeting in private. What was unknown to her family at the time, was that the young fisherman was working with his uncle for the summer, and his father was a wealthy and respected businessman."

"So, Joseph was wealthy and well educated?"

"He was, and when the couple couldn't be together, they would write letters to one another. Especially, when he was out on the boat, he would use his free time to write her letters expressing his love for her. At home, Amy, between writing him letters, painted a portrait of Joseph. One day, shortly after his return, they were caught together and her father chased Joseph off, threatening him that if he came near her again, he would kill him. Unfazed by her father's threat, they decide to continue to meet, and soon realized that the only way they could ever be together was by getting married. So they did, and consummated it," said Liam, pausing to take a sip of his drink.

"I bet her father's not going to be too happy," said Rebecca looking at Mia.

"No, it's not looking good," admitted Mia. "Have you heard this story, Becky?"

"Not in its entirety," she replied honestly, and intrigued.

"Please, Liam, continue?"

"The following morning, Joseph gives his young wife a letter in a sealed envelope, making her promise to wait till he gets back before opening it. He kisses her goodbye before leaving on his final voyage, vowing upon his return, to run away with her. The following day, news reaches Amy about his boat sinking, and Joseph drowning. Nine months later she has a baby boy and names him Joseph. With no proof she was ever married, she is shunned by society, and can't even tell her husband's family about their boy because she doesn't even know who they are. So, with the help of her mother she raises the child."

"That's so sad, to lose your husband, and be left alone with a baby," said Mia.

"Especially back then, to be unwed and pregnant, was definitely frowned upon," stated Rebecca.

"Now fast forward to nine months ago," said Liam. "The family believes if they can find the letters, it may help prove the heritage of their grandfather and clear their great-grandmother's name. I agree, but I only have three days to locate them. On the second day of my research, I come across a note that their great-grandmother had written in a copy of Shakespeare's *Romeo and Juliet*. It read, 'From betwixt mine legs, comes mine truth; Betwixt mine eye and heart a league is took.' So, I look around the house for a picture, portrait, or painting of Joseph, and there are none. I ask the family if they have any old pictures, portraits, or paintings that they may have packed away. They said they had two, and had been advised to throw them out, but hadn't yet. One was by Amy, and it was a painting of Joseph. I ask the family where the picture used to hang, and they take me to her room and show me the wall. I remove the painting from the frame, and there on the backing, is a drawing of an arrow pointing up. I go upstairs to the attic, pull up the wood flooring, and find a box right above where the arrow had pointed to. A box that contained Amy and Joseph's love letters and her diary."

"So, he gave her the copy of *Romeo and Juliet*?" asked Rebecca.

"He did, as a wedding gift."

"Is what she wrote a quote from that play?" asked Mia.

"No, the first part, 'From betwixt mine legs, comes mine truth,' she wrote herself, and she was referring to their son coming from between her legs and him being her truth."

"Truth that she was married?"

"Married, in love, was his wife, and that he was their son," stated Rebecca.

"Right," said Liam. "Now the line, 'Betwixt mine eye and heart a league is took,' is from the opening line of Shakespeare's 'Sonnet 47' and when translated it means, between my eye and heart a pact, an alliance, is made, which on its own, really didn't help me that much. But after I analyzed 'Sonnet 47' I realized that the line she had written was only to direct me to that sonnet."

"So she only wrote that line in hopes that one day someone would pick up on her clue and go to that sonnet?"

"Not someone, Liam," clarified Rebecca.

"Yes, Liam," sighed Mia.

Rebecca smiled at him as he continued.

"'Sonnet 47' from Amy's point of view, revealed how her heart and eye work together and do good things for the other, and when her eye is starved for a look at him, Joseph, and her heart misses and desires him, her eye feasts upon her love's picture and bids her heart to join it in this painted banquet; her eyes are her heart's guests and in thoughts of love they share a part. So, either by his picture or her love, he is still with her when he is away, and that he is no further than her thoughts, and she is always with them, as they are with him. Or, if they are asleep, Joseph's picture in her sight awakes her heart to heart's and eye's delight." Liam stopped and took a drink of his beer. "In summation, when she misses him, her eyes look at her portrait of him, which inspires her heart to think of him. So, either by her painting or her love for him, he is still with her when he is away, and he is always in her thoughts, as she is in his. And when they are asleep, his portrait in her sight awakens her heart to both her heart's and eyes delight."

"So, she wasn't only talking about 'Sonnet 47' and her looking at the portrait she painted of him, she was also leaving a clue as to where the letters were hidden using that portrait," said Rebecca.

"Exactly!"

"But why hide them?" asked Mia,

"Back then, she probably didn't want her parents to find them and throw them out," suggested Rebecca, "and then have her father hunt down Joseph and kill him."

"Then why not just give them to her son when he was old enough?" continued Mia.

Rebecca looked over at Liam wondering the same thing.

"There's no definite answer to that question," he replied glancing back and forth at them. "Mia, why do you think she didn't?"

She contemplated momentarily. "Amy wanted her secret to die with her and to come to light when the time was right."

"That's well said," complimented Rebecca, impressed and nodding her head. "That's what I believe also."

"So do I," admitted Liam.

"What was in the final letter Joseph wrote to her, the one she promised she wouldn't open until he got back?" questioned Rebecca.

"It was a letter for his parents telling them who Amy was, his love for her, and if anything were to ever happen to him to take care of her," answered Liam, "and it also contained their marriage license."

"What the envelope opened? Did Amy open it?"

"Yes, was it?" asked Mia excitedly.

"What do you guys think?"

"No," said Rebecca slowly, "she wouldn't want to break her promise to him."

"I was going to say yes, but Becky just reminded me of the promise, so I'll say no as well."

"You're right, she never opened it and kept her promise."

"It's so sad, but so romantic," sighed Mia. "Thank you, Liam."

"Yeah, thanks," said Rebecca, falling for him.

"You're welcome," he replied, took a sip of his beer, then changed the subject. "How's your aunt and uncle doing?"

"Oh, I meant to tell you as soon as I saw you!" said Mia sitting up animatedly. "Your interview in the Banner came, out and Arthur did such a nice piece on them, then there was a…I don't want to say weird, but geeky guy who did a small article on them and their restaurant. It was in

The Boston Globe and on their website, as well as the newspapers in Albany, Syracuse, Rochester, and Buffalo, and their websites."

"That weird, geeky guy is Johnny Lens, he's Liam's buddy," said Rebecca with a chuckle and glancing over at him. "I didn't know he worked for the Globe."

"Yeah, he does freelance," replied Liam. "So, they're happy?"

"They're over the moon, and they want you guys to drop in tomorrow," she said then remembered something. "I almost forgot. I was supposed to do this as soon as I saw you at the museum." She leaned over and kissed Rebecca on either cheek, then, Liam. "That's from my uncle Marco. So, just tell him I gave it to you earlier."

"We will," said Rebecca with a smile then noticed Mia suddenly looking past her. "Is everything okay?"

"Everything's fine, it looks like my friends just got here."

"Then go join them," stated Rebecca, "and take your drink with you."

"Are you sure?"

"Of course."

"Okay, I think I will," she said standing and motioning to them she was on her way over. "Do you mind if we take a selfie?'

"No," said Rebecca as Liam got up and stood with them.

"Thanks, got it!" she said putting her phone away. "I'll see you guys soon, bye."

"Bye, Mia," they replied.

"She's such a sweet girl," said Rebecca watching her leaving then turning to Liam. "She really appreciated you taking the time to talk with her and tell her that story. She's probably sharing it with her friend as we speak."

"There's nothing mediocre about me," he said candidly and casually looked around.

"I see, unlike mediocre Rebecca Anderson from Amare," she recalled.

"If the shoe fits."

"This shoe fits and is going to be kicking you in the ass if you keep that up," she joked and went to grab his hand but caught herself. "Do you want to get out of here and have a drink on my porch swing?"

"I would love to," he replied, wanting to be somewhere quiet with her.

On the way out, they said bye to Mia and met her friends, then walked down William Street to Rebecca's.

75

Chapter Fourteen

Liam waited on the swing, while Rebecca went inside, got two bottles of beer, and joined him.

"Before I forget, James Childwall wants to meet you tomorrow morning at eleven for coffee and pastries."

"Are you coming?"

"No, he just wants to meet you," she explained. "He lives off of Oak Boulevard in the long-term facility."

"Facility?"

"Trust me, it's more like a five-star hotel and spa," she clarified. "It's a ten-minute walk from the mansion and I'll give you the address before you leave."

"Do you know what he wants?"

"Probably to introduce himself, ask how the house is house, if you need anything, that kind of stuff."

"How come he doesn't live in the house?"

"He was up until a month ago," she replied. "Over the last eight months, he's been going away for at least one week each month, and there was gossip that he was sick and sorting out his affairs. Anyway, the last time he came back he announced he was moving out, and that his mansion was going to be given to one of the Historical Society board members. And that the museum could have all its contents, except the wine cellar, and code-locked room."

"What is in that room?"

"I heard he built it about a year ago, and its climate controlled. So I'm thinking he took personal items from the warehouse and put them in there."

"How did I end up there?"

"When he heard you were coming, he was adamant that you stayed there, and wouldn't take no for an answer."

"Why?"

"I don't know…to be hospitable," she suggested. "Maybe he just wants to impress the great Liam Wilson!"

"Yeah, you're probably right," he sighed stretching out his arms and placing his hands behind his head.

Seeing her opportunity, she laid her head on his shoulder, and he responded by putting his arm around her.

"What was the feedback you were going to give me about my exhibit?" she asked.

"With the amount of time you will be spending with me reviewing the exhibit, the tight deadline, I think you need a third person to help you out," he suggested. "Actually, someone like Mia, an exhibit designer, who can work with Brittany."

"I would have liked to have hired Mia for the summer?"

"Why don't you?"

"She's not in the budget?"

"Can't you add her in?"

"I can, but there's this whole process I would have to go through - posting the job for at least a week, sifting through resumes, conducting interviews – it would be a month before she would even start, even if she was the only candidate.

Liam thought for a moment. "How did you do my contract?"

"We wrote it up first, got it approval, I called you, and you accepted. Not at first, I might add. But that was different because we were hiring you, with her, we have to post the position."

"What about my assistant?"

She sat up. "You don't have one."

"No, I don't, but after speaking with you and looking at my workload, I believe I'm going to need one."

"Is her name Mia by any chance?"

"Why, yes, it is."

"How would I go about doing it?"

"Did you do my contract?"

"I did?"

"Then do another for Mia, send it to me in the morning, and I will tell Mr. Childwall that I need an assistant, ASAP, and hand him the contract. If he asks why, I'll will explain it's due to my workload and tight deadline."

"Just like that?"

"Just like that," he replied. "It cuts through the red tape, and if anyone questions you, you can tell them she's my assistant and it has nothing to do with you. Besides, the worst he can say is no, but I'm guessing he won't."

"No, I don't think he will, and I could need the extra pair of hands," she replied admiring his resourcefulness. "I'll send it to you in the morning."

Good," he said, as she placed her head back on his shoulder.

"Who's the board member receiving his mansion?"

"First, let me explain something," she said collecting her thought. "About a month ago, before we asked you to come here, I found out about him moving to Florida and leaving the mansion to one of the board members. Originally it was going to be given to her last week, but when Mr. Childwall found out that we wanted to hire you, he said that he was postponing giving her the house because he wanted you to stay there, and she would get it after you left."

"Who is she?"

"The board member he is referring to is my mother."

Liam looked at her confused. "He's giving the house to your mother, why?"

"Mr. Childwall, knew he wasn't going to be around much longer, so he said he could trust my mother, and let her decide what was best, as long as his conditions regarding the property were met."

"What conditions?"

"Not altering its structure or landscape, knocking it down, and so on, and he hoped my mother would respect his wishes."

"Hoped?"

"He was giving her the house, so he couldn't really force her," she answered, "but he trusted my mother to do the right thing."

"Which was?"

"I've had several discussions with her about what to do with it, and one was to turn the house into a museum," she explained.

"A museum?"

"It was one of the ideas, and I was planning on discussing it with you to get your input. Personally, I can see the positives in turning it into a museum and having tours."

"What are the other ones?"

"When I think back about the reasons Victoria and William built their house here, and what this town meant to her, I believe she would prefer it to be a home for people to stay in while enjoying Amare."

"You're talking about a B&B?"

"Or an inn," she replied. "Visitors can stay in the mansion, experience Amare, and visit the exhibits five minutes away at the museum."

"And you want to know my opinion?"

"I do."

"If it was a museum, the mansion would have antique pictures and photos of what it looked like back in the day, with a few pieces of furniture scattered around?"

"It would, because we need the space for people to walk around the rooms," she replied. "The B&B or inn would have a mixture of antique furnishing plus the modern amenities that you are currently enjoying today."

"So, you're asking if I would turn the mansion into a historic museum or a historic B&B or Inn?"

She nodded her head and sipped her beer.

"Before I answer, what's your mother's take on this?"

Rebecca let out a heavy sigh. "She said we will take your opinion under advisement and doesn't want me to talk about it again till after you've finished here."

"I guess there's nothing you can do inside the place till I leave."

"No," she answered, "which means there's no rush for you to answer today."

Liam sat back. "The pieces that are, and where, in the mansion you've already catalogued and researched, and you know exactly where you're putting them in the museum. Right?

"That's right."

"The only piece that will be missing to complete your exhibit is whether you will be adding a picture of the mansion as a historical museum, B&B, or inn."

"Yes, and also what to do with the items that we don't use, like the furniture."

Liam knew she wasn't going to disregard or sell the furniture. Rebecca also said Victoria would prefer it to be a home for people to stay in while enjoying Amare. "I think you've already made up your mind."

"Maybe," she said giving him a smile.

"Here goes," he said leaning forward. "I think you should place those items from the mansion that you have already decided on into the exhibit and set up the mansion as a B&B or an inn. That way people can view the 'History of the Childwalls' exhibit, then experience it firsthand by staying in the Childwall Mansion…and you can even offer packages."

"And if I have my way, it's going to be a B&B or an inn, and I want to call it, 'Cor Eius,'" she conceded. "I'm glad I have your support."

"And if you didn't?" he asked.

"I would have taken your decision into consideration," she responded with a grin.

"Are there any other board members in the event there's a tie?"

"There's three, it's my aunt Tammy," she answered.

"Your mother's sister," stated Liam. "Why didn't you tell me?

Rebecca drank a mouthful of beer and looked at him anxiously. "I didn't want you to think I got to be the curator because of my mother and aunt."

"Is that it?"

"When I first asked you to come here, you said no, and I took it that you didn't want to waste your time helping someone like me."

"Like you?" he asked. "The reason I said no initially, is that I didn't believe you needed my help. I've seen all the work you have done and it's flawless."

Rebecca couldn't keep the smile off of her face. "But you ended up coming anyway, why?"

"I told my parents about your request, and that I wasn't going to go, because I didn't think you required my help. The next day my mother called me out of the blue and said that she I should go, I might learn something."

"Like what?"

"I'm guessing from you, maybe about myself, maybe both," he suggested. "She's always told me you're never too young to learn."

"I think I would like you mother."

"I know she would like you," he said kissing the top of her head.

She glanced up, smiled, and kissed him on the lips.

Chapter Fifteen

Liam was pouring a coffee when he heard a knock at his door and answered it.

"Morning Sandra."

"Good morning, Liam," she said pleasantly, "I hope I'm not disturbing you; I know it's early."

"Not at all, I was just pouring a coffee. Would you like one?"

"No thank you, I'm off to a meeting, and wanted to drop these off," she revealed unfolding the cloth and displaying a basket full of muffins. "They're oatmeal chocolate chip, the boys' favorite."

"That's awfully nice of you. I'll have one with my coffee," he said taking them from her.

"I have to run, have a nice day."

"You too," he replied and remembered something. "I heard your boys playing along the side of your house yesterday afternoon. Sounded like they were having a lot of fun."

Sandra gave him an odd look.

"Maybe, it was in the backyard?" suggested Liam.

"Are you sure it was yesterday?"

"Yeah, around five thirty," he confirmed.

"Hmm," she said thinking. "We were at my parents yesterday afternoon, and got home very late, so it couldn't have been them."

Liam wondered who it could have been.

"I know," said Sandra slowly nodding her head. "Essentia has a lot of families eating in their garden on Sunday afternoons, and all the kids get together and run around playing, you probably heard them."

"Ah, maybe."

"These big hedges can be a maze for acoustics," she said motioning towards them.

"You're probably right," he agreed, "I wasn't a hundred percent sure where the sound was coming from."

"If you do hear the boys playing too loudly outside, please let me know."

"Oh, don't worry about that, I like hearing them laughing, and they can make as much noise as they want," he revealed. "It breaks up the silence of the house."

"It's big for one person," she admitted wondering if he was single but knowing it was rude to ask.

"It is, and it will take me some time to get used to, and by then, it will probably be time for me to leave," he kidded.

She smiled at his joke. "I should get going," she suggested leaving then swiftly turning around, "there's no rush returning the cloth and basket."

"Okay, thanks again."

"My pleasure, bye."

"Bye," he replied then closed the door and smelled the fresh baked goods on the way to the kitchen. He picked one out, grabbed his coffee, and went out onto the deck. He stopped, took a bite, and headed down the stairs to the gazebo.

"Hi, there," said a young girl sitting on the swing inside and taking Liam by surprise.

He quickly moved his body to avoid spilling coffee on it, then walked over to the gazebo's steps. "Hi, there, who are you?"

"I live here," she replied.

"In Amare?" clarified Liam.

"Uh-huh," she answered. "Do you live here now?"

"Well, I'm staying here for a few weeks to do some work, so I will be for a little while."

"With Mr. Childwall?"

"No, he lives at a place where elderly people live who need help taking care of themselves."

"He lets me play back here with my friend," she explained. "Is that okay?"

"Sure, as long as your mom is okay with it?"

"Okay," she answered. "What's your name?"

"Liam. What's yours?"

"My mommy told me not to tell strangers my name because once you do people may think we know each other."

"That's good advice," he said smiling at her. "Where's your friend?"

"She's shy around people she doesn't know, so I told her I would come and see you and let her know what I think."

"And, what's the verdict?"

"Verdict? What's that?"

"It means, what's your decision?"

"I'm going to let her know that I like you and can trust you."

"Well, thank you for that," he said and was about to take another bite of his muffin.

"Would you like one? The neighbor just dropped them off."

"No thank you, I need to get going now," she said standing up and walking past him. "Bye, Liam."

"Bye," he replied and watched her happily skip down the driveway. He took her spot in the gazebo, finished his muffin and coffee, then went inside and got ready for his meeting.

"Oak Boulevard Manor," Liam read walking through the sliding doors. He signed in at the reception area, and was told to go to the fifth floor, where he went to room 504 and knocked.

"Mr. Liam Morris?" asked a man formally.

"Yes," he answered, and guessed he was a lawyer.

"I'm Mr. MacDonald, Mr. Childwall's lawyer," he revealed, "please follow me."

Liam walked behind him into a large living room.

"Mr. Morris," said James Childwall in a voice that made Liam feel like they were old chums.

"Please, call me Liam."

"Liam it is, and please let me extend your kindness and ask that you call me James," he said cordially. "Take a seat. Would you like a coffee?"

"I would, thank you."

A maid came out of the kitchen holding a tray containing two coffees and fresh pastries. She asked Liam what he wanted with it then added the cream and sugar before passing the cup to him. She added milk to James's, passed it to him, then offered them each a pastry.

Liam took a sip of his coffee and wondered why Mr. MacDonald was still standing.

"David needs to leave for Syracuse shortly, I thought we could get that business part out of the way first, so he can leave," explained James.

Business, thought Liam. "Sure."

"Ms. Moore informed me that she met with you on Friday, showed you around the home, and explained to you no gardening?"

"Yes, she did, and she was very thorough," responded Liam. "And as I told her, which I'm sure you relayed to you, I'm not a gardener."

"More of a digger," quipped James referring to his archeology background.

"I am," he said laughing and feeling more at ease. "Do you need me to sign something?"

"No, of course not," stressed James. "David is just doing his due diligence. We are more interested in how Ms. Moore did, and from what you are saying, she was exceptional."

"Definitely, and if I, or someone I knew, was buying or renting in the area, I would highly recommend her in a heartbeat."

"Excellent! David, please see to it that she gets that bonus we talked about," he said looking at him then Liam. "I believe when I employee someone, and they do exemplary work, they should be justly rewarded."

Liam nodded his agreement before sipping his coffee.

"Before David leaves, is there anything you need at the house?"

"No."

"For you to complete your work here?"

"No," he replied too quickly. "Wait, actually there is. I need an assistant to help me filter through the workload."

James had noticed the envelope when he had walked in, and momentarily studied him. "I take it you have someone in mind?"

"I do," he said taking out the contract. "It's Ms. Mia Romano, she's a Syracuse University graduate student who is studying for her Master of Arts degree in Museum Studies. She has worked several times throughout the year with Ms. Anderson and has come highly recommended. I have met with her and find her more than capable of the task at hand. Plus, it will give her an opportunity to receive hands-on experience in at town she calls home."

James looked impressed. "Did you rehearse that?"

"No," said Liam with a chuckle. "My plan was only to tell you her name, the college she was attending, and program."

"Well done," he said satisfied.

"David?"

Mr. Macdonald walked over, took the contract and envelope from Liam, and looked it over before passing it to James who skimmed over it.

"Her title is Exhibit Designer?"

"Yes."

"Eight weeks?" queried James.

"Once I'm gone, Ms. Anderson will need her help setting up and finalizing the exhibit in order to meet the September 9 deadline and the Amare Museum's Grand Opening on September 11."

"Looks like Ms. Romano has already started," suggested James noticing her hire date.

"No time, like the present," offered Liam.

"Absolutely," agreed James liking him, and passing the document to his lawyer. "David, please add to this that if Ms. Romano helps meet the deadline, that she will receive a substantial bonus. Let's say, fifty percent of what the assistant curator will be receiving."

"Consider it done."

"I want to share something with you before David leaves," said James with a pensive look and playing nervously with the gold signet ring on his finger. "For health reasons, at the end of the month I will be leaving Amare for good and moving down to Florida to live out the rest of my days. As you are probably aware, the home you currently occupy will be given to one of my fellow board members, Christine Anderson. She, with the help of Rebecca, will oversee turning the property either into a museum, B&B, or an inn," he explained. "The reason that I bring all this to your attention, is that I want to stress to you how important it is that my family's legacy is shown in the most positive light possible, and that their integrity and love for Amare, brightly shines through in the exhibit, and the mansion," he expressed, then looked directly into Liam's eyes. "It's very important to me that what they have accomplished is not overshadowed in anyway."

"I understand, and I can guarantee that Ms. Anderson's exhibit, will not only fulfil your wishes but exceed your expectations," he replied, reinforcing Rebecca's work ethic. "As will their decision with the mansion."

"Thank you, I want you to know how important it is for me to hear that assurance from you," he said sincerely, then turned to David. "Is there anything else before you go?"

"The key," replied David producing it.

"Oh, yes," he said taking it from him and passing it to Liam. "This is the key to the wine cellar, please help yourself to as much of the wine as you would like and take anything that is left home with you as I have no need for it."

"Thank you."

"And make sure you drink the most expensive bottles first, like you said, there's nothing like the present."

"I'll try," said Liam, wondering what he had in his stock.

"David, I guess you can go."

"Just give me one minute," said David leaving.

They waited in silence for him to return.

"I've made the inclusion you asked for, and signed it," he stated passing the contract to James who signed it and passed it back to him. James placed it in the envelope then gave it to Liam. "It was nice meeting you, if you need anything during your stay, feel free to contact me," he said handing him his business card. "Goodbye, Liam, James."

"Goodbye," said Liam and watched him leave.

"Now I won't keep you much longer," promised James, "but there is something important that I need to ask you, and it is imperative that you are honest with me?"

"Okay," replied Liam wondering what it could be.

"You want me to tell Liam why he's really here?" asked Rebecca.

"We have no choice," replied her mother. "It would have been nice to ease him into it but I'm afraid were running out of time."

"Do you think James Childwall is going to leave for Florida sooner than the end of the month?"

"I do, and I would like us to have this wrapped up before then."

"Why?" asked Rebecca unsure of the urgency. "We can always forward on our findings."

"I would prefer we present them to him while he's still here and get his input."

"Okay," she agreed hesitantly. "What do I say to Liam?"

"I'm sure you will find the right words," she said supportively. "Just be honest."

"Mom, I brought him here under false pretenses, so me being honest with him is basically admitting that I lied to get him here," she said shaking her head at the thought of telling him. "What makes you so sure he will agree to what I ask?"

"Trust me, he was undecided about coming here initially, but someone changed his mind."

"Who?" asked Rebecca. "And how do you know that?"

"Don't concern yourself with those details right now. He's here, and that's all that matters, you just concentrate on making sure he stays and helps us."

Rebecca looked at her curiously. "Mom, what aren't you telling me?"

"You and I both know why we asked him to come to Amare, how we did it is unimportant."

"We?" asked Rebecca. "I know I only asked him to come here, who's this 'we' you keep talking about?"

"It's of no great concern," said her mother not answering her question. "After you speak with him, just make sure he promises to keep this between the three of us, we don't want this getting out," she emphasized. "Your interviews in the newspapers and posted on social media about why Liam is here, will hopefully keep them off our backs until we get our answers. So, it's imperative that you keep them believing that by showing up at the museum with him occasionally and giving updates on your progress once in a while."

"You know, we could still do the work on the exhibit, and I can ask him for his help on this other matter?"

"Rebecca, he's seen your exhibits, and if he hasn't already figured it out that you don't need his help, he soon will. Do you want to wait till it gets to that point?" she asked walking over and gently moving a strand of hair away from her daughter's face.

"No," whispered Rebecca.

"I owe it to Jason to at least try and find out the truth, you understand that, don't you?"

"I do." she replied. I just don't want Liam to be disappointed with me, she thought.

Chapter Sixteen

"Liam!" cried Liz, walking over, and kissing him on either cheek. "Marco, it's Liam!" she shouted towards the kitchen then turned back to him. "Thank you, thank you, thank you, for asking your friend to do a story on us."

"Where is he?" asked Marco opening the kitchen door, walking quickly towards him, and kissing both cheeks. "We were excited about us being in the local paper, but all those major cities, too. Our phone has been ringing off the hook for reservations, and for some reason, we've been booked to cater several weddings over at the winery."

"And it wasn't even mentioned in the interviews," added Liz.

"We're guessing word of mouth," suggested Marco.

"Whatever it was, we aren't complaining," said Liz, happily smiling with Marco. "He's going to have the articles framed."

"I'm putting them right over there by the reception area so everyone can see them when they come in," confirmed Marco.

"I'm happy for you both, you deserve it, your cuisine and restaurant are amazing."

"Look at this guy, so modest," said Marco with a grin.

"Rebecca said you're meeting her here for a working lunch?" asked Liz.

"I am, has she arrived?"

"Not yet, but I'm sure she will be here soon," she replied. "Would you like to wait for her in the garden?"

"That would great," said Liam.

"And how about I make you one of my famous full-loaded pizzas?" asked Marco.

"That would be wonderful."

Liz showed him to a shaded table outside on the grass and came back momentarily to drop off a glass of wine. Liam watched her leave, sipped his wine, then noticed a young girl coming out by the hedges and heading his way.

"Hello."

"Hi, there," he replied.

"Are you Liam?"

"I am," he replied unsure how she knew him.

"You met my friend yesterday in the gazebo and she told me your name," she explained. "She said you were nice and that I could speak with you."

"Well, I'm glad you did."

"I thought she might have been out here?" she said looking around.

"No, only me."

"Okay, I'm going to go inside and see if she's there. I'll see you later," she said skipping away.

A minute later, Rebecca came out onto the deck and sat next to him.

"Did the young girl find her friend?"

"What young girl?"

Liam told Rebecca about her.

"I didn't see her," she replied, "but I was in the bathroom then came outside, maybe she went by when I was in there."

"She seemed to come out from those hedges over there?" queried Liam, pointing.

"There restaurant has a side entrance that people can use if they're meeting someone out here," she explained.

"Did you get the Italian thank you?" asked Liam smiling.

"I did," she said giggling. "I'm said I was happy for them."

"Me too."

"How did your meeting go with James Childwall?" she asked as Liz dropped off her wine.

Liam told her everything except the last question that James had asked him.

"Can I ask you something personal?" said Rebecca putting her laptop on the desk in the library.

"Sure," he replied. "Does this have something to do with what you are going to tell me?"

"Somewhat," she replied uncertainly, and tried to find the right way to say it but there wasn't one. "Do you hear or see apparitions?"

"You're the second person to ask me that question today, the other was James Childwall."

"Did he say why?"

"He said he's a fan of the supernatural, and likes watching the documentaries on TV, and was interested to see if the stories he read about me were true."

"What did you tell him?"

"I told him, sometimes I wake up from a dream that seems real, like visions, in which I've talked to deceased people, and they tell me things. I've also woken up in places and don't know how I got there. And other times I just get a sensation, a feeling."

"Do they tell you things that help you find what you are looking for?"

"Usual it's more like clues that I have to decipher."

"The story you told us, about the quote in the book that led you to look for the portrait. How did you know?"

"I was told that they wrote love letters, which meant they were educated, and studied literature. When I saw the old books on the shelf, I went directly to *Romeo and Juliet* because it was similar to their story, and I had a feeling what I was looking for would be somewhere in that book."

"An intuition," suggested Rebecca.

"I guess."

"But no dreams of Amy talking to you or waking up in the room where the books where kept?"

"No, that only happens when I visit a place or area where the people have died under questionable circumstances, and by questionable, I mean some type of supernatural circumstances."

"Does it happen when you touch something?"

"No," he replied, "and it hasn't happened all that often, maybe six times. One time the newspaper blew it out of proportion because I mentioned dreaming about a dead woman who told me things I shouldn't have known. As you know, one of the tabloids called me a 'Ghost Whisper.' I quickly responded by saying I had researched the woman's history, and my subconscious dreamt about her, and what I had revealed was general knowledge. It eventually blew over."

"Was it general knowledge?"

He studied her momentarily. "No, it wasn't, and from that point on I never shared any future experience like that with anyone, and the only ones who know the truth are my parents, Mr. Childwall, and now you."

"Why tell him?"

"He seemed interested in me, and he didn't seem the type who was going to pick up the phone and call the media as soon as I left," he admitted with a chuckle.

"True," she said laughing with him. "Does it scare you when you see them in your dreams?"

"Not really, they're not evil people, more like lost souls."

"Why did you tell me?"

"I don't want us to have any secrets."

Rebecca looked at him and smiled at what he said. She now knew she needed to tell him why he was really here.

"Here is your pizza," said Liz dropping it off with a smile, "and two more glasses of wine."

"Thank you," they replied and waited for her to leave.

"After we eat, we need to go to the mansion, there's something I need to tell you then show you."

"All right, sounds important."

"It is."

Chapter Seventeen

Rebecca opened up her laptop, searched for the files, and when she located them glanced up at him wondering how she was going to tell him. "I didn't ask you to come to Amare to help me with the exhibit."

"I had a feeling I wasn't here for the reasons that you told me."

"An intuition?" she joked nervously.

"More like a superpower," he replied.

"Please, let me show you a couple of things first, then we can talk about it?"

"All right."

She continued to gaze at him deep in thought before looking down and clicking on the first file. "All right, this is a newspaper article from The Post-Standard dated September 7, 1980."

"1980?" whispered Liam. "Suspected child killer Jason Campbell commits suicide by William Duncan." He wasn't sure where she was going with this, and the look he gave her revealed that.

"Please, just read it."

Liam did. "Town of Amare - The body of twenty-nine-year-old Jason Campbell was found last night at his place of residence in Seneca County. Deputies arrived at his home last night at 10 p.m. to arrest him for the murder of two young girls, when they found the gruesome discovery. Sources close to the investigation said that the suspect had carved himself with a knife from pubic mound to chin, and from ear to ear. The knife used was found at the scene, along with a suicide note left on top of several witchcraft and black magic books. Deputy Sheriff Lee Davidson summarized the note by saying it stated his sorrow for killing Amanda Peterson aged 11, and Heather Downs aged 12, who had gone missing two and six months earlier, respectively. A reliable source revealed that Jason Campbell also wrote in his wordy note, that he was a 'Servant of Satan,' and 'was called to sacrifice innocence in His name.' The local townspeople were shocked, not only to learn of his being charged with the murders, but his admission of guilt, and that he had actively practiced witchcraft and black magic, and had offered the young girls to Satan. It was also confirmed by Deputy Sheriff Lee Davidson, that there was nothing in his note disclosing the location of the young girls' bodies. The investigation is still ongoing, and a news conference with further details is scheduled today at 2 p.m., at the Amare Townhall." He finished the article and looked over at her.

"Watch this," she said playing the video.

"Good afternoon and thank you for coming. For those of you that don't know me, my name is Sheriff Baker," he said picking up a piece of paper and reading from it. "I want to confirm that the body of twenty-nine-year-old Jason Campbell was found last night at his place of residence in Amare, Seneca County. Deputies arrived at his home at 10 p.m. to arrest him for the abduction and murder of Amanda Peterson, aged 11, and Heather Downs, aged 12. After entering his home, they found the deceased, and next to his body, a suicide note, in which he admitted to taking and killing Amanda Peterson and Heather Downs, two and six months earlier." The sheriff paused briefly then continued. "After a thorough search of his residence and the surrounding area, inside his camper, which was located next to his home, we found articles of clothing belonging to the two young girls. Clothing that they had been wearing on the day of their disappearance," he said looking up momentarily. "At this time, I can confirm that the investigation into finding Amanda and Heather's abductor and murderer is closed, and we will now concentrate our efforts on locating the missing girls' bodies," he declared before putting down his statement and looking up at the group of reporters. "I will be glad to answer any questions you may have." Then pointed to one with her hand raised.

"Is it true that the suspect had carved himself with a knife from pubic mound to chin, and from ear to ear?"

"Mr. Campbell died severing his carotid arteries with a knife. Next question?"

"Is it true that he practiced witchcraft and black magic?"

"No. Next question?" he asked swiftly signaling to another.

"A reliable source has revealed that Jason Campbell wrote in his wordy suicide note that he was, and I quote, a 'Servant of Satan' and that he was 'called to sacrifice innocence in His name.' Can you confirm this?"

"Mr. Campbell was a very sick man on medication, which, if not administered regularly left him confused and hallucinatory. Yes?" he asked motioning to another.

"Can you tell us what type of knife was found at the scene, and was it his?"

"It was a steel-bladed Bowie knife, and yes, it was his. Final question?"

"Many people in this town have stated that they were not only shocked to learn Mr. Campbell was being charged with these murders, but to his admission of guilt, that he actively practiced witchcraft and black magic, and had offered these young girls to Satan. They say, and I quote, 'Jason was a nice, respectable young man,' that, 'he was very well-liked in the community,' and, 'I think they have the wrong person; Jason wouldn't do such a thing.' Can you comment on these?"

"For the record, we have no evidence of him practicing the occult or sacrificing these young girls to Satan," confirmed Sheriff Baker. "In regard to the charges against him, here in Seneca County, our Sheriff's Department sticks with the facts, not local gossip. And the facts are as follows: first, the accused, Jason Campbell, committed suicide; second, in his hand was the knife that he used to take his own life; third, a suicide note was written by the accused confessing to the abduction and murders of Amanda Peterson and Heather Downs; and lastly, we recovered several articles of the girls' clothing from his residence…Thank you."

Rebecca closed the file and her laptop.

"I'm not sure what you want me to do? I'm not a detective and I don't solve crimes."

"I'm not asking you to do that. I just want you to research the knife wound and find out the truth."

"The knife wound?" he questioned. "The sheriff said he cut his own throat."

"The sheriff's right, he did."

"I don't understand?"

"Prior to that, Jason Campbell stuck the knife into his pubic mound then cut upwards to the bottom of his chin, then sliced himself from ear to ear."

"Rebecca, that was the media embellishing the facts," suggested Liam, "you heard the sheriff dismiss them."

Rebecca opened up a large brown envelope, took out photos, and gave them to him. Liam looked at the three pictures of Jason Campbell with the cuts that Rebecca had described.

"Why would the sheriff lie about him slicing his body?"

"He didn't, he said he died from cutting his own throat, which is true. He just decided to leave this out," she said pointing to the cut on his body.

Liam glanced at her then stared at the picture.

"I just want you to research the wound, see what you can find out, and if it means something?" she requested. "You must admit it's odd."

"I do," he agreed.

"Was he sick and on medication?"

"No."

"Do you think he was mixed up in witchcraft, black magic, the occult, like they reported?"

"Definitely not," she said resolutely.

"How can you be so sure?"

"I just am."

Liam reviewed the pictures again, and as he did, he thought about the newspaper article and the news conference; something didn't sit right. "They found him at 10 p.m., the story ran the following morning, and the news conference was 2 p.m. that afternoon?"

"Yes," she said with a slow nod, and realized his mind was turning, and waited patiently.

"It looks like a ritual suicide?"

"It does."

"And he left a note saying as much?"

"He did."

"But if what you're saying is true and he wasn't into the occult, why would he cut himself up like that and leave a note?" he wondered. "There has to be a reason why he did that? Is that the truth part you're referring to?"

"Yes, it is."

Liam let out a big sigh. "Rebecca, you didn't invite me to Amare to evaluate your exhibit, you wanted me to come here and help you with this."

"I did," she replied. "I'm sorry I deceived you, but I didn't know what else to say to get you here."

"And me coming her under the radar, and doing the newspaper interviews, they're just a cover story for me."

"I'm afraid so," she confessed. "We wanted to keep the media out of what we were doing and limit it to a select group."

"I must admit I had my suspicions when you asked me to come here and help you, because your prior work is exceptional, and after showing me around the museum last night, I realized your current work is too and that you didn't need my help."

"My mother said that would give me away."

"Well, she was right," he said looking at her. "Why do you even care about Jason Campbell? Who's he to you?"

"Jason Campbell was my grandparent's good friend, he ate dinners at their home, and played board games with my mother and aunt when they were young girls. They all adored him," she revealed, then paused for a moment. "He also lived on my grandparent's property and worked on their farm."

"Is that where they found him?"

"Yes," she whispered and glanced up at him with watery eyes. "My mother said he wasn't capable of doing this, and we really need your help."

"I know," he said contemplating, "but I'm not sure how I can. I think you may have this notion that Jason spirit is going to appear in my dreams and point me to clues."

"I'm not asking you to conjure the dead, all I'm asking is that you research the knife wound and maybe uncover the truth."

"And if this truth is what has already been reported, what then?"

"I will deal with that, then," she replied. "But looking at your reaction, I can tell you know there is something unnatural about that wound."

"I must admit, there is."

"Don't you want to find out what it means?"

"I'd be lying if I said no," he confessed and studied her. "So, you want me to pretend that I'm helping you with your exhibit but off secretly researching Jason Campbell's knife wound."

"No, we need to pretend we're working on my exhibit while we are off secretly researching the knife wound," she stated. "You'll need my help, and besides I can't have you galivanting off on your own, it will blow your cover."

"True."

"What do you say? Will you help me? Will you help us?"

"I would need to talk to people who were around when this happened, preferably first-hand witnesses, but are there any?" he asked doubtfully.

"Deputy Sheriff Lee Davidson, who was first on the scene, is now Sheriff Lee Davidson, and lives here in Amare. He's Vanessa's dad."

Liam recalled Vanessa mentioning that.

"There are also a couple of others who knew him very well that you can speak with," she said hoping to convince him. "One of them, you can meet tonight."

"I'll help, but on one condition?"

"Okay," she replied liking the sound of that.

"If we come up empty, we stop researching, and go back to working on your exhibit."

"Deal," she said reaching out her hand.

Liam pulled her over onto his lap.

"Thank you," she said kissing him on the cheek.

Chapter Eighteen

"Please, come in," she said warmly.

"Mom, Liam," said Rebecca. "Liam, my mom, Christine."

"A pleasure to meet you, Christine."

"I've been looking forward to meeting you, Liam," she said enthusiastically. "Please, follow me, I thought we'd sit outside on the deck."

"This is beautiful," said Liam looking over the landscape.

"Before my sister and I sold the farmland, we both agreed to keep several acres of land each, and have our own homes built on it," she explained then pointed. "Those trees go right along the back of our property, and behind them is a subdivision. The tree line to the north, separate our properties, and the one to the south, separates my property from a subdivision which is part of downtown."

"You could walk to the center of town from here," noted Liam.

"It takes about twenty minutes," she replied. "I wanted mine as close to town as possible, my sister wanted hers closer to the winery."

"They built my aunt's house first, and then my mother's," said Rebecca, "then they tore down the farmhouse."

"I didn't want to, but it needed so much work done to it, and besides, I wanted a new home to raise Rebecca and Glen, one with a pool with a large deck," she said with a smile.

"The farmhouse used to be right there, where the guest house and swimming pool are now," stated Rebecca motioning to them. "Personally, I think she made the right decision."

"The pool's amazing," sighed Liam.

"Did you bring your bathing suits?" asked Christine.

"We did, Mom," replied Rebecca, "but maybe we should talk first."

"Nonsense, you two go for a swim while I cook dinner, and we can eat down by the pool, and talk later."

Rebecca followed Liam to the guest room, where they changed before jumping into the water. Through the kitchen window, Christine watched them intently as she prepared the salad.

"You're not worried about your mom seeing us?"

"Seeing what?" she asked mischievously.

"For starters, you with your arms and legs around me, and kissing me."

"It's my mom, and I don't want to lie to her about you, us," she said frankly, then realized what she had said. "I'm sorry, I never thought about you, are you okay with it?"

"I was until I saw your mother taking photos on the deck," he noted. "Are they for the newspaper?"

"What!" cried Rebecca letting go, turning towards the house, and not seeing her. "Why you…?" she whispered noticing his grin. She jumped up and pushed his head under the water, when he surfaced, she put her arms around him and kissed him passionately "Are you sure you're okay with this?"

"I am," he replied, "and to be honest with you, it been difficult keeping my distance from you."

"Me too," she replied, wishing they didn't have to.

As they ate dinner, they talked about the town, and Christine apologized for her husband, Phil, being away.

"He says it's a conference, but I think it's more of an excuse to play a few rounds of golf with his friends," she revealed.

"You didn't want to go, Mom?"

"No, I was more interested in meeting Liam," she answered looking at him, "because I've heard so much about you."

"You have?" he asked glancing over at Rebecca.

"Just professionally," clarified Rebecca.

"Of course," agreed her mother, "although I've seen how you are both getting along privately."

"Mom!" screamed Rebecca melodramatically. "You're embarrassing me!"

"Really, you Rebecca?" asked Christine skeptically. "I severely doubt it. What do you think Liam, is she?"

"No," he replied with a laugh, "but she tried her best to act upset."

"Oh, so you're on my mom's side, and ganging up on me," she stated leaning towards him. "You wait and see, Mister!"

He tilted close to her, and kissed her, taking her by surprise. When she pulled away, she was blushing, and smiling.

After dinner, they changed and met Christine on the deck where she handed them each a glass of wine.

"On the phone, Rebecca updated me on what you two had spoken about earlier, and I just want to thank you for helping us out and looking into this for me."

"I'll do my best," replied Liam truthfully, "and hopefully we can get some answers for you."

"Thank you," she said sincerely.

"Can you tell me when you first met him?" asked Liam.

Christine took a sip of her wine and began. "1979, late July, early in the morning, there was a knock on the door, and I opened it, it was Jason Campbell and he asked to speak to my parents, so I called for them. He said he was wondering if they were looking for anyone to work on the farm or a handyman to fix it the place. During this time, my father was running the farm more as a hobby than a business and would sell excess goods to the local stores or at the farmer's market. We also had the winery up and running at this time, but he wasn't involved in that, nor was he interested. My parents took him around the farm, and when they came back, they told Tammy and I that they had hired him for the remainder of the summer and fall. Jason had a truck with a camper hitched to it, and my father told him to park it next to the worker's cabin and set it up there."

"What's a worker's cabin?" asked Liam.

"Years ago, we had farm workers that would stay for the summer and live in the cabin. It had several bedrooms, a kitchen, and a shower. But it hadn't been used for several years and was in disrepair," she explained, then continued. "He was a good worker and helped out on the farm and repaired whatever needed fixing. Before harvest, my father asked him if he wanted to stay on for the winter and spring. He told him he could live in the cabin and fix it up before the weather turned, and help with tending to the livestock, and repairing the barn and fences. Jason agreed, and worked throughout the winter and spring, then my father asked him to stay on for the summer and fall. And was going to ask him to stay on permanently and give him the cabin."

"Your parents liked him," stated Liam.

"They did," she agreed, "and they didn't like him being on his own, so they would invite him for dinner often. Eventually, he was so comfortable that he would drop by whenever he wanted and used to play board games with Tammy and I, he even watched us once in a while if my parents needed to be somewhere. Jason was like one of the family. When I saw him that first morning, he had a beard, long hair and looked like a hippie, but over time he shaved it off and cut it short. He was very handsome, and caught the eye of quite a few local girls, but never seemed to be interested. He made a few friends, and the one he became closest with was James Childwall. James was a few years older, but they had the same interests, and were both well-educated so they talked a lot about, well, everything."

Well educated, thought Liam, and working on a farm.

"Jason had a degree, and worked for a law firm," answered Rebecca as if reading his mind, "and yet, here he was, working on a farm."

Liam gave her an uneasy look.

"I'll get to that in a minute," confirmed Christine. "Saturday March 29, 1980, Heather Downs came to our house to play for the day. Before dinner, we walked with her through the field towards her house in town. On the way we passed Jason, who talked with us for a while, before leaving and heading back towards our house. We only walked with her as far as the dirt road, watched her cross it, and started back home. She was supposed to walk through the field for ten minutes, come out the other side into her subdivision, then walk another ten minutes to her house. An hour later, my mom received a call asking if Heather was staying for dinner; Heather never made it home. Everyone looked for her, but she was never found."

"Did they suspect Jason?"

"Someone had said that they had seen his white cube van driving down the dirt road around that time. They questioned him, and he confirmed he had driven that way but never saw her or anyone else," replied Christine. "You see he was running an errand for my father and always used are van."

"When he came back from talking with you in the field, he met your father?"

"He did. My father said he could run the errand tomorrow, but he said he would go now. They questioned him again, even searched the van and his place, but found nothing. The sheriff told him, and my parents, that they were just following procedure" explained Christine. "You must understand, the van was the only lead they had. There were no other leads to follow up on or suspects to interrogate. All they had was a drifter driving a van who was new to the town, and they knew as soon as they dropped Jason as a suspect, the case would go cold, and it did. He was never questioned again."

"Do you remember where he was coming from when you met him on the path?" asked Rebecca.

"If he told me, I don't remember," replied her mother. "Why do you ask?"

"It just seems odd, that where he was coming from, was where she went missing," replied Rebecca. "Did you always walk that way with Heather?"

"We did, almost every other Saturday. On the opposite Saturdays, we would go to her house and my father would pick us up, or sometimes Jason."

"Had you ever bumped into Jason on that path any other Saturday?"

"No, never, he usually had Saturdays off and would hang around his cabin," she answered. "Why are you asking Rebecca?"

"It feels like too much of a coincidence, just to be a coincidence."

"Are you saying he had something to do with it?" asked Christine surprised.

"I'm not sure, Mom. It's just that serial killers have been known to stalk their pray, learn their habits, that's all."

"But there were only two girls," stated her mom.

"That we know of?" suggested Rebecca. "Did they check other counties for missing girls.

"I don't know about that, you will need to ask the sheriff," said Christine, recognizing what was happening to her daughter.

"What do you think Liam?" asked Rebecca.

"I think it's a clever observation, and you've brought up questions that need to be answered."

Rebecca proudly smiled, then thought of something. "Mom, tell us about Amanda."

Her mother let out a deep sigh. "Amanda Peterson went missing on Tuesday July 15, on her way home from soccer practice. After practice, her and her friends would stop off at the candy shop on Main Street, then walk down Park Street, where she would leave them to cut through the Town Park; Amanda was never seen again."

"How did Jason become a suspect?" asked Liam.

"The girls had seen him on Victoria Street crossing over Park, he even honked his horn, and waved as he drove by. They brought him in for questioning, searched his place, and the van. They found nothing. He said he had passed all three girls, waved to them, then drove back to his cabin. By this time, he was well-known and liked by the townspeople, and no one could ever see him doing such a thing."

"What changed everyone's mind?" queried Liam.

"About six weeks later, someone called saying they had seen Amanda getting into a white cube van after she crossed Town Park. The witness also said she gave the driver her backpack, and he put it under the driver's seat, and that the driver was Jason. The police came to our farm, took the van, and searched it again. A backpack was found stuffed under the seat and it was hers. When they checked for fingerprints, they found hers and his on it. With the eyewitness, the bag, and fingerprints they went over to Jason's cabin to arrest him. The police said that he must have caught wind of the evidence they had and took his own life. When they searched his camper, they found clothing items belonging to the girls."

"Hold on, hold on, Mom! They searched the van and found nothing the first time then they receive an anonymous tip, and voila, they find the bag."

"Apparently, it was small and stuffed under the seat."

"Let's assume that was the case, and it was him. He just forgot about putting it under the seat?"

"Maybe," suggested her mother, "and it did have his fingerprints on it."

"What about the fact, that six weeks later, someone anonymously called this in," said Rebecca. "Are you telling me that isn't a strange coincidence?"

"I never said it was unanimous," stated her mother.

"You would have said their name if you had known who it was, you know everything about everyone. Plus, this town has an extremely healthy gossip line."

Christine smiled at her daughter.

"I'm with Rebecca on this," said Liam, "something doesn't add up."

"Oh, now your own my side," she teased.

"For now," he replied with a smile. "Do you have any background on Jason?"

"My parents said he was educated, a lawyer, and lived in Boston. He had a fiancé who lived in Worcester, who was killed at home during a robbery gone wrong. After that, he decided that he didn't want to live in the city anymore, and wanted to travel across New York, and work odd jobs. He definitely wasn't short of money."

"Do you think he may have been on the run?" asked Liam.

"No, he had no warrant out for his arrest, no criminal record, not even a ticket."

"I think he was hiding from someone," stated Rebecca adamantly.

Liam glanced over at her. "And you think they found him?"

"And targeted him," she added.

"Then why wouldn't he just leave?" wondered Liam.

"Maybe he didn't know who they were or what he was hiding from?"

"Before you two solve the mystery, today," said Christine tongue-in-cheek, "you should speak to Sheriff Davidson and James Childwall, and get the whole story."

"We will," replied Rebecca realizing they were speculating. "Mom, I've noticed you haven't disagreed with anything we've said."

"Fresh eyes, offer a fresh perspective," she answered.

"That's something my mother would say," divulged Liam.

"Then they'd probably get along like a house on fire," suggested Rebecca.

"Just one last question," declared Liam. "Why did the police buy into it so quickly?"

"I think it's better if you ask the sheriff that question," she replied, and stared at him curiously. "I don't want to put you on the spot, and it's okay if you don't have an answer or don't want to tell me, but what was your first impression of the wound?"

"It seemed an excessive way to kill yourself," he replied. "Which makes me believe it means something more, something unnatural, maybe even something supernatural."

"All right," said Christine nodding her head and content with his response. "I'm going to grab us another bottle of wine, and by the way, you two can stay in the guest house tonight."

"Who said we were staying?" asked Rebecca.

"I did. Besides, I think it might be a good idea to show Liam around the property tomorrow morning."

Rebecca waited for her to leave. "I think she's hoping you may see a spirit or have a premonition," she joked. "Can you see them during the day?"

"I don't think so."

Christine came back, filled their glasses, and took her seat. "Do you have any final questions about Jason Campbell?"

"I don't, Liam?"

He thought for a moment. "Can you give me any factual reasons why you believe he's innocent?"

"You two make a good team," she said admiringly. "How about I give you three, but don't ask me to explain them, you will need to figure them out on your own, okay?"

Liam nodded his head intrigued.

"First, his faith; second, he's right; and third, his note."

"Mother! That's it! And you're not going tell us?" she asked rhetorically before glancing over at Liam "I'm guessing she wants us to see if we uncover what she did, and in doing so, prove she's correct."

"You're definitely your mother's daughter," said Liam playfully.

"I'll take that as a compliment," she replied cheerfully then turned to her mother. "Liam's mom likes giving him riddles to figure out, too. You two should meet one day."

Christine smiled uneasily and refilled their wine glasses.

Chapter Nineteen

"That's strange," noted Rebecca.

"What is?" asked Liam.

"This chest is always in the spare room," she said looking at it then him. "It only contains blankets, maybe she didn't want you getting cold sleeping on the sofa."

"Well, you should pull one out for me," he replied humorously.

Rebecca strolled over to him, grabbed his hand, and led him to the bed. "Not tonight," she said kissing and undressing him.

Something woke Rebecca up. She glanced over at the clock, read 3 A.M., and noticed Liam wasn't lying next to her, A voice softly called her name. She got out of bed, slowly walked over to the open chest, and looked inside at the ladder. Rebecca heard her name being called again and proceeded down into the darkness. She noticed a light in the distance and strolled over to it. "Liam?"

"Rebecca?"

"What are we doing here?"

"Minutes ago, I heard my name being called and came down her."

"Are we alone?"

"No," answered a voice approaching from the darkness and stopping in front of them.

"Jason?" queried Rebecca.

"Yes," he replied, "please, follow the light."

"Rebecca are we in the basement?" whispered Liam.

"There is no basement," she confirmed, "but we are in a room."

Suddenly the room lit up, changed into a street, and they followed a couple talking as they climbed up stairs to the front door of a house.

"It's a lovely evening," said the girl.

"It is, Alicia," agreed the young man who they recognized as Jason.

"It's locked," she said with a puzzled look. "Didn't Maggie say she was leaving it unlocked?"

"She did," replied Jason trying it. "Wait, I have the spare." He pulled the key out and placed it in the lock. "Did you hear that?"

"What?"

Jason unlocked the door, and the four of them walked into the living room. Noticing the turned-over furniture, Jason and Alicia quickly ran into the bedroom, with Rebecca and Liam in tow Alicia screamed, as Jason looked on in horror at his fiancé's hands and feet bound to the bedposts, duct tape covering her mouth, and her robe open to reveal her young body sliced from her pubic mound to her chin, and the slit across her throat from ear to ear.

"Oh my god!" said Rebecca turning away and finding comfort in Liam's arms.

The room faded away and they followed Jason's voice inside a cabin where he was looking down at a large, black book resting on the kitchen table with a pentacle on its cover. "I've hid this, and you have to find it urgently," said the voice behind them. "Now we must hurry, come with me."

Rebecca and Liam followed him back to the ladder.

"I can only let you in here this one time," he explained. "I need you to remember what you saw and help me before it's too late. If White Witches can't free me, we can't free Maggie and the children, and we will be lost forever under an eternal spell of Darkness…Liam this is for you, it's mine…and this is for you to wear Rebecca, it's Maggie's," he said handing them each an item. "You have been chosen. Go, and trust no one. Darkness is coming, and he will be looking for you, be careful."

"Will we see you again?" asked Liam.

"Yes, but I will look much different," he replied. "Make sure you recognize me and remember Darkness will always try to trick and manipulate you." He stopped and listened momentarily. "I'm sorry to put such a dangerous burden on you, but you need to leave…Now!" he screamed.

Rebecca woke to the sounds of birds chirping and the sunlight on her face. She cuddled into Liam's chest as he gently put his arm around her.

Suddenly, she sat upright. "I had the scariest, weirdest dream," she said and briefly glanced over at the closed chest.

Liam sat up next to her. "Was I in it?"

"You were," she replied. I climbed down a ladder inside the chest, to a light, and—"

"I was there," he said. "I also climbed down the ladder."

Rebecca slowly opened her hand to reveal a black pentacle necklace. Liam lifted up his and showed her the Bible.

"Fuck me!" said Rebecca scared. "Is this the way it happens?"

"Sometimes, but not as vivid, and never with another living person."

"What should we do?" she asked anxiously.

"Get your laptop, and let's go to the desk," he instructed, "we need to type everything we heard and saw before we forget."

"I can't believe we remembered every detail, usually with dream you forget them shortly after or only remember bits and pieces," she said closing her laptop and strolling over to the chest with Liam. He carefully opened it, and proceeded to remove the blankets until it was empty. "Liam, was it real, a dream, a nightmare?"

"It has to be real, how else could we explain this," he said lifting up the Bible.

"I know," she whispered. "I'm really frightened, Liam."

Liam held her in his arms. "Don't worry, you will be safe with me."

"Did that really happen to his fiancé, Maggie?"

"That's one of the things we need to find out," stated Liam contemplating. "Let's get dressed."

"Can we take a swim first, I'm sweaty and a little freaked out, and I'm hoping the water will calm me down."

"All right," he said, and as they put their bathing suits on, he wondered about the origin of the chest.

"What shall we tell my mother?" asked Rebecca. "Jason said not to trust anyone."

"Well, it's your mother, what do you think we should do?"

"She won't say anything to anyone, so we should tell her, and maybe she can tell us something that can help us."

"Okay, but let me talk first," suggested Liam.

Rebecca nodded her head.

They ate breakfast in the solarium, talked about the house, the winery, and then the guest house. After Christine took the plates away, she filled up their coffees, and rejoined them.

"In the guest house, there's an antique chest, is that a family heirloom?"

"No, it was a gift for my mother from Jason. He gave it to her a week before he died," she revealed. "He asked her to take very good care of it and never throw it out. She said the same to me, and one day I will say the same to Rebecca."

"You've only used it to store blankets?" asked Rebecca.

"That's it."

"Nothing else we should know about it?" she probed.

"He made it by hand, and it took him a few weeks," she replied wondering where she was going with her questions.

"Do you know why he specifically asked you to keep it around?" asked Liam.

"No, I never really thought about it."

"Why did you move it to the guest house?" queried Rebecca.

"I thought it would remind you of the farmhouse that once sat there," she revealed not being completely honest.

Rebecca picked up on it immediately. "That may have been one reason why you put it there, but was the another?"

"What do you mean?" she asked.

"Oh, I don't know…maybe so Liam might connect with it…and go inside it and talk to a dead guy!"

"You talked with Jason inside the chest?" asked her mother, now glad she had put it there.

"No," answered Liam.

"No," repeated her mother confused.

"We both went down the rabbit hole, Mom, and it was fucking scary!"

"Watch your language young lady," said her mom sternly, then swiftly changed her tone. "Now, tell me everything."

They did, except what he had given them.

"Mom, do you know what any of it means?" asked Rebecca.

"I don't," she replied, realizing their journey had to be their own. "I knew she had been killed, but nothing more."

"Did you know he has a fu…a big, black book with a pentacle on it?"

"It's called a grimoire, and no, I didn't."

"What? A grimoire, as in a witch's magic spell book?"

"A Black Witch's magic spell book," corrected Christine.

"So he was a Black Witch?" asked Liam.

"I don't know for sure. Maybe he was, his fiancé was, or he was taking care of it for someone," suggested her mother. "But from what you've told me, I would say both of them probably were."

"Mom, witches don't exist!"

"You asked me my opinion," she said to her in her defense. "You've seen the book, you talked to him, he showed you things that happened before you were even born. How else could he have done that?"

Rebecca had no answer. "But how could he pull it off over forty-three years later?"

"The only way," said Liam thinking out loud, "is if he put a spell on the chest."

"But why pick us?" asked Rebecca looking at him.

"I honestly don't know," he replied.

"Mom?" she asked turning to her.

"Did he give you anything?"

"This is his," said Liam showing her the Bible.

"And this is Maggie's pentacle necklace," she said lifting it up from around her neckline.

Christine looked on and concealed her happiness. "They've chosen you to help them."

"Mom, we know that, he told us," stated Rebecca matter-of-fact.

Christine didn't expand on what she knew. "I can't offer you any more advice except to carry on as you see fit to do so, and the answers will come to you, and under no circumstances, do you tell anyone what we talked about this morning or last night.

"We won't," confirmed Rebecca quickly glancing over at Liam.

"Did you get your work at the museum sorted out?"

"We did, we spoke with Mia and offered her the position, then had a meeting with her and Brittany, and went through what they needed to do. Then explained to them that we would be reviewing the catalogue at the mansion, and coming in periodically to the museum," she explained. "So, we're covered."

"Sheriff Davidson wants to meet you tomorrow morning at nine at Burt's Diner, and James Childwall on Friday afternoon at three at his place. Make sure you call them both today and confirm."

"Will do," said Rebecca.

"What are your plans today?" asked Christine looking at Rebecca, who looked at Liam.

"Research."

Chapter Twenty

"Okay, where do we start?" asked Rebecca putting her laptop on the desk in the den.

"Let's go through the…encounter, unless you want to choose another word, and list key questions."

"Encounter is fine," she replied and read out the details as Liam wrote the questions.

"When I read them, you type them."

"All right…ready."

"Who is the woman entering with Jason? Maggie's murder: the where, when, why, and what was stolen? When and why did Jason start his trek across New York State? Do only witches' own grimoires? Who owned the grimoire on the kitchen table? Where did Jason hide it? Who are the White Witches and how can they help us? Why did he give you Maggie's pentacle necklace? Why did he give me the Bible?"

"Did you look inside it?"

"I didn't, good point," said Liam undoing the clasp, opening it, and catching three photographs before they fell out, then reviewed them with Rebecca.

"That's Jason and Maggie," she said as she watched him put it at the back. "That's them with Alicia," she said. "And there's Maggie, Jason, Alicia, and a woman we don't know, another woman with a young girl that we don't know, and a man we don't know. The adults look like they are all in their late twenties, except this woman, she looks a little bit older, the man as well. The girl looks around ten."

Liam looked at the photo, then closely at the younger unknown women, then glanced up at Rebecca with a peculiar look.

"Liam, what is it?"

"This woman in the picture, it's my mother, Anna," he whispered in disbelief.

"Are you sure?" asked Rebecca looking at her.

"I'm sure."

"So, she knows them."

"I guess."

"Did she ever talk about Jason or Maggie?"

"Never."

"What are we going to do?"

"We have to go to Worcester?"

"When?"

Liam went silent and thought for a few minutes about the best way to proceed. "For now, we'll add my mom to our list of questions, and meet with her in person when necessary."

"Okay," she said. "We should also add my mother's three facts: his faith, he's right, and his note."

"And on another page add our general questions for the sheriff, about the coincidences, the caller—"

"I remember them," she said jotting them done.

"And add Darkness, and the knife wounds."

"Done. Now let me quickly categorize them," she said taking a minute. "People – Jason, Alicia, Anna; Murders – Maggie's, Jason's; Witches – Black, White, Darkness, knife wounds; Items – grimoire, necklace, Bible, photographs," she read off. "And, if we are meeting the sheriff and James Childwall regarding Jason, we should eliminate researching him and his murder for now. And, your mom, and I am also going to suggest Alicia, too, because we can look into her when we meet with your mom. Which just leaves us Maggie's murder, the Witches, and the Items, to research. What do you think?"

"I think that's a good start,"

"Do you want to research them together or split them up?"

"We have all day, so no rush, let's do it together."

"I was hoping you were going to say that," she said relieved. "Let's start with Maggie's robbery end murder."

They went online, searched, and found several news articles on the murder of Maggie O'Brien, dated July 6, 1978, and read them. Once they finished, Rebecca printed them, then looked over at Liam.

"I know you weren't born when this happened, but did you ever hear about this?"

"No."

"Do you know the road?"

"I do, and it's not far from where my parents live."

"All right" she said then reviewed the articles. "They all say the same thing: a burglary gone wrong, that the individual panicked, and stabbed her. They believe he was probably a junkie because they found needles in the backyard. That it was meant to be a quick grab and run, and the items that he stole, were going to be sold for drugs to feed his addiction."

"What where the items he took?"

"Money from her wallet, jewelry, antique silverware, and rare gold coins."

"Does that sound like a grab and run to you?"

"No, not really."

"I would say yeah, if he only took the cash, maybe the jewelry, but the silverware and coins? He would have to go to a pawn shop to sell those, which he definitely wouldn't want to do."

"It says that he came through the bedroom window, which means he climbed over the neighbor's fence. And this article states she had no bruises on her body or skin under her fingernails, which means she didn't put up a fight. It also says that she didn't have any cuts or bruises on her head, which means he didn't knock her out, and must have taken her by surprise. Which would suggest, he used something like chloroform to render her unconscious," suggested Rebecca. "Implying it was planned and the thief was lucid."

"Maggie's unconscious. He carries her onto the bed, ties her up, tapes her mouth, then robs the place," said Liam piecing it together. "Let's assume he was wearing a mask, why kill her?"

"Maybe his face wasn't covered?" suggested Rebecca.

"Okay, say he wasn't, same question, why kill her? He didn't hurt her, rape her, he just robbed her. Is she going to be so worried about those items that she'll want the police to make it a priority, and on the other hand, are the police going to comb the city looking for him, if it is a him."

"No, not for a robbery," admitted Rebecca, "they would probably wait and see it the silverware or coins showed up at a pawn shop."

"So why kill her?" asked Liam knowing the answer.

"To make it look like a robbery gone wrong," stated Rebecca. "Which would mean…? He was there to kill her," whispered Rebecca.

"Yes, he took those items and tossed furniture around the place only to make it look like a robbery and not a murder."

"And he planted the needles to make the thief look like a desperate junkie."

"So, we both agree it was an intentional, planned murder. Now, they reported it as only a stabbing, which it was, but he sliced her up. Why kill her up like that? Why not just cut her throat?" he asked looking over at Rebecca and thinking.

In her mind, Rebecca recalled how Maggie's body looked. "Ritual," she murmured slowly, then searched for the pictures of Jason's body. "He's performing a ritual!" she cried excitedly. "Look, both the exact same cuts!"

"A ritual," repeated Liam. "It's a ritual."

"But, why her? Why did he pick her?" asked Rebecca sitting down and playing with her necklace.

"Because she's a Black Witch," said Liam looking at the pentacle on her necklace.

"Black Witch?" asked Rebecca doubtfully. "I'm having a difficult time believing witches actually exist."

"We went down the rabbit hole and talked with her dead fiancé."

"I know what you're saying, if that can happen, then witches can be real too."

"I am, but also, how could it have happened?"

"Something magically, mystical, supernatural?" she said throwing out words. "You said, a spell."

"The grimoire contains a witch's spells," said Liam leading her on his train of thought, "and Jason had one. He also made that chest and told your family not to throw it out."

"All those years ago, he put a spell on the chest, and last night he put us under it and pulled us in."

"Which would explain why we he said we could only go into the chest once, and why he was so limited in what he could tell us."

"And why he was so desperate for our help. If we ignored him and passed it off as a bad dream, his spell would have been in vain, and they'd be lost forever," explained Rebecca.

"We know the how, when, and where of Maggie's murder. The questions are: Who is the thief? Why did they want her, a Black Witch, killed? And, why the ritual?"

"Liam, was Jason running away from this killer, and did he catch up with him?"

"Hmm," he said smiling at her. "I was only thinking about Maggie, but you're right, the killer found Jason and performed the same ritual on him."

"Does that make Jason a Black Witch too?"

"He has a grimoire and can cast spells."

"It does," she confirmed. "Which means the killer found and performed the same ritual on two Black Witches."

"Following this logically, if he made Maggie's murder look like a robbery gone wrong, then he would make Jason's murder look like a suicide."

"A killer's occult suicide, who was a 'Servant of Satan,'" she clarified. "He didn't abduct those girls and wasn't 'called to sacrifice innocence in His name.' It was meant to look that way."

Chapter Twenty-One

"There he is," said Rebeca leading Liam to the back of the diner. "Hey, Sheriff, this is Liam."

"Hello, Liam, nice to finally meet you, I've heard a lot about you."

"Pleasure to meet you, Sheriff."

"Please, call me Lee, and have a seat," he offered. Rebecca's mom contacted me about the information you are looking for regarding Jason Campbell, and I have it here in this file. She also said you may have some questions."

"We do," replied Rebecca.

"You were the first one to arrive at the scene?" asked Liam.

"I was." he confirmed. "We arrived around at his residence 10 p.m., the door was open, so we proceeded inside and found the deceased."

"We've reviewed the photos, was he on a table?"

"It was his kitchen table, and what was odd about that other than killing himself on it, was he had moved the table prior," he explained. It used to run the length of the kitchen, but he had placed it on angle."

"Do you know which direction?"

"I would say east to west."

"Were his feet facing east or west?"

"East," replied Lee, looking at him curiously. "Does that mean something?"

"I don't know, but you're right, it's strange that he would deliberately move the table," commented Liam.

"Is there anything else you found peculiar?"

"After he sliced his throat, the hand he was holding the knife in was on the left side of the table, on the floor."

"And?" queried Rebecca.

"He was right-handed," stated the sheriff.

"Didn't that raise suspicion?" asked Liam.

"Sure, but they said it was probably part of his ceremony that it had to be done with his right hand, like the moving of the table," he replied. "There was something else odd."

"What?" asked Rebecca enthusiastically.

"Where the knife cut the bone, there should have been some metal particles found in the autopsy."

"There wasn't any?"

"There was, but they were gold."

"Gold!" cried Rebecca "How did they get there?"

The sheriff said nothing and looked at them.

"The only way they could, is if the knife he used had a gold blade," answered Liam.

"So the knife at the scene wasn't the one he used?" asked Rebecca.

"No," replied Lee, "but it had his blood on it."

"To make it look like he had used it," declared Rebecca. "What did they say about that?"

"They said the knife didn't leave any metal shavings because it was too sharp."

"And just ignore the gold one?"

"Yeah, pretty much."

Rebecca glanced over at Liam, who was thinking, then at Lee. "Was there anything else suspicious?"

"There was one other thing. On the suicide note he left, his signature didn't match, Jason always connected the 'J' to the 'a.' I believe someone else wrote it and signed his name. And before you ask, they just said that people don't always sign their name the exact same way."

"Was him having black magic and witchcraft books wasn't unusual?" asked Liam.

"No, he liked reading them," he confirmed. "He also had books on UFO sightings, Bigfoot, that sort of thing, and was always watching documentaries about them."

"You knew him then?" asked Rebecca.

"I knew him, but we didn't hang out, he was a little older than me. When I did see him, he was always friendly to me, and he'd walk back to town with me after church on Sundays. We'd mostly talk about sports, and he'd ask me what it was like being a deputy, and if I had a girlfriend. He was a really nice guy."

"If you don't mind me asking, what religion was he?"

"Catholic," replied Lee, "a devout catholic. He didn't believe in missing mass, cheating, or divorce, and read his Bible a lot."

"He told you this?" asked Rebecca.

"Well," said the sheriff with a chuckle, "he would often tell me to keep going to church, never cheat on your girlfriend, and if I marry someone never get divorced. And it wasn't in a preachy-way, it was more like older-brother advice. Then he would quote something from the Bible which made us laugh." Lee stopped and remembered him fondly. "He couldn't have done that to those girls, or himself, I know that."

Liam looked on as Rebecca reached out her hand and squeezed Lee's. "We know that, and hopefully we can prove it."

Liam waited a few moments before continuing. "Were there any thoughts on the cut itself, what it meant?"

"No, we didn't see the relevance."

"How about the call you received about the backpack?" asked Rebecca.

"The call came from a payphone in Geneva. It was an older person, male. He said that he was in Amare working the day the girl went missing, and that had seen her girl getting into the van. He explained that he had been on vacation, just got back, and seen the pictures of the missing girls."

"He didn't leave a name or address?"

"The man said he didn't want the press hounding him or have to go and testify, and wanted to be left alone," answered Lee. "We had originally searched that van and his camper thoroughly. Sure, the backpack was stuffed under the seat, but I'm positive we have found it the first time."

"And the girls' clothes in the camper?"

"Assuming he had abducted them and buried their bodies, it didn't make sense he would have kept articles of their clothing in his camper. They said he was keeping them as souvenirs, which murderers have been known to do."

"When you say 'they,' I'm guessing the people in charge of the investigation?"

"Mostly Sheriff Baker, the mayor, and some town councilors."

"They wanted the investigation closed quickly, and for it to go away?" asked Liam.

"Amare depends on tourists, and girls going missing, and a murder on the loose, isn't good for businesses."

"So all these coincidences were overlooked?" asked Rebeca.

"And quickly forgotten," added Lee.

"Did you check in any other counties for missing girls?" she asked.

"We did, but there wasn't any."

"One last question for me," said Liam. "Did you look into his fiancé's murder?"

"I did. She was stabbed during a home burglary, and Jason and her best friend, Alicia, found her body."

"Could you get us the file on her?"

"Sure, I know someone, but I don't see the connection?"

"I'm interested in how she was stabbed," disclosed Liam.

"I'll make a call today," confirmed the sheriff leaning in, "and we're keeping this just between us and your mom, right?"

"Just the four of us," assured Rebecca.

Chapter Twenty-Two

"I'll grab my laptop, and meet you at the deck," said Rebecca walking toward the back door.

Liam walked to the kitchen, poured two glasses of juice, and headed outside. "Oh, I see you met my new friends," said Liam looking at the two young girls before sitting on the steps and turning to them.

"Hi, Liam," they both said.

"Hello."

"This is Mandy, and her friend Hetty," acknowledged Rebecca.

"Ah, you got their names."

"We like you Liam, and Rebecca, too," said Mandy, "and we were told we can trust you, right Hetty?"

Hetty nodded her head shyly.

"I'm glad to hear that," he replied with a grin. "Can I get you some juice?"

"No thank you, Liam," answered Mandy. "It was too hot in the sun, so we've been playing on this swing for a while, and we have to get going now. We just wanted to see you both before we left."

"That was nice of you," said Rebecca as she watched two girls jump off the swing, head down the steps passed Liam, and turn.

"Bye," they both said with a wave.

"Bye," replied Rebecca and Liam, watching them leave.

"Do you know them?"

"No," replied Rebecca, "they must be new in town."

"You don't know everyone?" teased Liam.

"Ha, ha," she replied sarcastically as she got up and sat next to him, then opened up the sheriff's file and reviewed it with him.

"Not much more than what we already know," suggested Liam. "The toxicology report says there was no alcohol or drugs present."

"It has the list of the witchcraft and black magic books, should I order them?"

"Yeah, that's a good idea, and we can see if there's something in them."

"Or should I ask Sheriff Lee and see if I can get Jason's copies?"

"Actually, that's a better idea, he may have written something in one of them."

"Okay," she replied making a note of it. "What did you think about our conversation with Lee?"

"It's obvious that Sheriff Baker and the mayor wanted to get this investigation closed quickly and move on, and he had some concerns that fell on deaf ears."

"Like Jason being right-handed and the knife," said Rebecca. "He also told us about his friendship with him and Jason's faith."

Liam looked over at her. "Faith?"

Rebecca looked at him, then searched through the file in her laptop. "His faith," she read out. "That's what my mom said."

"Sheriff Lee told us Jason was a devout Catholic."

"Wouldn't that make Maggie one, they were engaged?"

"Probably," replied Liam thinking. "Isn't suicide a mortal sin in the Catholic religion?"

"I believe it is," said Rebecca quickly looking it up. "Yeah, it is. So he wouldn't have killed himself knowing he would end up in hell."

"What does the Catholic religion say about seeing a loved one in Heaven?" asked Liam waiting for her to search for it.

"I'm paraphrasing, but the New Testament says that you will be reunited with your families and loved ones…which means he would never see Maggie again."

"I believe we've just strengthened our argument that he was murdered."

Maggie flipped through the sheriff's file. "Here's the note and his signature. Note, was my mom's second fact. Her third was, 'he's right,' right about what?"

Liam looked at her as they contemplated what Jason was right about.

"It's not what he's right about, but that he's right-handed!" stated Rebecca.

"Of course," said Liam nodding approvingly.

"My mom also believed Jason couldn't have done this either."

"Okay, so now we all agree he was murdered, but by whom and why?"

"Maybe we should wait and see what James Childwall has to say before we tackle those questions?"

"That a good point," agreed Liam. "Let's review the other outstanding items."

"Well, we looked up Black Witches, White Witches, and Darkness, but it was general information. We said we needed to find someone who is a Black or White witch. The question is how? Next, the pentacle necklace, it's available to buy online. We said that it has a special meaning because it's Maggie's, but not sure what it's for or why I have to wear it. The Bible, again, we know it belonged to Jason. It was special to him because he was religious, and Lee said he used to read it often and quote from it. We also now know he was a devout catholic who wouldn't commit suicide. We reviewed the photos, and there was nothing with the individuals or in the background that stood out, with the exception of your mother being in one of them. We did find out Alicia was Maggie's best friend and agreed we would talk to her and your mom in person. In regard to the grimoire, it is a witch's spell book, but we had a couple of issues: finding Jason's and what we need to do with it when we do? That's it."

"Okay, add gold-bladed knife, positioning of the table, Jason's books, Maggie's file, and knife-wound meaning, to it," he said glanced over at her typing. "Am I missing anything?"

"I'm thinking we may need to talk with my mom again, I get the feeling she's hiding something."

"All right, add her to the list."

"You think so, too?"

"I do," he confirmed. "She did set up the meeting with the sheriff, knowing he would share what he knew, which is probably the same person she got her information from. So I don't believe she's hiding something from us about the case, it's something else, and I'm not sure what."

"I get that feeling, too," she said. "What's next?"

"You phone the sheriff and ask if we can borrow the books, and maybe call it a day, and start early tomorrow morning?" he suggested.

"I like that plan," she said standing "While I call the sheriff, you grab your bathing suit."

They walked down Park Street to her place, changed, then headed to the beach.

"Hi, guys," said Vanessa, who introduced her children to Liam before letting them go and play with their friends. "I heard you had breakfast with my dad this morning?"

"We did?" replied Rebecca.

"He said he wanted to meet Liam and welcome him to the town."

"Yeah, my mom was speaking with him, and he told her, so she let me know and I called him."

"He's a very nice man," said Liam.

"Yeah, he likes you, too" replied Vanessa. "He said you have a 'good head on your shoulders,' and trust me, that's a huge compliment coming from him."

"Thank you, that's very kind of him," said Liam giving Rebecca a look-at-me go expression.

"Liam, I don't think there's enough room on this beach for us and your ego," joked Rebecca and tenderly touched his arm.

Which didn't go unnoticed by Vanessa. "What are you two up to tonight?"

"Not much, just going to take it easy."

"I'll probably take the kids to the concert in the park and let them run around the playground."

"I forgot that was on," admitted Rebecca, and talked about who was performing.

"The lasagna will take about an hour to heat up," said Liam.

"Good, then we have time to go buy a good bottle of wine."

"Wait a second?" asked Liam going to the library, returning, and showing her what he had in his hand.

"A key?"

"Not just a key, but a key to the wine cellar."

"No way! He gave you that?"

"He most certainly did," he said as she followed him to the basement. "He also told me to help myself to as much of the wine as I wanted, and to take anything that was left home with me, as he had no need for it. So, I'm guessing there are only a few bottles." Liam opened the door, turned on the light, and looked down at the rows of bottles then at Rebecca.

"You're going to need to rent a truck to take all this home," she gasped before walking between the rows, "there must be over two thousand bottles. There are reds, whites, rosés, dessert, sparkling...come here, look at all the different champagnes he has."

Liam looked over her shoulder. "I'm no sommelier, but I'm guessing these are excellent and expensive."

"Me neither, but I think you're right," confirmed Rebecca. "I'm thinking red." She walked to the red section looked down and picked one out.

"Why that one?"

"Because I like the bottle design, the name 'Château Mouton Rothschild,' the year, 1945, the 'V' with 'Année de la Victoire' written within it, and it's a Bordeaux."

"The year of victory," he translated.

"Yes," she replied, "and hopefully, this will be our year…you know what? Let's take two bottles."

They locked the cellar, stopped by the kitchen, then climbed the stairs and went outside onto the front terrace. Liam put the glasses on the table, took one of the bottles from Rebecca, opened it, and filled their glasses.

"Cheers."

"Cheers," said Liam clinking her glass.

"Mm, this is quite good," sighed Rebecca, "and perfect for admiring such a lovely sunset."

Liam gazed at the setting sun's rays lighting up her face. "You look beautiful."

"Thank you," she said happily. "Come and move a little closer to me."

Liam did, and with her free hand, held his. He slowly lifted it, softly kissed it, before placing it back onto his thigh. She smiled, kissed his cheek, then put her head on his shoulder.

Chapter Twenty-Three

"Rebecca, wake up…wake up, Rebecca," pleaded a quiet, young voice. "Rebecca…wake up."

Rebecca stirred and looked over at Liam who was still sleeping.

"Rebecca, follow me, follow me."

She sat up in bed and looked at the young girl standing in the doorway. "Hetty, is that you?"

"Quickly," begged Hetty walking out the room.

Rebecca got out of bed, followed her out, and down the stairs.

"We don't have much," said Hetty grabbing her hand and leading her into the den. "The picture, the girl, you need to ask about the girl in the picture." Hetty looked towards the door. "It's here."

"What's here?"

"Darkness," she said in a scared voice. "Take the picture and show it to your mom. We have to go."

Hetty pulled her out of the room, up the stairs, and ran with Rebecca towards the room. A black mist seeped through the back door, chased after them, and grabbed Hetty.

"Don't let go of me, Rebecca!" cried Hetty. "Don't let go!"

Rebecca tried to pull the young girl free.

Suddenly, an evil spirit with a demonic face and black eyes appeared. "Let her go!" it screamed in a satanic voice.

Rebecca fell back to the floor in fear, let go of the picture, then crawled into the room before running and jumping onto the bed screaming for Liam.

Rebecca abruptly woke up, sat upright, and promptly looked over at the closed door, then carefully around the room, before stopping on Liam who was sleeping peacefully. She lay down next to him, placed her head on his chest, then took his arm and put it around her. She eventually fell asleep. When she woke the following morning, she was alone in the bed. and was about to call out his name.

"I made us some coffee," he said coming towards her then suddenly stopping. "What's wrong?"

"Hold me," she said.

Liam put the coffees on a table, lay next to her, and held her as she told him about her nightmare.

"It was a dream, right?" she asked nervously.

Liam didn't answer and sat up.

"Liam?"

"Wait here."

Rebecca watched him get out of bed, walk out of the room, and when he returned, hand her the photo. "This was just outside the room on the floor."

"Oh fuck!" she cried. "Liam, I'm scared."

Liam comforted her.

"If it wasn't a dream, then that Darkness, that Demon, whatever the fuck you want to call it, is real."

"I'm afraid so," he replied.

"And Hetty, what the fuck is that about?"

"I don't know, but we'll find out, okay?"

"She was terrified, and I let go of her."

"We'll help her."

"How?"

"We'll find where he took her and get her back."

Rebecca nodded her head. "I don't want to be alone."

"I'm here," he said reassuring her.

She looked at the picture. "Who's this girl?"

"I don't know, but apparently your mom does."

Liam went to the chest of drawers, took out a T-shirt, and handed it to her. "Come on, I'll make us some breakfast."

Rebecca put on the shirt, picked up her coffee, and quietly followed him downstairs. In silence, she sat and watched him cook.

"Are you okay?" he asked putting a plate of food in front of her.

"I feel better now," she replied with a smile.

They had just finished eating when they heard a knock on the door. Rebecca peeked around the corner.

"It's the sheriff," she said panicking. "What should I do?"

"Go upstairs, get dressed, and I'll bring him into the kitchen."

Liam waited till she was in the bedroom before opening the door. "Morning, Sheriff."

"Good morning, Liam."

"Would you like to come in, I just made some coffee."

"I'd love to," he replied.

"How do you like it?"

"Cream, and two sugars, please," he replied looking around. "Is Rebecca here?"

"Yeah, she just in the bathroom," he answered then noticed her coming. "Here she is."

"Morning, Lee."

"Hey, Rebecca, you decided to enjoy the weather this morning?"

"Hmm?" she asked confused.

"You left your car at home?"

"Oh yes, yes I did, it was a wonderful walk," she lied. "Can I get a cup?"

Liam gave them their coffees then sat with them.

"I've got that file for you," said Sheriff Lee, "before I hand it to you, how did you know?"

"That she would have the same wounds?" asked Rebecca.

"Yeah."

"We had our suspicions," said Liam.

"Well, here it is," he said handing it to them.

"This someone, who got you this?" asked Liam.

"He's a detective in Boston, and also my cousin," said Lee. "Why, is there something else you need?"

"Do you think you can ask him if there were any murders or suicides that have similar wounds to this, maybe involving witchcraft or the supernatural?"

"Around the same time as this?"

"Yeah, in the seventies, early eighties."

"Okay," he replied then glanced over at Rebecca. "I brought all the books from his cabin, including the ones you asked for, they're in a box by the front door."

"Thanks, Lee."

"How are things going?"

"We think Maggie's death was not a robbery gone wrong, but planned and deliberate.

"Do you believe there's a connection between the two killings?"

"We do, and we also think it's the same killer," replied Rebecca.

"I'm getting the feeling that you don't believe it's some crazy, fanatic, Satan worshipper looking for attention?"

"No," said Liam, "these killings have purpose and meaning to him, with an end result."

"End result?" asked the sheriff.

"If he's not crazy, then he's getting something out of it, otherwise why do it?"

"He's benefiting somehow?"

"It's just a theory," stated Rebecca, "but we think so."

"All right," said the sheriff standing, "I'll let you two get back to it, and if there is anything else you need, don't hesitate to call me."

"Thanks, we will," said Rebecca getting ready to stand.

"Please stay seated and finish your coffee, I can see myself out," he said starting to leave, stopping halfway, and turning. "I want you both to know I hope you find this son of a bitch, for their sake, and mine…Have a nice morning."

They opened the file and reviewed it.

"It says here that gold particles were found on her bones and were from the knife used," noted Rebecca.

"Did the toxicology report anything unusual?"

"Same as Jason's, no alcohol or drugs present," she replied closing the file. "At least we've got proof that she was murdered the same way, with probably the same weapon, which means we have a connection between to the two killings."

"We do," Liam agreed looking at her. "Before we go online, why don't you give your mom a call first?"

Rebecca grabbed her phone, called her mom, and put it on speaker. "Hey, Mom, you're on speaker, and I have Liam next to me. How are you doing?"

"Good, dear, how are you?"

"Fine, there's something I need to ask you something."

"All right."

"We found three old pictures in the Bible, and it looks like they were taken in the late seventies. One is of Maggie and Jason, the other is of them and Alicia, and the last one is of the three of them, plus Liam's mom, Anna, another slightly older lady with a young girl, and a man. I was wondering if you know anything about it?"

Her mom was silent.

"Mom, are you there?"

"I am Rebecca, I was just thinking," she said tentatively. "Can you bring the photo over; I would need to see it?"

"Sure, when?"

"How about Sunday afternoon?"

"Mom, it's only Thursday?"

"I know, I know, but I have plans today, your busy tomorrow, and I have plans Saturday."

"All right, what time?"

"Say around three, and we can have an early dinner."

"Sounds good, see you then. Love you, bye."

"Love you too, bye."

Rebecca hung up and looked at Liam. "She knows something, she seemed nervous, didn't she?"

"She did."

"She seemed hesitant to meet us sooner?"

"I would say so."

"I guess we'll find out Sunday," she said letting it go. "I need a shower and some fresh clothes. How about we go to my place, and we can do the research there? You can even take a shower with me," she offered with a kiss.

Chapter Twenty-Four

"Let's do a search on the knife first," said Liam. As Rebecca turned on her laptop, he looked out at the families enjoying the beach.

"Maybe we can go for a swim or a walk after we finished?" she suggested, noticing his gaze.

"I think that's a great idea," he said smiling at her, "but first, the gold-bladed knife."

Rebecca quickly typed in the words. "Liam, there are hundreds on here, you can even get them custom made."

"Search and see if any were found in an archeological dig in the 1900s, actually try the 1970s first."

"Here, in the US?"

"Yeah."

"Okay," she replied doubtfully. "Nothing."

"Look and see if there were any digs around that same time in New York State…or Massachusetts."

"Hmm, that's odd," she replied. "It says there were a few in both, but what antiquities could they possibly be digging for there."

"Is it the same archeologist?"

"It is, a Dr. Edmund Brown," she replied, "but it says he died ten years ago."

"Did your parents know him?"

"Probably. Let's make a note of his name, the dig locations, and dates."

"Done, next, the knife wound," she said looking at him. "Maybe we should find a symbologist and ask them?"

"That's a good idea, put that down," he said thinking. "For now, let's wait and see if the sheriff comes back with any additional information before contacting one."

"Okay," she said making a notation. "The positioning of Jason's table. Do you think that's important?"

"I do, because the killer did it deliberately, although it's not a priority for us right now."

"Do you want me to put that down?"

"I do, and that we will eventually need to get a map of the Finger Lakes, Massachusetts, and the Northeast States."

"Done, finding Jason's grimoire, we can't research that online," she said glancing up. "I believe that answer will present itself when its ready to."

Liam smiled at her. "Vanessa was right, you are quite astute."

"I will take that as a compliment," she said reaching over and kissing him before returning to the last item. "Oh, you may want to take that back, I forgot the books at your place," she said wondering why she had. "Actually, I don't remember seeing the box by the front door."

"I moved it to the Library, I thought we had enough on our plate today, and could review them tomorrow morning."

"Good, then let me wrap this up then," she said happily. "Review the books tomorrow morning, meet James Childwall tomorrow afternoon, and my mother on Sunday afternoon. What about your mother and Alicia?"

"I'll wait till after we meet with your mom before calling her."

"Duly noted," she said turning off her laptop and closing it. "Swim?"

"Let's go," he confirmed as they went inside and changed.

"The water's so refreshing," said Rebecca dunking the back of her head and staring up at the sky, "and it's such a beautiful day."

"Not a cloud in the sky," stated Liam laying on his back.

"Tonight, why don't we have dinner on the boardwalk, watch the sunset, and you can crash at my place?" she suggested. "I'm still a little shaken from last night to go back to the mansion."

"I understand," he said supportively, "but I'd have to go back and get changed, all I have are the shorts and shirt I wore here."

"You'll be fine, besides it's summertime, and casual is in. Which is why I am going to wear a cute, light, short summer dress, just for you," said Rebecca swimming up to Liam and putting her arms around him."

"I like you in a dress."

"I know you do," she said with a mischievous smile, "and before you say it, dinner is my treat. It's the least I can do, after cooking me lasagna, and helping you drink two bottles of delicious wine."

"I didn't actually make the lasagna; I just heated it up."

"But it was the thought that counts."

"All right," he replied. "I just hope the restaurant is an expensive one?"

"Why do you say that?"

"Those two delicious bottles of wine you downed—"

"With your help."

"With my help, on the open market, start at fourteen thousand dollars up to twenty thousand."

"What?" she asked giggling. "You're kidding me, right?"

"I kid you not," he replied. "I looked it up while you were putting on your bikini."

"I wonder how much all that wine in the cellar is worth?" she wondered "And they're all yours."

"Are they? I wasn't expecting to take them."

"He told you to take what you don't drink."

"Won't your mother want them for the potential B&B or inn?"

"No, she'll stock the cellar with wines from her vineyard, and force the guests to drink it," she revealed with a chuckle.

"I'd have to get rid of some of my furniture at my home to fit it all in," joked Liam.

Rebecca laughed with him, and when they stopped, kissed him full on the mouth before slowly pulling away.

"I think people on the beach can see you?"

"Then I better not disappoint them," she replied kissing him again.

Chapter Twenty-Five

"I was so pleased to see the great job Brittany and Mia are doing at the museum," said Rebecca following Liam inside the mansion.

"It looks amazing," replied Liam as his phone rang. "It's my sister."

She left him, went into the library, and started to unpack the books.

"My sister is dropping off my niece and nephew off tomorrow at ten and picking them up Sunday evening."

"Do you think that's wise?" asked Rebecca watching him walk towards her.

"I really can't say no, now, I promised her weeks ago."

"I didn't mean watching them, I meant them staying here?" she asked with an uncomfortable look.

"Are you suggesting we should stay in a hotel?"

"Yeah, maybe for the night."

"I'll think about it," he said considering her recommendation before looking at the books.

"These are the occult books, there are six of them," she said pointing. "Over here, we have books on UFO sightings, Roswell, Bigfoot, the Egyptian Pyramids, Renaissance painters—"

"Well, he had a broad range of interests."

"That's an understatement," she declared picking up a book, "and last but not least, a book on how to make chests."

Liam took it from her. "Your mom said he was handy building things, I guess he needed a little help with making her chest."

"What should I do with them?"

"Let's put everything except the occult books back in the box," replied Liam throwing the chest one in, "I don't think we will find anything in them that will help us."

Rebecca threw the last one in, sat, and gazed at the six books. "How about we take three books each and then swap them?"

"All right," he replied giving her three, sitting down, and opening the first one.

Three hours later Rebecca turned the last page. "Nothing," she said frustrated. "These are just general information books on witch hunts, witchcraft, Salem, black magic."

"It's a bust," confirmed Liam sitting back in his chair.

Suddenly, there was a knock on the door. Liam left and walked back in with the sheriff.

"Hi. Lee."

"Hey, Rebecca, how's things?"

"Not bad for a Friday," she replied pleasantly.

"I can't stay long, I just wanted to drop this file off as soon as possible, I think it may be very helpful."

"What is it?" asked Rebecca.

"In 1976 in Boston, there was a case nicknamed 'The Witch Trial,' where three men were charged with killing a woman which the defense argued was a suicide." The sheriff paused momentarily. "The woman's body had been sliced the same way as Maggie and Jason's."

"Really? I don't believe it," she said taking it from him opening the file.

"Was there a knife found at the scene?" asked Liam.

"Yes, and I believe she was still clutching it," he replied. "The full transcripts are in there."

"Thank you, Sheriff," said Liam, "we'll go through it."

"If you do have any questions or need additional information, please don't hesitate to call me," he said starting for the door.

"We will," said Rebecca watching Liam leave the library with him and waiting patiently for him to return.

They reviewed the documents, made notes, identified key issues, then created a high-level summary.

"Let's recap," said Liam leaning back in his chair.

"The high-level summary," clarified Rebecca. "The defense claimed that the female, Eleanor Peabody, was partying with the three men around town that evening, then invited them back to her place for booze, drugs, and group sex. When they left her apartment, she was heard saying goodbye to the three men, indicating she was still alive. The following morning, her twenty-five-year-old daughter, Lenore, found her naked body on the floor, lying on top of a white sheet with a black pentacle sprayed on it. The defense stated that throughout the evening she had been heard claiming to be a witch, who practiced witchcraft and black magic, and had sacrificed her body to Satan,"

"That's excellent," said Liam. "What are there the key issues we identified, start with the two witnesses?"

"In point form," she said and began. "A young man returning home from work saw the three men leaving Eleanor's apartment, and her saying goodbye to them before closing her door…Prosecution argued that the witness never saw the victim, only heard a female voice, and therefore only observed the three accused men walking by him… The defense countered that by saying, in either case, the men were heard and seen leaving while the victim was still alive…The prosecution rebutted that without facial recognition, the voice may have not been Eleanor Peabody's but a fourth individual inside the apartment impersonating her, and that she had been murdered prior to the three men seen leaving." She stopped and looked at him.

"Okay, good, the second witness."

"There was a witness, Gordy Jacobs, who said he had seen someone leaving from the back-window apartment on the third floor, apparently Eleanor Peabody's apartment, and then walking down the alley…Which supported the prosecution's argument that a fourth individual was involved in her murder and left via the back stairwell… Gordy Jacobs, a homeless alcoholic, was stabbed and killed three months prior to the trial from an apparent burglary gone wrong…His testimony was allowed but not having him appear in person was a blow to the prosecution."

"Now, the daughter finding her."

"Eleanor Peabody was discovered around seven by her twenty-five-year-old daughter, Lenore, in her bedroom lying naked on a white sheet with a black pentacle sprayed on it. Her body had been cut with a knife from her pubic mound up to her chin, and then from ear to ear. Her hand was clutching the knife that was used…The defense said it only strengthened their claims that she was a witch, who practiced witchcraft and black magic, and ultimately sacrificed her body, and in the words of the defense, 'to Satan'…The prosecution had several witnesses testify that they were very close to Eleanor Peabody and maintained she never practiced witchcraft or black magic."

"The closing arguments."

"The prosecution still maintained that the three men, along with a fourth who was let in through the back window, were responsible for Eleanor Peabody's 'thrill-kill' murder. Which came across as weak, unsubstantiated, and inconclusive…The defense stood behind what they considered to be the facts: the three men were invited to Eleanor Peabody's apartment, partied with her, had consensual sex, and left early the following morning while she was alive…That the prosecution had failed to conclusively provide any substantial evidence that the three accused men had killed Eleanor Peabody, or a motive as to why, and were desperately clutching at straws with their 'thrill-kill' murder theory…The defense continued by saying, that the reason the prosecution was struggling to find a motive, was because the three men were innocent. And that, on the morning of August 6, 1975, Eleanor Peabody took her own life.

"The scandals."

There were several scandals surrounding it, the most notable ones being: questions arising of witnesses being paid off, tampering of evidence, and the sudden death of the homeless man, Gordy Jacobs…Even with none of them ever proven, it did leave a tarnish on this trial and its proceedings.

"The verdict."

Boston Municipal Courthouse, a verdict of 'not guilty' against all three men charged in the first-degree murder of Eleanor Peabody that took place almost a year prior, on August 6, 1975…there was only several hours of deliberations."

"The lead defense attorney."

"Mr. Ernest Cartwright, said he always maintained that these men were innocent, and it was his responsibility to show, not convince, the jury of that…that the jury's swift response of a 'not guilty' verdict on all counts, stated to him and the public, that they believed these men were, without a doubt, innocent…He also said it was not only a triumphant day for these three men, but for the city of Boston, the state of Massachusetts, and our country's legal system; the best in the world."

"Is that everything?"

"There was no mention about gold particles in the wound autopsy," she revealed, "and they did have a symbolist review the cuts, and she said it could be a 'lowercase t, a capital T, a Cross, or a sword.' It was never brought up at the trial, I guess they felt it was irrelevant."

Liam studied her momentarily. "What do you think?"

"If I didn't know about Maggie and Jason's murders, I would say that the defense had a strong argument - especially with her inviting them over, her saying goodbye to them, and them having no motive to kill her – and there was reasonable doubt. But the talk of witnesses being paid off, tampering of evidence, and the sudden death of the homeless man, Gordy Jacobs, is suspicious."

"What do you think now, knowing what you do about Maggie and Jason?"

"Putting me on the spot, eh?" she asked playfully, not minding at all. "I believe when the three men left, she was alive, and they didn't kill her. I think the so called 'fourth man' seen leaving from her back window and going down the alley, was in fact the murderer, and he made it look like a ritualistic suicide." she explained. "I'd say she is probably a Black Witch, like Jason and Maggie, and would never own a white sheet with a black pentacle sprayed on it, instead, hers would have been a family heirloom passed down. I also believe that the people who testified she wasn't one, either lied, or didn't know."

"I agree" said Liam, then contemplated the trial itself. "Overall, the evidence against her flowed too easily as if it was scripted, and the scandals, whether true or not were strategic and added a Hollywood-style drama to the proceedings." He paused and looked at her. "If we are in agreement that the same person orchestrated abducting Heather and Amanda, and Jason's suicide, and Maggie's burglary gone wrong murder, as well as killing Eleanor Peabody, right?"

"We are."

"Then it is a very safe assumption to say that this same person also orchestrated Eleanor's night out with those men, her suicide, and her trail," he concluded.

"But to pull off something of the magnitude, he would have to be very influential, powerful, and wealthy," suggested Rebecca.

"And more importantly, at the same time, unsuspecting, unseen, and stealthy," added Liam.

"Okay, I'm freaking out," she said standing and pacing the room. "So, this man killed three Black Witches, made two of them look like suicides, and the other, a junkie's robbery gone wrong. That he killed two young girls just to set up Jason, and a homeless man to protect himself. And while he was doing this, you're saying he's walking around freely in social circles with nobody knowing any differently," she recapped anxiously.

"I am."

"Is this person Darkness itself?" she asked nervously.

"I believe some part of him is, how much I don't know."

"Why did this person kill these people then suddenly stop?"

Liam let out a heavy sigh. "I don't know, but the answer can't be good."

"Oh thanks," said Rebecca stopping and giving him a look.

Liam got up and put his arms around her.

"Why are we involved? Why are we doing this?" she asked upset and resting her head on his shoulder.

"We're involved because your mom asked us for our help," he replied, "and we're doing this to help Jason, Maggie, Amanda, Heather—"

"Eleanor Peabody and Gordy Jacob, and to uncover the truth" she said with a sigh. "You just know how to say the right things at the time."

Liam smiled affectionately and gently moved her hair from her face.

Rebecca glanced up and kissed him. "Thank you," she whispered.

"Do you feel better?"

"I do," she said gently pulling away, strolling towards the table, and sitting at her laptop. "I'll just add what we talked about."

Liam stood beside her and watched her type.

After she finished, she turned it off, and glanced up at him. "Do you think the killer is from Massachusetts?"

"I don't know, maybe."
"Do you think he's still alive?"
"Definitely."

Chapter Twenty-Six

"Please come in," offered the maid, then led them into the living room.

Liam and Rebecca were shocked to see how much James Childwall had aged.

"Ignore the wheelchair, it's more of a precaution than a necessity. I had a fall in the bathroom and hurt my hip," he explained. "Please, sit, sit. Would you like some tea?"

"Yes," they replied.

"I always find tea soothing and relaxing."

"It is," agreed Rebecca politely.

"Now, Christine has brought me up to speed on your progress, how can I help you?"

"We're hoping you can answer some questions on Jason that may help us with our… research?" asked Liam.

James chuckled. "Research," he repeated, "don't you mean investigation?"

"We're not interested in solving the mystery around his suicide, more the way he committed it," replied Rebecca cleverly.

"But in doing so, the answer to why, will also be uncovered?"

"Potentially."

"Let's cut to the chase," said James bluntly. "You and I both know he did not commit suicide. Jason was a good man and deeply religious, he would never have taken his own life, even if they wrongly convicted and sentenced him."

"You believe he was murdered?" asked Liam.

"I do, as does Christine, and Lee. Why do you think Christine and I asked Rebecca to request you come here? Rebecca is more than capable of setting up the museum's new exhibit on her own," he divulged. "The reason you are both sitting in front of me, is because we all want to know who killed our good friend Jason, and why. And we're hoping your research, investigation, whatever you want to call it, will answer these questions."

"James, I hope you don't think we are taking this lightly or being insensitive by calling it research, because we aren't," said Rebecca sincerely. "Believe me, when I say we are giving this one hundred and ten percent, but we are not criminal investigators."

James, teary eyed, momentarily gazed off to the distance before reestablishing eye contact with Rebecca. "I'm sorry dear, my emotions are getting the better of me, and I apologize to you and Liam."

"We understand," replied Rebecca looking over at Liam nodding in agreement.

"Well, let's start over," suggested James composing himself. "What would you like to know?"

"When did you meet Jason?" she asked.

"He used to help deliver produce with your grandfather to the local stores and restaurant, and they would come to mine several times throughout the week," he explained. "We became friends and started hanging out."

"You didn't know him before that, maybe from college?" asked Liam.

"No."

"But you two did share the same interests?"

"If you're referring to Roswell, pyramids, painters, Bigfoot? Then yes, we did, we actually had quite a range of interests and he was the only person in town I could discuss them with intellectually," answered James. "Early one spring, he even helped me start a garden in my backyard. I tried my best, but unfortunately, I failed miserably because I didn't have a green thumb like him."

"What about his books on witchcraft and black magic?" asked Rebecca.

"The occult was a topic that we both enjoyed reading books on and discussing, and back then, lots of people were interested in the subject matter but it didn't mean we all belonged to a cult," clarified James. "Today, it's more popular than ever, look at the books and movies based on Halloween and witches for example. Are those who participate in the

October 31 ritual of dressing up and partying, reading the books, or watching the movies, part of a cult? Of course not, my point is, because Jason had several books on witchcraft and black magic didn't make him a member of a Satanic cult."

"We understand," said Rebecca appreciating his candidness. "Can you give us your thoughts on the police questioning him when the girls went missing?

"Hogwash, pure hogwash. The only lead they had was someone saying they had seen the white delivery truck in the vicinity," stated James shaking his head in disbelief. "He drove that truck all around town and fifty people could have said they'd seen him it that day."

"What about the backpack?" asked Liam.

"I will say what you two already know, somebody planted it, then called the police."

"Do you think the man who abducted the girls and killed Jason, was the caller from Geneva who tipped them off about it?"

"I don't think, I know."

"You know?" asked Rebecca surprised.

James let out a heavy sigh. "How else would he have had access to her backpack and the girls' clothes that they found in the camper?"

Liam and Rebecca glanced at one another and realized they were back to square one: who and why?

"What about the suicide note?"

"As you probably know, Jason connected the letter 'J' with 'a' in his signature, and if he was writing something as serious as a suicide note he would have signed his name that way. So, I believe the killer slipped up."

"With all the information proving his innocence, why didn't someone do something with it?"

"I did. I hired a private investigator to look into it."

"And?" she asked leaning in.

"Nothing. He couldn't find the caller."

"What about the physical evidence, like him being right-handed?"

"They said it could have been part of the ritual that he needed to use his left hand, and there was no evidence to suggest otherwise."

"What about the signature on the suicide note?"

"Although it's true he usually signed his name that way, he didn't always, and this was their argument," revealed James. "For instance, he bought me a book for my birthday, just days before he was murdered, and in it had signed my name and his with the 'J' not connected to the 'a.'"

"Do you still have the book?" asked Liam.

"It's in my library, feel free to look at it," he offered. "It's a book on garden patios of all things. Jason said that if I couldn't be successfully at gardening that I may have better luck at building a charming patio in its place. Seems he was right, I picked one of the English designs in the book and started building one at the beginning of fall. It reminded me of Jason, so I sat on it often to read, and think about him," he said sorrowfully.

Rebecca quickly looked over at Liam indicating she was out of questions, he indicated he had one more.

"Where was Jason buried?"

"He was buried in unconsecrated ground in the Catholic cemetery. I purchased a small section of land allocated for future plots that hadn't been blessed yet. It's right by the brick wall close to the woods, and has a beautiful headstone," explained James sadly then looked over at Rebecca. "I purchased his casket and had a viewing for him right in my front parlor. Your grandparents came, your mom and aunt, Sheriff Lee, and a dozen or so townspeople. Many others, who thought he was innocent, kept away out of respect for the girls' families."

"Was it a closed coffin?" she asked.

"It wasn't for the adults. I made sure he was clothed in a way that hid the scare on his neck," he described. "But the day we removed the casket for the funeral it was closed, because your mother and her sister were in the house, and they were very young."

"He never had a Catholic burial?" queried Liam.

"No, after he was placed in the ground, family and individuals who wanted to say a few words, did, then we all said the Lord's Prayer."

"How sad," said Rebecca."

"Indeed," agreed James wiping away the tears.

They changed the conversation and spoke about the museum for several minutes, before saying goodbye, and leaving.

"He was really emotional, they must have been close," said Rebecca as they turned onto Main Street.

"I believe so," replied Liam.

"He didn't appear well at all, and looked like he was on death's door."

"I must admit, since I saw him last week, his health has turned, and he's aged."

Chapter Twenty-Seven

"Liam, wake up, Liam," whispered a young girl's voice. "Wake up, Liam."

Liam slowly stirred, looked down at Rebecca sleeping on his chest, then over at the apparition standing in the doorway waving him over.

"Mandy?" he asked gently moving Rebecca off his chest, standing, and walking over to her.

"You need to come with me and see this?" she asked taking his hand and leading him downstairs into the parlor.

The parlor transformed back in time to a room full of people quietly talking. Mandy led him to the open casket, inside was Jason. Time fast forwarded, and the room emptied, went dark, filled, then emptied, and eventually slowed down to nighttime. Jason sat up in the casket, climbed out, closed it, stripped to his underwear, and left the room. They followed him out the back door to the garden where a black mist surrounded him, and he disappeared with it. The black mist came from the ground, and as it came closer to them, a demonic face with black eyes appeared, and grabbed Mandy pulling her from him.

"Liam, help me!" she cried in fear. "Don't let him take me!"

The demon looked at him, swung his arm, and knocked him to the ground before disappearing with Mandy. Liam lay on his back, suddenly it was daytime, and standing in front of him was Jason in a vest and shorts raising a pickaxe and bringing it down on him. Liam quickly rolled out of the way, got up, and ran to the door while Jason gave chase. Jason threw the pickaxe to one side and with two hands grabbed Liam on the steps. Liam turned around and kicked him off onto the grass.

Jason, in his underwear, got up on two knees. "Liam, you're running out of time, Darkness will never let me leave, you need to hurry," he begged, then looked over his shoulder at the demon approaching before turning to Liam. "It you don't, we will be lost forever."

The demon grabbed Jason, threw him towards the back fence where he disintegrated, and then headed towards Liam snarling. Liam ran through the door slamming it behind him. It was daylight, and the casket was getting carried out of the house as the door behind him blew up knocking Liam onto the floor.

Unexpectedly, Liam woke up in bed with a loud gasp. He quickly realized where he was and looked down at Rebecca sleeping on his chest. "Fuck me," he whispered and eventually fell back to sleep.

The following morning, he woke up to an empty bed, and on the nightstand was a note from Rebecca saying she would be back by eleven.

"Hey, are they here?" asked Rebecca.

"They're in the family room playing PlayStation on the big screen."

"How's your sister and her husband?"

"Doing good. I took them for a tour around, stopped in the wine cellar, and told them to grab a couple of bottles."

"They'll be the talk of the anniversary dinner party," suggested Rebecca.

"They sure will. The two they took are worth six and eight grand. Janice just had to look them up," he said with grin. "Come and meet my niece and nephew…Guys, please pause the game for a second, this is Rebecca."

"Rebecca, this is Sophia, and that's Isaac."

"Hi," they replied in unison.

"Hello, nice to me you."

"Do you two want some lunch?" asked Liam.

"Yeah, we're starving," said Isaac pressing play.

"All right, I will be in the kitchen with Rebecca if you need me."

She followed him into the kitchen and noticed he wasn't himself. "What's wrong? Is everything okay?"

As Liam told her about his encounter, he took her to the parlor describing what he witnessed, then outside and back inside.

"Did Mandy give you anything?"

"No," he replied quietly before walking back to the parlor, running the sequence of events in his head, then going back outside to the deck. All of a sudden, something twigged. "Hold on a minute, he had a pickaxe, he must have thrown it to one side," he said walking down the steps and looking in the grass. "Rebecca?"

She looked on as he picked it up and showed it to her.

"Good morning," said a man turning the corner and heading towards them.

"Hey, Frankie, how are you doing?"

"Good Rebecca," he replied cheerfully. "This must be Liam."

"It is," she replied, "this is Frankie, the landscaper."

"Nice to meet you," said Liam.

"Likewise," he replied, "although Mr. Childwall prefers the term, gardener, I guess it sounds posher. I'm sorry to bother you, but I was just checking the lawn in the front to see if it needs to be cut and thought I should come around back and check the grass here," he explained looking at it the turning to Liam. "Probably middle of the week."

Liam noticed him looking at the pickaxe. "Is this yours?"

Frankie took it from him and studied it. "No, this is an antique, made over forty years ago."

"How do you know that?" asked Rebecca.

"This is handmade by the Frey family in Pennsylvania. Their hand-held tools were well-known for their durability, but weren't cheap, I believe they stopped making them in the late seventies, early eighties," he explained. "If you look here, you can see their family name carved in the wooden handle."

Liam and Rebecca examined it.

"It is mostly used for landscaping and breaking up hard surfaces. If you clean it up, remove the rust, it could be a nice addition to the museum," he suggested.

"That's a thought," replied Rebecca considering it.

"How long have you been the Childwall's landscaper?" asked Liam.

"Me, personally, thirty years. My family, seventy," revealed Frankie. "I took over the family business from my parents when they retired. My first job helping my dad was when I was ten. Mr. Childwall wanted a line of granite rocks, similar to the deck's color, over there under the deck where the lawn ends. My father tried to convince him to plant a garden, or some rose bushes, but he was dead set on having eight rocks spread out.

So the next day, I helped my dad carry them from the pickup to the deck. They were only the size of large melons, but they were heavy, well, for me. Anyway, it was my birthday that weekend and Mr. Childwall gave me twenty dollars, and said it was because I did the job of two ten-year old's. It was a lot of money back," acknowledged Frankie. "Anyway, about a week later, my dad came home ticked off and tells my mother that Mr. Childwall had given the rocks to the neighbor and decided to go with his idea of bushes."

"Was your father upset because he didn't listen to him?" asked Rebecca.

"No, it was because he gave the rocks to the neighbor, and could have sold them to another customer," replied Frankie chuckling and looking around. "I just hope when he does sell it, the new owner will plant more flowers and rose bushes around the place and brighten it up a little."

"It could definitely use more color," admitted Rebecca assessing the garden.

"Well, I have to be off," said Frankie turning to them "Is it okay if I come by early next week to cut the lawn, say Tuesday?"

"Tuesday's fine," said Liam.

"Fantastic. It was nice meeting you, Liam, see you around Rebecca."

"You too, Frankie," she said pleasantly.

They watched him leave then looked at the pickaxe.

"What's this mean?" wondered Liam.

"Jason had it, was he aiming it at you when he brought it down?"

"At first, I thought he was, but after speaking with Frankie I think he was using it to dig with."

"Was he using it to bury something?"

"I'm not sure," said Liam walking onto the deck and placing it against the wall.

"What about him sitting up, getting out of the coffin, and walking out here?"

"Maybe that was his spirit leaving his body and being taken away by the black mist, the Demon, the Darkness?"

"Unfortunately, more questions than answers," noted Rebecca.

"True, and hopefully we will get the answers sooner than later," he replied remembering Jason's warning about running out of time.

They went into the kitchen and started to make sandwiches, hearing the children laughing in the other room, Rebecca moved closer to him. "You can't let the children stay here," she whispered.

"I know."

"Why don't you stay at my place tonight?" she suggested. "There's more than enough room, and they can each have their own bedroom. After lunch, we can take them to the beach, eat dinner on the boardwalk, and they can play games in the arcade," she said trying to convince him. "Tomorrow morning, we can eat breakfast on the front porch, go the beach again, then take them swimming at my mom's later and have dinner there."

"You're quite the salesperson," he said with a smile. "Where do I sleep?"

"I have four bedrooms, so you can have your own, and in the middle of the night you can sneak into mine," she said with a naughty smile, then embraced him, and gave him a loving kiss.

Chapter Twenty-Eight

"I'm glad we took a couple of days off, and spent time with Sophia and Isaac, I needed the break."

"It was a good distraction," conceded Liam, "and I also got to see some of the town that I otherwise wouldn't have if we hadn't."

"I think you liked the arcades more than the children did!"

"You didn't seem to mind playing the games, either."

"That's because us girls ruled, right Sophia?"

"You know we did," she said happily.

"Liam, do you believe these two?" asked Isaac.

"They're only saying that because they know we kicked their butts," stated Liam giving Isaac a high five.

Rebecca opened the door, and they followed her in. "Mom?"

"In her, honey," she shouted from the living room.

"Grandma, Grandad," shouted the kids running to greet them.

"Mom, Dad, what are you doing here?" asked Liam confused.

"No, hello, how are doing?" asked his father.

"Sorry, Dad, how are you?" he said giving him a hug. "This is Rebecca. Rebecca, my dad, Kenneth."

"Please to meet you," she said.

"Hi, Mom," he said reaching down and giving her a kiss. "Rebecca, my mom, Anna."

"Nice to finally meet you," said Rebecca with a smile.

"You too, dear."

"Liam, my father, Gerald."

"Call me, Ged," he clarified shaking Liam's hand.

"Nice to meet you."

"And who are these adorable children?" asked Christine.

"This is Isaac and Sophia," said Anna. "Say hello to Christine and Ged."

"Hi," they replied shyly.

"Do you guys want to go for a swim?" asked Ged.

"Yes!" screamed the children.

"Okay, follow me and your grandpa down to the pool, and you guys can get changed in the guest house," said Ged leading the way.

"Mom, do you know Anna?"

"How about we go sit at the kitchen table?" suggested Christine standing up. "And I'll make some coffee."

"I'm going to need something a little stronger," said Rebecca, "Liam, want a beer?"

"Yeah, definitely!"

Christine made a pot of coffee, gave a cup to Anna, then sat next to her. "Can you update us on how things are going with Jason?"

Rebecca looked at Liam then their moms.

"After, we can talk about the photo?" promised Christine.

Rebecca and Liam brought them up to speed.

"Eleanor Peabody, that poor woman," said Anna.

"It such a shame what happened to her," added Christine.

"All right, you're both freaking me out," cried Rebecca going to the fridge, grabbing two more beers, and handing one to Liam.

"Do you have the photo?" asked her mom.

Rebecca handed it to her, then watched as she showed Anna. They both chuckled.

"I was so young then," said Anna.

"Look at me," said Christine, "I must admit I was pretty trendy for my age."

"That's because of your mom, she was always up on the latest fashion, look at her."

"Mom, you and Grandma are in this picture?" asked Rebecca with a startled look.

"I'm the young girl, and the woman behind me is grandma," she confirmed.

"Oh, I see, of course you are," said Rebecca sarcastically before glancing over at Liam who was quiet then at her mom. "And you know each other, how?"

"We're friends, not best friends, more like good friends," she answered.

"I was friends with Alicia, and your grandmother was friends with Maggie, and we all met," explained Anna. "I was the youngest adult at twenty-five, and your grandmother was the oldest at thirty-three, Maggie and Alicia were in their late twenties."

"And I was about ten," revealed Christine.

"Okay, what are us two idiots missing, and why is the picture so important?" asked Rebecca anxiously cutting to the chase.

Liam laughed at what she said, and Rebecca joined him.

"This is unbelievable!" she said smiling at Liam who shook his head in disbelief.

"There's something I need to tell you," said Christine leaving the table and coming back with a rectangular box.

"Your wedding album? Let me guess, Anna and Kenneth are in the photos," said Rebecca unamused as she watched her mom open it, remove something wrapped in a blanket, unfold it, and reveal a white grimoire with a pentacle engraved on it. Rebecca looked up at her mother wide eyed.

"Yes, Rebecca, I'm a White Witch, and come October you will be Blessed, and take ownership of this book."

Rebecca took a deep breath and let out a heavy sigh. "You're messing with me, right?"

"No, I'm not," said her mother sternly. "You have a great gift, greater than any White Witch, well, except one."

"Oh yeah, this will be good, who?"

"Anna?" said Christine.

"I'm dating a White Witch," teased Liam trying to lighten up the tension.

"Yeah, and I'm in love with a mere mortal," she snapped back.

Everyone looked at her silently.

"Oh! Me being in love with Liam makes everyone's jaw drop, but finding out my mother and I are White Witches, doesn't?"

"Come here," said Liam pulling her close and kissing her. "I love you, too," he whispered.

"You do?" she asked happily.

"That's if you don't mind me being a mere mortal?" he teased.

"I don't, wait, Mom, is Dad?"

"No," she replied.

"Then Mortal, I guess it's your lucky day," said Rebecca kissing him.

Christine cleared her throat to get their attention. "Go ahead, Anna."

Anna pulled out a small suitcase from under the table, opened it, unwrapped the blanket, and placed a white grimoire on the table. "Surprise!"

"A guy can be a White Witch?" asked Liam. "Tell me I'm a White Warlock?"

"Your ancestry goes back to the 18th century here in the US, and well beyond the 14th century in England. Warlock is a 14th century term, and they are generally evil, sorry," she said shrugging her shoulders. "And before you ask, the term Wizard originated around 1550, and they sported long white beards, had flowing robes, and were either good or bad."

"I can see where you get your witty sense of humor from," said Rebecca chuckling. "Which, by the way Anna, is what I love about him."

"Thank you," replied Anna with a grin, then looked at Liam. "There's something else."

"I should tell him?" suggested Christine.

"Of course, you should," acknowledged Anna.

Rebecca looked at them peculiarly.

"Liam, your mother is the White Witch High Queen, which means, she is the Queen of all the White Queens," she said dramatically bowing to her.

Liam and Rebecca looked on in silence.

"Please," said Anna, "it's only a title, everyone is equal."

"She's right," said Christine trying not to laugh, "I just wanted to see your faces when I sounded so officially and bowed."

Rebecca looked at Liam unamused as their mothers laughed at them.

"Are you quite finished, Mother?" asked Rebecca good-naturedly.

"Yes, we are," she said with a smile.

"This means, Liam, come October you will be Blessed, and become the White Witch High King, and will take ownership of this book," disclosed Anna."

Rebecca playfully pushed his arm. "Can you explain this High King, High Queen, stuff?"

"For now, I'll give you a quick explanation, and when we have more time, we can go through it in more detail," offered Christine. "Simply, each of the eleven Northeast States have Black, Gray, and White Witches, each of these states has a Black, Gray, and White, King or Queen. Overseeing all eleven states, we have a Black, Gray, and White, High King or High Queen, they are the most direct bloodlines to the First Witch."

"Who is the First Witch" asked Rebecca.

"That would take too long to explain," she replied.

"Okay, why only the Northeast States?"

"The Epicenter of Darkness is somewhere near Plymouth, close to where the first pilgrims settled, and it becomes less of a threat the further away it is from its center," explained Anna. "The eleven Northeast States are the first, and only line of defense, stopping Darkness from spreading further."

"So, Darkness has been an issue before?

"Yes, back in the early 18th century, but not since, well, until now."

"What is Darkness?" quizzed Rebecca.

"Darkness it's a malevolent spirit that has been invited by a person to be its Host on Earth, and inside its Host, Darkness will patiently hide and wait to take on its final human form. Until then, the Host will slowly become Darkness' Servant, and work endlessly to make it become as powerful as possible, while recruiting other Hosts or killing those it deems a threat," described Anna. "Darkness has one purpose: to open up the Gates of Darkness on Earth, releasing its Lord and its occupants."

"Are you talking about Lucifer, his Devils and Demons?"

"He is the Lord of Darkness, and they his army," stated Christine, "but the only way Satan can physically walk on this Earth, is if Darkness succeeds in its objective."

"Can anyone summon Darkness?" asked Liam.

"No, it won't simply come to any person asking, it has to be someone with incredible powers and a deep knowledge of how to summon such an Entity from the depths."

"How does someone get that knowledge?" asked Rebecca.

"By researching how Darkness was summoned before, finding its Epicenter, then conducting a ritual offering their body as its Host," surmised Anna. "None of us know for certain, but we believe this to be quite accurate."

"Quite accurate?" questioned Rebecca.

"We've never had a need to research and verify it before," replied Anna, "and hopefully we never have to."

"Judging by the Demon I saw in my vision, and Liam in his, we may want to get on that ASAP!" cried Rebecca.

"I understand your concerns," said Anna calmly, "and we will cross that bridge when, and if, we need to, but for now you must concentrate your efforts on the task at hand."

Rebecca knew she was right. "I'm sorry, I'm just overwhelmed by all this."

"I know, dear," comforted her mother, "and I will be very frank with you, we believe you have handled yourself far better than any of us had expected. And what you and Liam have accomplished so far, is a true testament to the strength, the will, and the spirit of the White Witches. I'm very proud, Rebecca."

"Thanks, Mom," she said going over and hugging her.

Anna grabbed her son's hand and squeezed it. "Me, too."

Liam smiled at her, then decided it was a good time to lighten up the conversation. "So, can royalty date a mere White Witch?" he joked making everyone laugh except Rebecca.

"Ha, ha, Mr. Funny White Witch High King makes a joke, and everyone has to laugh, because he's the future king, ha, ha," she said acting bratty and pretending to be offended.

Liam put his arm around her. "Mom, if I were to marry, would my wife be the White Witch High Queen?"

"If she's a White Witch, yes, she would."

"See?" he said glancing over at her.

Rebecca blushed, and for some reason finding out she was a White Witch was suddenly okay, because she knew he would always be at her side. "All right, Mom, what make me, I guess us, so special?"

"You not only see innocent, lost, and trapped spirits, you can communicate with them, and have the power, not only to find them, but set them free—"

"Mom, I'm going to stop you there. They're more like dreams, where you come back with a souvenir; I got a photo, Liam got a pickaxe."

"You don't believe they actually happened?" asked Anna looking at her then Liam.

"I'm with Rebecca on this."

"Liam, maybe this will help," suggested his mom. "When we used to visit Aunty Ally, you used to tell me about the sad women in the bedroom. You were very young, too. Do you remember?"

"No, I don't."

"Aunty Ally is Alicia, and she moved into Maggie's place after she was murdered to keep her spirit company. She could never see or talk to Maggie, but you could."

"Is Aunty Ally a White Witch?"

"She is, and she's protecting, not only her best friend's spirit, but a Black Witch's. That's her gift."

"Maggie used to talk with me?"

"Yes, she did."

"Rebecca, you probably won't remember this either," said Christine smiling at her. "But when you were very young, I used to take you to the Childwall's to visit James, and you would go outside and play in the garden. On the way home, you would tell me about the two friends you met, and to you, they were as real as we are right now. I didn't want others to find out what you had seen, so from that point on when we visited there, I would keep you inside and only let you go outside with your brother to play. You see, they wouldn't appear to you in front of him, because he couldn't see them. Do you remember that?"

"No," she whispered.

"You've both seen spirits during the day and talked with them. What you are experiencing are not dreams, they are real," she revealed.

"Mom, we didn't, we were both young and had imaginary friends, that's all,."

Christine and Anna glanced at one another and realized it was time for them to know the truth.

"Rebecca," said her mom softly, "the two girls you played with in the Childwall's garden, you told me their names, Mandy and Hetty."

"That's impossible, we've seen them playing in the backyard just the other day, and they're as real as we are right now."

"Rebecca, Liam, this may be difficult for you to comprehend but Mandy's full name is Amanda Peterson, and Hetty's, is Heather Downs."

"The missing girls," gasped Rebecca covering her mouth as the tears started to stream down her face, she abruptly stood up, and took off outside.

Liam went after her and found her on the front porch, she ran into his arms.

"Those poor girls, they've been trapped there for so long, and are so scared," she sobbed. "We have to help them."

"We will," promised Liam comforting her.

"I don't think I could be doing this on my own, I'm so glad I have you," she said squeezing him tightly.

"I know, me neither," he replied honestly and kissed the top of her head. "Are you okay?"

"I am. Let's go back inside and figure out what we need to do," she said managing a smile. "I just need to wash my face first then I'll meet at the table."

"All right."

Rebecca went to the bathroom while Liam went to the fridge, grabbed a couple of beers, then joined his mother and Christine.

"How is she?"

"She's fine," replied Liam, "she's just upset about the two young girls, and wants us to help them."

Rebecca walked back to the room, hugged her mom, then Anna before sitting next to Liam. "Okay, the photo, when was that taken?"

"Just after Eleanor's murder," said Christine. "She was the Black Witch High Queen, and her daughter, Lenore, should have taken her place.

But because of what happened to her mother, she blamed the Black Witches for not helping her, and abandoned them."

"She was never seen again," added Anna.

"This meant Maggie was next in line, and we feared whoever killed Eleanor, would now come after Maggie. So, Alicia stayed with her as much as she could, well, you know what happened," said Christine.

"After that, we thought it was best that Jason lay low for a while, until the Gray Witches found the killer."

"Gray Witches?" asked Rebecca.

"Well, at a high level, the White Witches help people, souls, and spirits. The Black Witches protect us from evil, the Darkness. The Gray Witches are the fulcrum, they assist the Black and Witch Witches, and are problem solvers. They help keep the balance, and if need be, eliminate rogue witches."

"Do you mean kill them?"

"If that's the only option, and only Gray Witches can kill other Witches, but Black and Gray Witches can kill rogue witches," confirmed Anna.

"Rogue witches?" asked Rebecca.

"They're the ones who have turned to Darkness, use Dark spells, Black Magic spells, or their gifts for evil. Simply put, they us them to hurt or kill people."

"The person we are looking for is a witch?"

"Either that, or Darkness itself," said Anna.

"That sounds familiar," said Rebecca looking at Liam. Then at her mother "Continue with Jason."

"After Maggie's murder, he left Boston and started to head west living in hotels and taking odd jobs, and eventually ended up in Amare. He thought with your grandmother and James being here, they could protect him, and he could have somewhat of a normal life until the Gray Witches found the murderer. They couldn't, and he was killed."

"James, James Childwall?" queried Rebecca.

"He's the man in the picture," said Christine showing them. "He is, was, a Black Witch and came with my mother to help Maggie."

"You said he was?" asked Liam.

"He was next in line to be the High King, but with the death of Jason refused, and said that he would never have an heir to pass it down to. Now the Black Witches were in disarray and decided to function temporarily as a committee until they found Lenore or hopefully her child, if she even had one."

"From what you said earlier, they didn't find her?" asked Liam.

"No, they didn't."

"Does James know we will be White Witches?" questioned Rebecca.

"He does, and only knows what Liam has shared with him about waking up from a dream that seems real, having visions in which he's talked to deceased people, waking up in places and not knowing how he got there, and getting sensations, feelings. And he believes, like us, that it will help you find the answers we are looking for," explained Christine. "He doesn't know about your special gifts, and what you have been both been experiencing lately, only us and your fathers do. Anna and I believe they are the key to finding out the truth."

"Why didn't you tell us about all this up front?" challenged Rebecca.

"You both needed to discover who you were and what you are capable of, you couldn't be told or led, it was your journey," replied Christine, "and look how far you have come."

"I understand," said Rebecca realizing she was right and turning to Liam. "I'm glad I have you, Sam."

"You too, Frodo," replied Liam, making them laugh.

"At least you've kept your sense of humor," said Anna. So, what's next for you two?"

"We don't have much to go on," admitted Rebecca. "We need to figure out who wrote the note, find Jason's grimoire, then locate their bodies so we can set them free. The question is, how?"

"Christine, regarding the note, did Jason ever sign his name without connecting the first two letters."

"Never," she replied adamantly, "he even joined his initials. Jason would say that if a lawyer was to sign his name on a legal document, he should be proud of his signature. So, whoever wrote that note slipped up."

"That's what James said, and probably Lee believes that too," said Rebecca.

"So, he was a lawyer?" asked Liam.

"He was, just before he got engaged to Maggie and up to her death, then he had to resign and flee."

"Up to the day of the funeral, did anything peculiar happen in the parlor or with his casket?" probed Liam.

"Not that I can recall," said his mom.

"Me neither," said Christine. "Rebecca's grandfather was a pallbearer, and when I asked him what it was like, he winked and said it was heavier than he expected."

"That's Grandad for you."

They sat in silence momentarily.

"Do you have any more questions?" asked Christine.

"No," they replied.

"We'll have to go back and review our notes," stated Liam. "See if we missed something."

"Before I forget, regarding setting their spirits free, there's one important detail you need to know," said Anna. "Only a White Witch, specifically chosen by a Black Witch, can read a spell from that Black Witch's grimoire."

"Jason gave Liam his Bible; has he been chosen?" asked Rebecca.

"Yes," replied Anna, "he was given something very dear to Jason."

"I was given Maggie's necklace, does that mean I have been chosen, too?"

"No, Maggie has to personally give you something that she cherishes," clarified her mom.

"You said we need to be White Witches to read the spell, but we won't be one till we are Blessed?" queried Liam.

"Being Blessed is only a ceremony, during which we transfer the grimoire and our responsibilities on to you," said Anna. "Before then, both of you have to truly believe in your heart, mind, and soul, that you are White Witches. Then, and only then, will you be able to set them free."

Chapter Twenty-Nine

"It's great that your parents and the children are staying around for another day," said Rebecca closing the car door.

"Yeah, your parents are taking them sightseeing today."

"They're going to Watkins Glen State Park to see the waterfalls, then taking the kids swimming in the Olympic-size pool."

"I wouldn't mind doing that, I've never been there before."

"Really? I'll make a point of taking you," she promised. "You'll love it! It has three hiking trails, stone bridges, and nineteen waterfalls; it's gorgeous!"

"Like you," he said kissing her.

"You say the sweetest things," she replied responding passionately. "I missed making love to you last night."

"Me too, but your parents did have a full house, and us sleeping with Sophia and Isaac in the guest house was problematic."

"At least we got to sleep together for a while, which was wonderful," she said smiling. "I'm actually looking forward to spending the day working at the museum."

"So am I, and we also get to remove this from the mansion," said Liam lifting the pickaxe out of the trunk.

"True. I wouldn't want to stay over with that on the back deck."

"Oh, I should put it back," joked Liam.

"Stop it!" she replied pushing him.

.

"That was great of you to take us all out for dinner."

"After such a long day, and with all the work that Brittany and Mia have been doing on their own, it's the least I could do," stated Liam.

"They were over the moon working with you today. You made their day. I'm sure they're telling their family and friends about it as we speak, and sharing all the photos we took," she said happily. "I also sent some to Arthur to post online."

"Keeping up appearances?"

"I have to make people believe we are busily working on the exhibit and not fighting demon," she replied.

"Well, between us working at the museum and you taking photos, you're doing a great job of that."

"Thank you," she said graciously before opening her front door then suddenly stopped. "Do you remember when we first met and I told you that I had promised Agnes that if she kept a lid on you coming, Arthur would have the exclusive for his newspaper, and could post it on social media."

"I do," he replied wondering why she was bringing it up.

"You asked me what I had promised Edith. I said that we would conduct the interview in her goddaughter and husband's new restaurant, that we would mention their restaurant in the piece, and it would be a good photo op for them," she reiterated. "I lied to you, originally I was planning on having the interview at the mansion and moved it."

"Why are you telling me this?"

"Because I lied to you, and I don't want there to be any dishonesty between us."

"It was only a white lie," he suggested.

"I know, but I wanted to come clean with you, and promise I won't deceive you ever again."

"All right," he said holding her.

"I love you, and I always want us to be honest with each other.

"I love you, and I agree," he said kissing her. "You know, it actually worked out better for your cover story having the interview there and us going back for dinner."

"It did, didn't it," she replied smiling and happy she had told him. "I just need to pick up a change of clothing and won't be a minute."

"Okay, I'll wait out here."

Thirty minutes later they walked out onto the mansion's front terrace, sipping their beers, and admiring the view.

"It's such a romantic, starry night," cooed Rebecca moving close to Liam as he put his arm around her.

167

Chapter Thirty

"Rebecca, wake up," whispered Hetty standing next to the bed. "Wake up."

Rebecca stirred and noticed her. "Hetty?"

"Come with me, we don't have much time," she said reaching out her hand.

Rebecca grabbed it, got out of bed, and followed her downstairs and out the back door. "Where are we going?"

"Shh," mouthed Hetty placing her index finger over her lips.

It went pitch black, then the sun quickly rose, and they were standing in the backyard of Rebecca's mom's farmhouse. They slowly walked towards three young girls who were playing and laughing.

"Hetty, your mom called, and asked that you start for home," said Rebecca's grandmother from the back door. "Do you want a ride?"

"No thanks, Mrs. Anderson," replied Hetty.

"Me and Tammy will walk her to the dirt road," shouted Christine.

"Okay, be safe," she replied watching them go into the field and out of sight.

"Follow them," whispered Hetty's apparition, and disappeared.

Rebecca followed the three girls through the field as they talked and giggled.

"Hey, ladies," said Jason approaching. "How are you today?"

"Jason!" shouted the three girls running to hug him.

"Where are you off to?"

"We're just walking Hetty to the dirt road," replied Christine.

"All right, I won't keep you then," he said with a kind smile, and continued on in the direction of the farmhouse.

The three girls arrived at the dirt road, said goodbye to Hetty, and watched her cross safely before turning around and heading for home. On the other side of the street, Rebecca watched as a car with tinted windows pulled up alongside Hetty, rolled down the passenger side window, and talked to her. Hetty opened the door and jumped into the car.

"Put on your seatbelt," said the voice.

Hetty did as he said and took the bag of candies from him.

Rebecca was now sitting in the back of the car.

Unexpectedly, the gloved man put a cloth over her mouth. Hetty reacted, and tried to push his arms away, but he was too strong, and she fell into a deep sleep. The man undid her seatbelt, pushed her limp body onto the floor, then drove. Rebecca tried desperately to see his face, but it was hidden from her point of view. The man drove for thirty minutes before entering a deep forest and stopping. From over his shoulder, Rebecca watched him pick up Hetty's body, place it into the backseat, then strangle the unconscious girl. He removed her coat and T-Shirt, put it into a clear plastic bag, then placed the girl's body inside a large black garbage bag, tying it up before putting it and the plastic bag into the trunk and driving. Time sped up, and it quickly turned to the middle of the night. Rebecca followed the killer as he carried the garbage bag to a hole, casually threw it in, and filled it worth dirt.

"You bastard!" cried Rebecca.

The man with demonic black eyes turned and came towards here. Rebecca felt Hetty grab her hand.

"This way, Rebecca," begged Hetty. "Run, Rebecca, run!"

They ran for what seemed like an eternity, as the Demon leisurely walked behind them. When they arrived at the back of the mansion Hetty let go.

"What are you doing?"

"I can't come with you, Rebecca, you need to go…Darkness, it's getting stronger, and if you don't hurry, I won't see you ever again."

Rebecca turned and ran up the steps to the deck, behind her, she could hear Hetty's terrified screams. Tears streamed down her face as she ran into the mansion. It was now afternoon, she saw a group of people in the parlor, and gradually strolled towards them and noticed the open casket.

"Liam, wake up," whispered Mandy. "You have to wake up, Liam."

He roused, realized Rebecca wasn't there, then looked over at Mandy's standing by the door.

"Hurry up Liam," she pleaded as he went toward her, held her hand, and descended the stairs. They went out the front door into the late afternoon sun.

Like a dream, they wandered down Victoria Street to Park Street. On the opposite corner, waiting to cross over Victoria Street, was Mandy with her two friends wearing soccer shirts.

"You must follow them," whispered Mandy as she faded away.

Liam crossed the road, stood behind the girls, and watched as a white van slowed down and listened as the driver shouted out of the passenger side.

"How was soccer practice?"

"It was hot!" shouted Mandy.

Jason gave them a friendly wave as he drove away.

Liam followed them down Park Street, watched Mandy say bye to her friends before cutting through the Town Park. Arriving on the other side, a voice called out to her from a car with tinted windows. She spoke to the man momentarily, threw her backpack onto the car floor, before sitting in the passenger seat. Liam was now sitting in the back seat. The gloved man told her to put her seatbelt on, gave her the bag of candies, then covered her mouth with a cloth. Mandy frantically tried to fight him off but was unsuccessful. The man undid her seatbelt, pushed her limp body onto the floor, then drove. Forty minutes later, they entered a deep forest and stopped. From over his shoulder, Liam watched him pick up Mandy's body, place it into the backseat, then strangle the unconscious girl. He removed her soccer jersey and headband, then grabbed her backpack, and put it into a clear plastic bag. He then placed the girl's body inside a large black garbage bag and tied it up, before putting it and the plastic bag into the trunk and driving. Time sped up, and it quickly turned to the middle of the night. Liam followed the killer as he carried the garbage bag to a hole, casually threw it in, and filled it worth dirt. Liam went toward him, but Mandy appeared, grabbed his hand, and held him back. The man with demonic black eyes turned and came towards them.

"Follow me, quickly," implored Mandy. "Now!"

They ran for what seemed like an eternity, as the Demon leisurely walked behind them. When they arrived at the back of the mansion Mandy let go.

"What are you doing?"

"I can't come with you, Liam, you need to go…Darkness, it's getting stronger, and if you don't hurry, I won't see you ever again."

Liam stood in front of Mandy, and turned to face the Demon, who picked him up and threw him through the back door into the mansion. In the distance, he could hear Mandy's frightened screams. All of a sudden it was the afternoon, he looked around and noticed a group of people in the parlor, spotting Rebecca he walked over and stood next to her.

"Rebecca," he whispered.

"Liam," she said happily. "What are we doing here?"

"I don't know, but I think it's best that we don't talk."

"Okay," she replied in a low voice, not wanting to see the Demon again, and holding his hand.

The people who were stationary, slowly started to move around the room, then faster, and faster, as the clock sped forward. Evening fell, and the mourners eventually departed. In the middle of the night, Jason sat up, climbed out of his casket, and stripped to his underwear. He slowly moved towards Rebecca and Liam, and as he passed between them, grabbed their hands. As they walked with him out the back door and across the garden it went black. They arrived at the burial site of Hetty and Mandy, Jason let go of their hands, walked on alone, and collapsed. The gloved man picked him up, tossed him in the hole, and filled it with dirt.

Unexpectantly, the man with demonic black eyes swiftly spun around and faced them. "Leave the mansion now and never come back!" he growled. "Otherwise, I will bury your corpses out here, and you will be my servants for all eternity!"

The Demon suddenly charged them; they turned and ran. They could hear it galloping behind them, and in the distance, see the mansion rapidly approaching. Rebecca and Liam quickly climbed the steps, as the Demon leapt and jumped on them, tackling them to the ground.

Rebecca and Liam simultaneously sat up in bed.

"Fuck me!" cried Rebecca. "What's happening?"

Liam looked over at her frightened face. "Either we're getting stronger, or the Darkness is getting weaker."

"But the Demon tried to grab us?"

"It did, but it can't."

"Why not?"

"We're not dead."

"Oh thanks, that makes me feel so much better," she said sarcastically.

Liam pulled her down and put his arm around him. "Let's try get some sleep."

Rebecca nestled safely into his chest and eventually fell asleep.

Chapter Thirty-One

Liam put the coffees on the counter as Rebecca joined him.

"I feel much better after that shower," she divulged taking a seat, sipping her coffee, and studying him deep in thought. "What did you mean, either we're getting stronger, or he is getting weaker?"

"I was just thinking about that," said Liam sitting next to her. "I believe it's a bit of both, as our powers are getting stronger, the Darkness is getting weaker. Which is why we are seeing past events clearer and communicating with Jason and the girls more often."

"How come we always wake up back in bed?"

"I'm guessing when the vision ends, we are taken back to the present, and the last place we were before it started," he explained. "I don't think we're waking up; I believe we're already awake, and just sitting up."

"Speaking of sitting up, tell me your vision," she said listening to him. "So, when you got up, I wasn't in bed?"

"No, you were gone" he replied. "Tell me about yours."

Rebecca did. "And then you joined me in the parlor, and you know the rest," she concluded taking a sip of her coffee. "I tried to look at his face, the car, and the surroundings, but they were blurry. His voice was distorted but I could understand him."

"Me too."

"I tried to hold on to Hetty but couldn't, the Demon, pulled her away," continued Rebecca. "It was like a dream, but not, it seemed so real."

"It's real, all right," confirmed Liam. "We can't pull them in to our world, but we can help them get out from under that Dark spell," said Liam.

"We need to find the grimoire, so you can read the spell."

"Let's go the den, and review what else we need to do besides finding Jason's grimoire."

Rebecca opened her laptop and quickly read the list. "Besides the grimoire, we need to find out who the killer is and why he killed them, and we talked about focusing on his signature on the note. We know where Jason is buried at the cemetery, but not the girls, we need to find them," she said glancing over at him. "They could be miles from here, the killer drove out into the country."

"That's an issue, there's a lot of land out there."

"Unfortunately, that's it," she sighed. "Do you want me to add he information from our visions in point form."

"Yeah," he said thinking. "If you casted a Dark spell, it was weakening, and someone like us could potentially find out who you were, what would you do?"

Rebecca sat back and looked at him. "I would either recast the original spell, strengthen it, or replace it with a stronger one, why?"

"Jason, Mandy, and Hetty, are telling us to hurry, that we don't have time, and if we don't, they will be lost forever."

"Are they telling us that the killer knows we are getting closer and that he needs to do something to keep them trapped and protect his identity?"

"They are. The question is, why hasn't he?"

"Because…he can't."

"But they know he is going to do it?"

"He can't, yet."

"I think you're on to something there, and that would align with them telling us that we don't have a lot of time," said Liam standing. "We can't waste time worrying about why he can't, we just need to realize that it buys us time, and that we need to get moving on this."

"Let me add the information first, then we can brainstorm," she said leaning over her laptop.

Liam left and came back a few minutes later with the Elegant Garden Patios book and flipped through it. "It's in here."

"What?"

"The English patio deign that's in the backyard, and it looks the exact same as the photo."

"I'm almost done."

After looking at most of the pictures, he went to the first page, and read aloud. "To James, Happy Birthday, Jason Campbell."

Rebecca turned off her laptop and looked at it. "He's right about the 'J' and the 'a' not being connected in either of their names. Although, my mother did say he was a stickler for writing his signature."

"I know, but I've signed my name different times on numerous occasions," he said closing the book.

"So have I," she admitted.

"Although, if you were writing a well thought out suicide note, wouldn't you be a stickler with your signature, especially under the circumstances?"

"You would think so."

"Yet he didn't. Why not?"

"Because we said he didn't write it, the murderer did."

"We did," agreed Liam opening it and studying the names. "If you were the killer, wouldn't you make sure you got his signature right, you know, to eliminate any suspicions that he was murdered?"

"Yeah, you would."

"Unless?" said Liam running the scenery quickly in his head. "Humor me for a minute?"

"Okay," she said with a cute smile.

Liam got a piece of paper, signed his name, and gave it to her along with a blank piece. "Write a quick note on the blank piece and sign my name as best as you can?"

Rebecca did and handed it to him.

"Rebecca, you are far more the superior White Witch, your humble servant, Liam Wilson…poetic," he said looking at her. "How did you know that was my signature?"

"If I had just written this note, and gave it to you, how would you know that this was my signature?" he asked pointing at it.

She lifted up the paper he had given her with only his signature on it. "Because I'd seen it before."

"So, if you wanted to forge my name, you would use that one on the blank page?"

"Yeah, because it's the only one I have."

"One last thing," he said containing his excitement. "Isn't it odd, Jason signed the book with his last name?"

"I thought that, too, they were friends."

Liam turned the book towards her. "Jason deliberately signed his full name, and incorrectly signed his first name, knowing the killer would believe that was his signature. Which means the killer had only seen his signature once and thought that was how he signed his name all the time…the killer slipped up," he whispered.

"Wait?" asked Rebecca, her mind turning, then suddenly stood. "That would mean James Childwall is the killer! He wrote the note and signed Jason's name incorrectly based on the signature in the book Jason gave him."

"He did," confirmed Liam.

"That smug bastard, the reason he knew the killer had slipped up, was because it was him," she said grabbing her phone. "We need to call the sheriff."

"And tell him what?"

"Well, what we found," she replied, then realized what he was actually saying. "We don't have enough on him?"

"No," he said with a grin, "but we know it was him, and he doesn't."

"We need to find the bodies, finding the grimoire is worthless without them."

"Grab Jason's report and look at what articles of girls' clothing they found in his camper."

She opened up the files and skimmed through the pages. "Hetty's coat, and T-shirt. Mandy's soccer shirt and headband. They items were confirmed by their mothers." It suddenly hit Rebecca. "Oh my God, James killed those poor girls," she said crying. "Why did he have to kill them? They did nothing wrong."

"Don't worry we'll find out, and we'll find them," comforted Liam.

"I'm sorry, I'm not being very professional," she sobbed.

"Our humanity is what connects us to them, it pulls their spirits toward us, and gives them the strength and courage they need to reach out and believe that we can help them. Without it, they would never trust us, and we would never succeed. It's what separates us from Darkness," he described. "So, without a doubt, you are acting extremely professional."

"Did that just come to you, or had you thought about it before?" she asked.

"I guess I've wondered why us before, and the answer just came to me now while I was holding you and listening to you cry."

"Thanks, that makes me feel a lot better," she confessed wiping her tears away then kissing him.

"That was pretty heavy, eh?"

"And follow it up with a joke, a hippy joke," she said giggling.

In the background they heard a lawnmower.

"Must be Frankie, the rock lifter," guessed Liam.

"Another kind of heavy," she said glancing up at him.

"You picked up on that?"

"I did, heavy, heavy rocks," she said gently pulling away. "Heavy, heavy rocks," she whispered slowly, "heavy…heavy rocks."

"Are you okay?"

"Quick, follow me," she said running out back. "Frankie, Frankie!" she yelled and waved.

He spotted her and turned off the lawnmower. "Rebecca, everything okay?"

"Yeah, I'm fine. Those rocks that you carried. What neighbor did Mr. Childwall give them to?"

"Sandra's mom next door?"

"Are you sure?"

"I'm positive."

"How did he get them over there?"

"I don't know," replied Frankie, "either they came over and took them or he dropped them off."

"Do you remember when it was you carried them in?"

"Sure, my tenth birthday was on the sixth, so it would have been the fourth of September."

"1980?"

"Yeah.

"And they were gone by the following week."

"My dad didn't know exactly when but when he came back on the twelfth, they weren't here."

"Thanks, Frankie," she said cheerfully and walked with Liam towards Sandra's home.

"What's going on?" he asked.

"Wait and see, and just hope I'm right," she replied knocking on the door.

"Rebecca!"

"Hi, Sandra, how are you doing?"

"Good, is everything okay?"

"Yeah, do you have a minute?"

"Sure."

"Do you mind if I look around your backyard?"

"No," answered Sandra closing the door, and taking them around the side of house into the yard.

"Did you ever have large melon-sized rocks back here that Mr. Childwall gave you? Now, it would have been back in the eighties, so he would have given them to your mom?"

"No, we never did."

"Are you positive?"

"My Mom liked our big lawn and loved watching us playing on it, she would never have had any rocks back here. But then again, I was young," she replied. "I could call her if it's important?"

"Would you, please?"

"Come inside."

They waited in the family room and listened as Sandra spoke with her mother.

"No," she said putting the phone down, "he never gave us any rocks for the garden."

"Thank you, Sandra, sorry to bother you," said Rebecca heading for the door.

"No problem, anytime," she said seeing them out.

Outside, Rebecca grabbed his hand, and quickly led him through the front door and into the den.

"Sit down and hear me out?" she asked nervously pacing in front of him. "You had a vision, and then we both shared one, where we saw Jason get out of the casket, take off his burial clothes and walk towards the back door. In the first one, you and Mandy followed him out to the garden where a black mist surrounded him, and he, along with the mist disappeared. In the one we both shared, Jason grabbed our hands, and we walked with him across the garden as it went black. Then we arrived at the burial site of Hetty and Mandy, where he let go of our hands, walked on alone, and collapsed. The gloved man picked him up, tossed him in the hole, and filled it with dirt. Right?"

"That's right."

"James Childwall told us that he purchased Jason's casket and had a viewing for him right in the front parlor. He told us that it was an open coffin for the for the adults and had made sure he was clothed in a way that hid the scare on his neck. But that day, it was closed, because my mother and aunt and were in the house and were very young. Remember?"

"I do."

"When I asked you why you were seeing the vision of him leaving his coffin and what it meant. You said, maybe it was his spirit leaving his body and being taken away by the black mist, the Demon, the Darkness? Right?"

"I did."

"You asked your mother when Jason's casket was in the parlor, did anything peculiar happen? Your mom replied, not that she could recall, and my mom said the same. Then my mom told us my grandfather was a pallbearer, and when she asked him what it was like, he winked and said it was heavier than he expected."

"Where are going with this?" asked Liam captivated.

"Four days before Jason's murder, James Childwall insists on having eight rocks brought into the garden. Then claims he doesn't like them, gives them to a neighbor, who says he never did. Where did the rocks go?"

Liam gave her an uncertain look.

"Okay, here it is," she said trying to contain her excitement. "The day before the funeral, the casket is open, then the day of the funeral it's closed, because of the children. I believe the night before the funeral, James

Childwall took Jason's body out of the casket, removed his clothes, and threw him in the trunk of his car then buried him next to Mandy and Hetty. Came home, put Jason's burial clothes in the casket, and filled them with the eight rocks from his garden. No one ever suspecting what he had done. The three bodies are now out in the wilderness trapped in a Darkness spell."

Liam was silent.

"What do you think?" she asked anxiously.

He studied her, smiled, and stood up. "I think you're brilliant," he said lifting her up, spinning her around, then putting her down.

"You think I'm right?"

"Without a doubt," he replied confidently. "Now we just have to prove it."

"By prove it, you mean dig up the grave and open the coffin?"

"That's the only way, unless you have another option?"

"No," she said knowing he was teasing her.

"But we need to do it as discreetly as possible?"

"We're not digging it up in the middle of the night, are we?"

"I didn't mean that discreet," he said with a chuckle.

"I don't know," she replied playfully pushing him.

"You need to call your mom and tell her we need a legal letter from Jason's family stating they want the casket moved to Boston, ASAP, and how long it will take."

"Okay, then what?"

"After we hear back from your mom, I'm going to call the sheriff, tell him about the document, and to meet us at the cemetery with the gravediggers."

"What if my mom asks me why?"

"Just tell her to do that first, and we'll explain later."

"All right."

Chapter Thirty-Two

"Good morning, Sheriff."

"Morning Rebecca, Liam," he replied. "Do you want to tell me what all this is about?"

"Once we get the coffin on the stand," replied Liam.

"Okay, said the sheriff reviewing the legal document, "looks like you got this signed in less than a day, it must be urgent."

"It is, trust us," assured Rebecca.

"Oh, I do, otherwise I wouldn't be standing here at six o'clock with three gravediggers," he said, and motioned for them to start.

Once they finished, they gently lifted the casket, placed it on the stand, then put up a large canvas tent around it before being told to go on a break. Rebecca Liam and Sheriff Lee walked into the tent and zipped it closed. They walked over to the casket, Liam took the top while the sheriff took the bottom, and Rebecca watched from the middle.

"Ready?" asked Liam.

"You want to open it?" asked the sheriff unsure.

"We do," confirmed Rebecca.

"All right, on three…one, two, three."

They opened the casket and looked inside at the rock-filled burial clothes.

"What the…?" asked the sheriff. "Where's the body?"

Rebecca smiled at Liam who proudly winked at her and motioned with his head to tell the sheriff what happened to the body.

Rebecca filled the sheriff in.

"James Childwall killed Jason, Amanda, and Heather, and buried them out in the wilderness miles from here," summarized the sheriff.

"He did," she replied.

"That son of a bitch!"

"What happens now?" asked Rebecca.

The sheriff glanced over at Liam, then they both looked at Rebecca.

"First, we need to put the coffin back," said Liam closing it.

"I'll tell the gravediggers to put it back in the ground and let them know there was an error with the document."

"Here's two hundred dollars each for them," said Liam handing the sheriff an envelope, "no one can know about this."

"I understand."

"What about James Childwall?" asked Rebecca.

"There's not much we can do?"

"What do you mean?"

"If we told James what you just told the sheriff. He would probably say Jason signed the signature in the suicide note like he did in his book. And that somebody, maybe a Satan worshipper, dug up the grave and robbed the body."

"We need more evidence?"

"You do," confirmed the sheriff. "Finding the bodies would be a good start, but it has to be directly connected to James Childwall."

"That's why we have to keep this quiet," emphasized Liam.

"You don't want James Childwall to catch wind of this?" she asked.

"On the contrary, after we speak with your mom, we're paying him a visit."

They walked out of the tent, the sheriff went over, spoke to the three men, and gave one of them the envelope.

"I wait here till they finish," he said returning. "Here's your document back."

"Thanks," said Liam. "We'll be in touch."

Chapter Thirty-Three

"Are you ready?"

"I am," she replied and knocked on the door.

"Good afternoon," said the maid. "Rebecca and Liam?"

"Yes."

"Please this way," she said and took them to the living room. "Please, try keep your visit short, he's hasn't been doing well these last couple of days."

Rebecca and Liam were shocked at the old man they saw.

"Take a seat, please," he offered then glanced up at the maid. "Some lemonade and cookies." Then waited till she dropped them off. "How can I help you two today?"

Liam and Rebecca told them what they had found out.

"And?" he asked.

"We also know you murdered Eleanor Peabody and Maggie O'Brien," stated Rebecca. "Although were not sure why you killed them all?"

"We originally thought it was so you could be the Black Witch High King, but when you had the opportunity to become one you refused," revealed Liam.

"Then we thought it was just to create fear and cause chaos within the Black Witches, but in the last forty-three years nothing else has happened, so we're guessing it wasn't that. Which leaves the questions why and was it worth it?" asked Rebecca. "Look at you, you're decaying."

"Not for long," he said with a chuckle. "I must admit, I'm pleasantly surprised how far you got in such short time, and with you being so open and honest with me let me indulge you and tell you why."

"Why would you want to do that?"

"I will answer that at the end," he confirmed. "Please, feel free to record what I'm going to tell you with your phone."

Rebecca pressed record and put it on the table.

"Both of you are right, I did want to be High King, and my original plan was to eliminate my competition, but something happened in 1972 that changed my mind. I hired an archeologist to find something for me, and he did, it was a Clunaclum."

"A sacrificial knife," translated Rebecca.

"Yes," replied James impressed, "with a black handle and gold blade, and it comes from the time Jesus walked the Earth."

Liam looked over at Rebecca doubtfully then at James. "How did it get here in the US?"

"That is too long of a story, and quite frankly, one you need to figure out on your own," he said, then continued. "For finding the Clunaclum, I paid Dr. Edmund Brown handsomely, and once I had this knife in my hand I realized that I had the power to invite the Dark Spirit into our world and be its Host. He completed his research and found the Epicenter of Darkness. I now knew where I must go. I sponsored his excavations in Egypt, and after he left, I went to Massachusetts—"

"Where in Massachusetts?"

"Nice try, my dear, but you need to do your own fieldwork," he stated. "Once there, I conducted a ritual and offered my body, which the Dark Spirit accepted. I realized with my new power, I could be the Dark Witch High King, and eliminate all the Black, Gray, and White Witches. So, I decided to start with the Black Witch High Queen, Eleanor Peabody."

"You're admitting that you killed her?" asked Liam.

"I am, I murdered Eleanor Peabody," he confessed. "That evening I went to her apartment, told her that I had kidnapped her daughter, and would kill her if Eleanor didn't do exactly what I told her. I had someone hire the three men to meet her, party, then go back to her place for drinks, drugs, and sex. They thought it was her idea. After they left, the Dark Spirit killed her."

"So, you didn't kidnap her daughter?"

"I met Lenore a few days earlier, told her I was a friend of her mother's, that I was a Black Witch visiting Boston, and wanted to surprise her. During which, I got my picture taken with her and showed it to her mother."

"She believed you based on that?"

"Eleanor had her doubts, so I also told her that I was once a Black Witch who was now a Dark Witch, and would kill her on the spot, and then her daughter. Then the Dark Spirit showed its black eyes."

"So you set up the whole night and manipulated the trial."

"Originally the trial was perfect, actually too perfect, so I had to throw some drama into it spice things up a little."

"You're referring to the scandals surrounding it?" suggested Rebecca. "What were they again? Oh, witnesses being paid off, tampering of evidence, and the sudden death of the homeless man, Gordy Jacobs."

"You've done your research," complimented James. "Unfortunately, Gordy was just in the wrong place at the wrong time, but his death did add intrigue to the proceedings."

"Weren't you worried that the three men would hear about what had happened to Elanor and tell the police."

"I paid them a lot of money, and I told them if they did, the high-priced lawyer that I hired for them would quit, and they would rot in jail," said James bluntly. "Besides, after the trial I comforted Lenore, and told her a secret about her mother that her grandmother could help her with," said James reeling them in.

"What secret?"

"Her mother could change into a feline, it's called ailuranthropy or werecat."

"Any cat?"

"Yes, but a panther running around Boston is sure to attract unwanted attention, but not a black house cat," he clarified. "Lenore, who felt betrayed by the Black Witches, turned her back on them. They warned her not seek revenge on the three men, but she didn't listen, and instead took my advice. Within a couple of years, the three men met horrible deaths. All were considered accidental and witnessed by a black house cat."

"Lenore, as a cat, killed those men?"

"It saved me the trouble," said James openly. "After that, she disappeared, and was never seen again."

"So Maggie O'Brien was next in line for High Queen?"

"Yes, and with what happened with Eleanor, there was fear that she was next. So, I was invited by your grandmother to offer advice on how to protect her. Instead, I figured out the best way to get into her house and kill her. I won't go through the details because you already have them, but I will go on record to say that what you have is accurate."

"And Jason?" asked Liam.

"After she was killed, they told him to resign from the law firm and disappear. Which he did. Then tired of being on his own, he knocked on your grandmother's door looking for some stability in his life."

"He knew you lived in Amare too?"

"He did, and while we became good friends, I plotted his demise."

"Now you're admitting killing him and the two young girls?" asked Rebecca.

"Yes, I sliced Jason up on his kitchen table while he was waking up from a sleeping potion. I grabbed Hetty on the dirt road, and Amanda at the Town Park, and lured them into my car with a bag of candies that contained a hypnotic spell. After I placed a sleeping potion over their mouths, I drove them into the woods, where I strangled their unconscious bodies and dumped them into a ditch."

"Why are you confessing to all this?" asked Rebecca.

"What are you going to do? Run to the sheriff and have him listen to the rantings of a crazy man who is talking about conjuring spells, murdering people, and summoning a Dark Spirit. And believes he's a Dark Witch, and knows Black, White, and Gray Witches," he said cackling. "Who's going to believe that?"

Rebecca and Liam quietly looked at one another.

"Besides, you have no bodies, and trust me you will never find them," he bragged. "And even if you did, you need to find a White Witch who Jason has chosen, to read a spell from his grimoire that has been missing for over forty-three years."

Rebecca was just about to tell him Liam had been chosen, and decided not to because she realized James was fishing for information. "Your arrogance will be your downfall," she warned.

"Well, I know it won't be due to you two," he replied derogatively.

"You're next in line, they offer you High King and you refuse, why?" asked Liam then realized the answer. "They didn't offer it to you, they decided to look for Lenore instead…The Black Witches must have suspected you."

"Very shrewd," he said slowly clapping his hands. "They did, so before they could approach me, I told them that with the death of my friend Jason, I refused to be High King, and would never have an heir to pass it on to. The Black Witches were in disarray and decided to function as a committee until they found Lenore or hopefully her child, if she even had one."

"Your plan was to become the Black Witch High King?" queried Rebecca.

"It was, and once I was, I would rename myself the Dark Witch High King, recruit Black Witches to join me as Dark Witches and eliminate those that didn't. After which, I would go after the Whites Witches, then the Gray."

"But you didn't become High King, so throwing them off your scent and creating chaos was your next best solution," queried Liam.

"It was, and the last thing I wanted have was a Gray Witch knocking on my door to eliminate me."

"Look at you," said Rebecca with disdain, "knocking on death's door. You die, and the Dark Spirit dies, and everyone is going to know what you did. You have no heir, no one to pass your Dark Spirit on to and fulfill your plan, only a disturbing legacy that will be quickly forgotten."

James laughed loudly.

"What's so funny?" asked Rebecca unamused.

"Oh, I forgot to tell you about my son."

"You have a son, sure?" she asked doubtfully.

"In 1973, after I got the Clunaclum, I realized that if anything were to happen to me, I would need someone to pass the Dark Spirit on to. I went to New York City, found a young attractive stripper who was working to save enough money to get out of the city, open a bakery, and live a better life. After I met with her several times, and made her a proposition, and asked her to have my child and raise it. In return, I would give her a lot of cash and buy her a beautiful home in a quaint town where she could open a bakery. I also told her I would pay for the child's upbringing and college, and that she could marry and have children. All I wanted to do was not leave this world without having left my mark. She thought I was just eccentric and agreed, had my son, and raised him not too far from Amare. He went to college, has a wonderful career, and is happily married with three children, and still lives in the town he was born in."

"And you're going to ruin it all, by passing the Dark Spirit on to him and making him a Dark Witch High King?"

"Of course not, he was just a vessel for the Dark Spirit over these last seven months."

"Just a vessel?" asked Liam nervously.

"No, of course not, but you will find out what he's been up to sooner or later," said James. "My grandson, will have that honor."

"One of his children?" asked Rebecca.

"No, when he was eighteen my company sent out letters to several individuals who had applied and were accepted to the same college he was planning on intending, saying we were interested in potentially hiring them after they graduated. We set up meet-and-greets, held seminars, that sort of thing. During the night they partied, and I had an ex-stripper pick him up, and sleep with him every night of the week he was here."

"Another stripper?"

"She was a college girl, stripping to pay for her education. The owner of the club said she could make a lot of money doing tricks for clients. I could tell she didn't want to, so I paid the owner to convince him to let me be her first customer. She reluctantly accepted my offer. When we met, she said she had made a mistake, and was going to leave, I said that I wanted to make her a proposition, and if she didn't like it, I would give her two thousand dollars and she could leave. She agreed to sleep with my son, get pregnant, and not contact him afterwards. Once she had the baby, she would give it to me, and in return, she could pick any college she wanted. I would guarantee her acceptance, pay for her tuition, buy her a house and car in the city where she attended school, and give her cash."

"Nine months later, she just gave you her baby?"

"Technically she gave it up for adoption to a good Catholic couple who couldn't have children," he clarified. "I made sure my grandson was well taken care of, went to the best schools, and university."

"You have a son who doesn't know you are his father—"

"And doesn't even know the Dark Spirit lives within him," James bragged.

"How does he not know?" probed Rebecca.

"Darkness hides, and only comes out when I say it needs to, without him even knowing. He then becomes its Host, and once Darkness is finished, he goes back into hiding."

"What does Darkness do for you?"

James went silent and offered no answer.

"And you have a grandson who doesn't know his father, mother, or grandfather?" continued Rebecca.

"He's well hidden, and when the time is right, and the fall's full moon is bright, we will meet at the Epicenter of Darkness where he will conduct his first sacrifice, and me, my thirteenth…and Darkness will live."

"Okay, crazy man," said Rebecca picking up her phone and standing. "Now these killings are sacrifices. Liam, I'm done, let's go."

Liam stood next to her. "We will find the bodies and the grimoire, we will free them, and you will die in jail."

"My immature White Witches, you have less than forty-eight hours. After that, my new Dark spell will be too strong for any Witch, and they will be stuck in Darkness for all eternity."

Rebecca and Liam turned around and left.

Chapter Thirty-Four

Outside, Rebecca waited till they turned onto Main Street before grabbing Liam and holding him. "I'm really scared," she whispered, "and he terrifies me."

"I wouldn't have guessed it with the way you stood up to him," said Liam reassuringly.

"I did do a pretty good, didn't I?"

"You did great," he said with a kind smile. "Why don't we take a walk before going to the mansion and talk about it?"

"I'd like that," she said grabbing his hand and contemplating what James had told them.

"Why do you think he told us all that?"

"Because he's arrogant and narcissistic and believes he will still get away with it."

"I can't argue with you there," said Rebecca. "Why do you think he confessed to everything so easily?"

"I was wondering the same thing," admitted Liam. "The problem with committing the perfect crime, is that the criminal never gets caught, therefore, he never gets the credit for that crime."

"And if he reveals himself as the criminal, it's no longer a perfect crime, but he gets the notoriety."

"Exactly, it's his legacy, and he wants everyone to know what he did."

"What did you make of him first admitting to killing them, then he said Darkness killed them, and at the end said they were actually sacrifices."

"Over the last couple of weeks, I believe James has been the one desperately trying to hold off our powers, and with his spell slowly deteriorating, it's affected his body physically and mind mentally. Now he's very weak, and I think he's mixing up his stories and lies," acknowledged Liam. "I believe originally, he wanted to be the Black

Witch High King, then become the Dark Witch High King. But like my mom said, he's actually Darkness' Servant, and has been murdering and sacrificing those people for Darkness' greater cause."

"All the people he's killed are sacrifices?"

"No, only the ones he cut up with his Clunaclum."

"Fucking Clunaclum, that freaked me out," she said with a shiver. "James said his last sacrifice would be his thirteenth, but he's only done three, and if we include him performing the last one that would make it four. Who are the other nine?"

"He did make it sound like the thirteenth was his last."

"Which would mean he's committed nine others?"

"It would, and we need to make a note of it when we get back, then worry about that another day," he recommended.

"You're right," she said and thought for a moment. "Is there anything he said that was helpful?"

"No, not really," admitted Liam.

"Well, we know why he murdered the Black Witches. They're sacrifices for Darkness, and to give it life, and potentially human form. And we know the who," she said thinking out loud. "We now need to find Jason's grimoire and the bodies."

"Jason said the grimoire was hidden and that we had to find it urgently," recalled Liam. "Which means he obviously wants us to find it, but where is it? I get the feel we're missing something very obvious."

"I agree, and how are we supposed to find their bodies in Seneca county, or worse, the Finger Lakes region?"

Liam opened the mansion door, and they walked in. "I'll make the coffees."

"And I'll set up the library," she said leaving him, going into the room, and organizing their findings on the wooden floor.

"Here you go," said Liam passing her a coffee. "What do we have?"

"Photos, books, police reports, printouts of the descriptions of our visions, printouts of our meeting notes, printouts of our list of questions and answers, and lastly the audio recording of James Childwall," she said walking down the line and pointing to them. "Finding Jason's grimoire and the bodies are the priorities."

"Let's concentrate on finding the grimoire first, and make that our main priority, without that we can't free them," suggested Liam looking down. "And I believe right now, there's something in one of these piles that holds the answer, we just need to find it quickly."

"Within thirty hours and sixteen minutes," confirmed Rebecca looking at her phone then up at Liam's grinning face. "What? I set up a timer on my phone."

"I can see that," he said favorably. "Now, let's go through each of the piles and remove those items that don't have any relevance to Jason's grimoire whatsoever."

Twenty minutes later, they looked at the four printouts and James's audio recording.

"This is all we have," said Rebecca. "The first printout describes our journey inside the chest, seeing it on his kitchen table, and Jason saying he has hidden it and to find it urgently. The second is when my mother told us that Jason had made a chest for my grandmother and said to my family never to throw it out. Third, is when we realized all those years ago, Jason had put a spell on the chest, and that night we stayed in the guest house, he put us under it and pulled us in. The fourth, is your mother informing us that only a White Witch chosen by a Black Witch can read a spell from that Black Witch's, Jason's, grimoire. The last, the audio recording, is James Childwall telling us we still need Jason to choose a White Witch to read the spell from his grimoire, and that his grimoire that has been missing for over forty-three years."

"And here's what we know. James Childwall doesn't have it because he said it has been missing for over forty-three years. That Jason put a spell on a chest that he gave to your grandmother over forty-three years ago and told her not to throw it out. The night in the guest house, we are put under his spell and pulled into the chest and see the grimoire in his cabin on the kitchen table. Jason said he has hidden it, a physical book, but where?"

"James probably searched the cabin and camper to guarantee no one else would find it, read the spell, and free him," suggested Rebecca. "The fact that he said it was missing means he didn't find it because it wasn't there."

"If we remove all we know, and just keep the physical, tangible items, what are we left with?" asked Liam thinking aloud. "The grimoire, the cabin, the camper, the guest house, and the chest.

"It's not in the cabin, nor the camper, and the guest house was built years later, so he couldn't have hidden it there."

"The chest?" asked Liam.

"We've emptied the chest, there's no book."

"Damn!" screamed Liam getting up and pacing, as he did a book caught his eye and he picked it up. "The book on how to make chests," said Liam looking at Rebecca. "Your mom said he was handy building things, and remember I joked that he must have needed a little help making the chest."

They sat on the floor and slowly flipped through it.

"That's it there!" said Rebecca pointing to it.

They read the description.

"I don't believe it!" she screamed excitedly.

Chapter Thirty-Five

"Mom, where are you?"

"In the living room."

"Where's the chest that was in the guest house?"

"Hello to you, too, dear," she said standing.

"Sorry Mom, just under the clock here," she said hugging her.

"Hello, Liam."

"Hi, Christine."

"I had your dad, and Liam's dad, move it back into the spare room for me," she replied as they followed her upstairs.

Rebecca opened the chest and removed the blankets, then Liam stuck his hand underneath, clicked a lock, and pulled out the secret compartment that was the width and length of the chest.

"Jason's grimoire?" asked Christine looking down.

Rebecca knelt down, picked up the item wrapped in a blanket and placed it on the floor, then a second. She slowly removed the blankets to reveal two Black Witches' grimoires. "Jason's, and I'm guessing Maggie's," she said glancing up at her mom, then over at Liam.

"They've been there all this time," said her mother teary eyed."

Rebecca stood and held her mom as she cried.

"I'm sorry, I need a minute alone, and then I need to call, Anna. Please, excuse me," she said departing.

"Will she be okay?" asked Liam.

"Yeah," sighed Rebecca sitting next to Liam. "It will be an emotional day for them both."

"I bet," agreed Liam. "I think we'll wait till your mom returns and find out what spell we need."

"Okay," she replied happily. "We did it!"

"We did," replied Liam with a smile, then leaned over and kissed her.

Christine eventually returned, and went through Jason's grimoire first, found the spell and marked it, then did the same with Maggie's.

"They're slightly different spells?" asked Rebecca.

"That's because they held under different Dark spells."

"What should we do with the grimoires?" queried Rebecca looking at Liam.

"Let's put them back where we found them," he suggested. "The safest place is here with your mom, and when we need them, we can come back and get them."

After they did, Christine replaced the blankets in the chest, closed it, then followed her daughter and Liam downstairs.

"Mom, what about Eleanor Peabody, doesn't she need to be set free?"

"Her daughter, Lenore, did that shortly after the trial ended."

"I thought you said only a chosen White Witch could perform that?"

"That's only true if Black Witches have no offspring," explained Christine. "You need to remember; we've never had this issue with Dark spells before."

"I understand, Mom."

"Rebecca, once Liam frees Jason and the girls, you will need to go to Worcester and meet Maggie," revealed Christine. "She still has to choose you before you can free her."

"Why wouldn't she?" asked Liam.

"She doesn't know Rebecca and may think she's a Dark Spirit trying to trick her."

"But can't Liam, Anna, or Alicia, vouch for me?"

"It doesn't work like that, dear, she has to believe you and trust you."

"Fuck Mom, you're freaking me out!"

"I'm just telling you like it is, and watch your language, young lady," said Christine moving her daughter's hair from her eyes and smiling. "I know you will do fine, and don't worry, Anna will be there to guide you through the steps."

Rebecca and Liam silently walked to the car and got inside.

"Why don't we take the rest of the afternoon off and start fresh tomorrow morning?" suggested Liam. "We've accomplished a lot these last few days and we could do with the break."

"I think that's a great idea. My head's just spinning."

"Why don't we go for a walk along the beach then grab a drink on the boardwalk."

"All right, then after we can make dinner at my house while enjoying a nice bottle of wine."

Chapter Thirty-Six

"That was the best sleep I've had in a while," said Rebecca walking into the mansion.

"What? Are you blaming this place?" joked Liam.

"You must admit, everything seems to happen here?"

"It does, and I'm sure having Jason's wake—"

"And his killer here…"

"Has something to do with it," finished Liam.

"Well, here we are, back in the library," she said flopping in the chair.

"Why don't we do the same thing as yesterday, go through all the items we have, and focus only on the information that will help us locate the bodies."

Rebecca stood and helped him set up the piles on the floor. Thirty minutes later they looked at the several printouts they had chosen.

"We've both agreed that the photos, books, police reports, and James Childwall's audio, contain no information that will be helpful to us finding their bodies," verified Rebecca. "Which leaves us with the printout descriptions of our visions, and no physical evidence…Actually, that's wrong, we have the pickaxe."

"I'd forgotten about that, too," said Liam sitting on the floor next to her. "Let's review our last visions, the ones where the girls are abducted, and we end up meeting in the parlor. First, we'll focus on Mandy and Hetty being taken, then James in the parlor."

"Here we go, they're almost the exact same," revealed Rebecca. "They get in the car, are put to sleep, the killer, James, undoes their seatbelt, pushes their limp body onto the floor, then drives. I said for thirty minutes, you said forty. He enters a deep forest, stops, places the unconscious girl on the backseat, and strangles her. He then removes articles of their clothing and places them in a clear plastic bag, then puts the girl's body inside a large black garbage bag and ties it up, before putting it and the plastic bag into the trunk and driving…Time speeds up, it's the middle of the night, neither of us know how long he drove for, but because it's nighttime, we assumed it was a great distance…We followed the killer as he carried the garbage bag to a hole, casually throws it in, then fills it with dirt…We each ran for what seemed like an eternity, as the Demon leisurely walked behind us…We arrive at the back of the mansion, and eventually end up inside…that's it," she said looking at him.

"When you walked from the car to the burial site, was it a long walk?"

"No, it was actually quite close, about twenty-five steps…and now that you mention it, it was close to the side of a paved road."

"It was," recalled Liam.

"Which could be any paved road in any area in any county," stated Rebecca discouraged. "I've got nothing."

"Neither do I," sighed Liam. "Here, I'll summarize Jason in the parlor, and give you a break."

"Here you go," she said handing him the printout.

"All right…In the middle of the night, Jason sat up, climbed out of his casket, and stripped to his underwear. He slowly moved towards us, and as he passed, grabbed our hands. We walked with him out the back door and across the garden as it went black. Then we arrived at the burial site, where the man, James, picked him up, tossed him in the hole, and filled it with dirt…The man with demonic black eyes turned to us and told us to leave the mansion now and never come back…Otherwise, he will bury us out here, and we will be his servants for all eternity…He charges us and we turn and run…We could hear the Demon galloping behind us, and in the distance we could see the mansion rapidly approaching…we swiftly climb the steps as the Demon jumps on us and tackles us to the ground…that's it."

"I'm glad you read that one, it's creepy," said Rebecca shivering. "Was that James chasing us or the Dark Spirit?"

"It was James possessed by the Dark Spirit killing the girls, and disposing their bodies, and James's. After that, it's the Demon, Dark Spirit, Darkness itself, chasing us; they are all one and the same."

"The only detail I found odd, is that we drove for a long time, but ran back to the rear of the mansion rather quickly. Even when we left the parlor with Jason, after he was thrown in the hole, we ran back rapidly."

"True," said Liam.

"The man with Demonic black eyes told us to leave the mansion now and never come back or he would bury us out there and be his servants for all eternity. Yet, when the Demon tackled us, we woke up in the bedroom, which would mean if it couldn't catch us, it couldn't bury us, right?"

"You're right," he agreed, contemplating.

"That's all I have," confessed Rebecca leaning forward and putting her head in her hands.

"So, we have two questions. First, why did we run back to the rear of the mansion so quickly? Second, why were we told to leave the mansion, and threatened, if we didn't? And we have one fact, we know ow that the Demon can't touch us," said Liam, hoping it would spark some insight.

"It definitely wants us to leave the mansion, but why? Why are we a threat?"

"Because we see most of our visions here," he replied. "The only exceptions are the guest house, but that was the chest, and me seeing Mandy in the Essentia garden, but that's very close to the mansion's backyard."

"I forgot about that. Mandy was looking for her friend?"

"That's what she said," replied Liam struggling to find something and becoming frustrated. "We've exhausted all the information we have here, and have nothing to show for it, and we're running out of time. Damn it!

Rebecca put her arm around him "Why don't we take a lunch break and pick up this conversation in a more…conducive setting and get out of this room."

"You know a place?"

"I know the perfect place."

Chapter Thirty-Seven

"Essentia?" asked Liam following her in.

"We were talking about it, and it's close, and I was hoping getting a different perspective on our problem may trigger something that we hadn't considered before. Which is why we are going to sit in the garden."

"Rebecca, Liam!" cried Liz. "How is my favorite couple?"

"We're fine," replied Rebecca with a smile.

"Lunch in the garden?" she asked.

"Please."

"Then follow me," she said walking away before turning her head towards them, "we have a lovely 'Ravioli di Zucca' today."

"That sounds wonderful, Liam?"

"Perfect," he replied.

"One second," said Liz stopping, going to the kitchen door, and opening it, "Marco, Rebecca and Liam are here." On her way back, he was right behind her.

"My good friends," he said happily. "How are you doing?"

"We're busy," replied Liam.

"And we needed a break, and what better place to come than here," added Rebecca, "where we can relax in your garden and eat a delectable, authentic Italian meal."

"Well, you won't be disappointed," promised Marco with a smile and hastily returning to the kitchen.

They followed Liz to the garden, were seated, and she quickly returned with two glasses of Chardonnay. Between sips, they talked about the delightful wine, the beautiful garden, and the gorgeous weather. When the meal arrived, as they ate, it prompted them to talk about how delicious it was. Once finished, without asking, Liz brought them each a bowl of gelato al pistachio and told them it was the perfect dessert for a hot summer's day, which they devoured appreciatively.

"When I saw Mandy here, and she asked me if I'd seen her friend," said Liam placing his spoon in his empty bowl, "I originally thought she came from behind those hedges. You said she probably came in from the restaurant's side entrance, and because I thought she was a little girl, I assumed she must have. But thinking back, and knowing that it was her spirit I saw, I believe she did come out from those hedges behind me."

"They back onto the mansion's back yard," said Rebecca glancing over his shoulder. "When I was younger and saw them in the backyard, I played with them, so I'm guessing they've been playing out there all these years. But James has never mentioned seeing them, which means he couldn't. Yet, they said he let them play in the garden, but how could he if he didn't even know they were there?"

"They didn't want us to ask James about them," suggested Liam.

"Or James to know that we'd seen them," she stated. Which brings me to my next point. We've only ever seen the girls in the mansion's backyard or inside the mansion. And every time they've taken us somewhere, we've left from the mansion, and came back to it. Even when you saw Mandy here, you believe she came from the hedges that back on to the mansion's backyard. And besides seeing Jason inside the chest, he's always appeared at the mansion," explained Rebecca. "We've stayed at my house numerous times, and they've never appeared, not once. Why not? Isn't that peculiar?"

"That's a great point. We've have been concentrating on the details of our visions, but never where they started or ended," said Liam thinking back. "And you're right, they always begin and finish at the mansion."

"We've believed the reason we've seen Jason was because he had his wake here, and therefore, his spirit remained here," she admitted. "But we know Jason was removed from his casket and buried with the girls somewhere out there," she said pointing out past Amare. "The girls were never here at the mansion, yet we see them here, and only here. Is it because James's spell on them has restricted them to the mansion and its backyard? Or are they able to flee the burial site and come here to us because James's spell is weakening? And when Darkness realizes their spirits have left, does he send the black mist or Demon to find them and bring them back?"

Liam contemplated what she had just said. She was right, but why would they come all the way here? Did Jason tell them to? Then he remembered something Jason had warned him about 'Darkness will always try to trick and manipulate you.' And also, when he and Mandy followed Jason out the back door to the garden, a black mist surrounded Jason and he disappeared along with the mist, then the black mist came from the ground and took Mandy. Another time the Demon grabbed Jason and threw him towards the back fence where he disintegrated…And the girls, they were always taken by Darkness from the mansion via the back door, and when they were out in the backyard, it vanished with them…What about the pickaxe? Why leave that?"

"Liam, what is it? You're deep in thought."

"The pickaxe, why leave that?" he asked trying to remember. "Jason was wearing a vest and using it on the ground."

"James said Jason helped him with his garden, you probably saw an image of Jason digging."

"That's right, James said early one spring Jason helped him but failed miserably, Jason must have been helping with the pickaxe."

"Frankie said it was mostly used for landscaping and breaking up hard surfaces."

"And what was the name of that book he signed for him?"

"Elegant Garden Patios."

Liam then recalled something James said that Jason had said to him, 'if he couldn't be successful at gardening, he may have better luck at building a charming patio in its place.' Then James admitted Jason was right and told us he picked one of the English designs in the book and started building it at the beginning of fall. 'It reminded me of Jason, so I sat on it often to read, and think about him.' "That clever, sharp, arrogant, deceitful, smug, narcissistic bastard," whispered Liam who, as upset as he was, couldn't help smiling at how easily they'd been duped.

"Who? James?"

"Yeah, James," confirmed Liam slowly. "We need to go, now."

They paid, said goodbye to Liz and Marco, and left. When they arrived at the mansion Liam stopped and turned to Rebecca.

"Where are your car keys?"

"Inside."

"Grab them, and a small towel."

When she returned, he took the keys from her. "I'm driving."

"All right."

"Do you have earbuds for your phone in the car?"

"I do," she replied puzzled.

"I want you to plug them in, select a play list, listen to your music, then use the towel to blindfold yourself. Once we get to our destination, I will stop, then tell you what to do next, okay?"

"All right, but where are we going?"

"To the burial site."

"Hold, hold on. How do you know where it is?"

"Just trust me," he replied with a cheeky smile and started to drive.

Rebecca did as he said, and forty minutes later the car stopped, and she felt him pulling off her earbuds.

"I'm going to help you out of the car, then take you to the back of the car, and tell you what to do, okay?"

"Okay," she replied intrigued.

Liam placed Rebecca by the trunk. "Now, when you followed James to the burial site, what do you remember?"

"The paved road," she said stamping her foot on the tarmac. "That's it."

"Good, now we are going to walk, how many steps?"

"I thought it was about twenty-five."

"All right, I'm going to grab your arm, and lead you. You try and remember if it feels the same."

Liam stopped on the twenty-fifth step. "Before I take the headband off, tell me what you thought."

"It was the exact same; the paved road, the soft grass, even the smell."

"So, for all intents and purposes, you're standing in front of the burial site?"

"I am."

"Okay, take off your blindfold."

Rebecca removed it and waited for her eyes to slowly adjust to the sunlight, before suddenly realizing she was looking at the English design patio in the backyard of the Childwall Mansion. "This is the burial site?" she asked looking at him unsurely, then it twigged. "You have proof it is."

"I do, let's go over to the gazebo."

She followed him and they sat.

"You were right, they were fleeing the burial site and the Demon was pulling them back, but something didn't sit right with me. Why did they come all the way here? Then I remembered something Jason had warned us about: how Darkness will try trick and manipulate us."

"So when we were driving with James, after he murdered the girls, we hadn't been driving a long time, time just sped up, and we were only watching James driving home in the middle of the night."

"Yes, and when the black mist surrounded Jason and he disappeared with the mist, then it came from the ground and took Mandy, it was only taking them back underneath the patio. When the Demon grabbed Jason and threw him towards the back fence, he disintegrated—"

"And went back under the patio," finished Rebecca. "The girls, they were always taken by Darkness out of the mansion by the back door or when they were out in the backyard, it vanished with them back under the patio.

"When I mentioned the pickaxe, you said that James said Jason helped him with his garden, and that I probably saw an image of him digging it. Jason told us that early one spring he helped him."

"Jason was only here for one spring," confirmed Rebecca. "Which means in March Jason helped James dig his garden, and at the end of that month after Hetty went missing, James buried her in his garden, and then Mandy in July."

"Correct," confirmed Liam letting Rebecca continue and confirm his theory.

"Then James said he failed miserably, and Jason gave him a book on Elegant Garden Patios and told him if he couldn't be successfully at gardening that he may have better luck at building a charming patio in its place."

"And James told us Jason was right, and he used one of the English designs in the book and built one at the beginning of fall."

"Jason was removed from his casket the night before his funeral, and was buried in the garden, a week prior to fall. James then covered up the garden by building the patio," concluded Rebecca.

"Exactly!"

"James said the patio reminded him of Jason, so he sat on it often to read, and think about him," she suddenly recalled, putting her head on Liam's shoulder, and crying. "What a cold-hearted bastard."

Liam comforted her until she stopped crying and composed herself.

"He fucked with us, Liam."

"Yes, he did."

"I want him to rot in jail."

"We both do," he agreed, "but first, we need to verify something."

"What's that?"

"We need to contact Frankie and have him ask his father the exact date he started the garden, how much Jason helped, and when they started the patio. Do you know how to get in touch with him?"

"I can call his landscaping company, he'll probably answer, if not they'll transfer me."

"Okay, do it."

Rebecca called, got through to him and asked him, then said goodbye and hung up. "He's going to call his dad and call me back within the hour. He said his dad was fairly good with dates, especially when James and Jason started to dig his garden, because he was ticked off James never asked for his help when they initially broke ground."

Chapter Thirty-Eight

"Okay, thanks, Frankie," said Rebecca hanging up and walking towards Liam. "His father said James started the garden on the third day of spring, he remembers that because they were talking about the nice spring weather."

"What about Jason helping him?"

"It was only for that one day, he helped James break the ground, and his father even recalled Jason using a pickaxe."

"Anything else?"

"His father said he only dropped by every other week to perform his gardening duties and was told not to touch it. Apparently, James said to Frankie's dad that he had sowed seeds, but he doesn't remember seeing anything grow."

"Either he was a terrible gardener or never planted seeds?" suggested Liam.

"Probably both," replied Rebecca. "Frankie's father said that he was asked to cover the garden with a patio late September, it was the first day of fall."

"Did James help him?"

"No, Frankie's father had one of his employees help him. James just picked out the design and the furniture."

Jason looked up the dates. "So, the first day of spring in 1980 was March 20, which means he started the garden on March 22, and then had it covered with the patio on the first day of fall, which was Monday September 22."

"And Hettie was abducted and killed on March 29, and Jason was murdered on September 6, giving him ample opportunity to bury them there," suggested Rebecca. "We have James's audio recording, and Frankie's father's information, should we go to the sheriff?"

Liam looked at her, deep in thought. "We have enough for the sheriff to obtain a search warrant, but do we want him to get one at this time?"

"What do you mean?"

"If we do, they will come and start digging up James's backyard, it's going to draw a lot of attention and chances are he'll hear about it."

"I don't believe we are," said Rebecca hesitantly, "but what if there's a chance we're wrong and he's just setting us up?"

"That's my thought," agreed Liam. "We need to be certain."

"Are you suggesting we dig up the garden?" she asked warily.

"We can put the patio furniture on the grass, put the stones next to the garage, and just dig a portion of it. Once we uncover a body, then we will contact the sheriff, and they can finish the remainder."

"I want to help, but I don't know if I can lift those stones or dig?"

"No, you're right," he replied. "I was really trying to keep it between us."

"I can call my mom and ask if they can send a couple of guys over from the vineyard?" she offered. "We'll give them a couple hundred bucks each, tell them to bring tool, and make sure they leave before we get close to locating a body."

"That's a great idea. We should start around dusk when it's cooler," he suggested. "Can you get your hands on a canvas tent, big enough to cover the patio and a portion of the yard, some flashlights, and tent lights?"

"I'm sure they will have them at the winery, if not I'll buy them."

"All right, call your mom."

At dusk, two men showed up, removed their tools from the pickup truck, and followed Rebecca and Liam to the backyard. They removed the patio furniture, then the stones, before putting up the tent. They dug in the area where they thought Hettie's body would be, and as they got deeper, Rebecca and the two men looked on while Liam continued. Realizing he may be getting close, Liam stopped, and was pulled up. Rebecca paid the men, and after they left, Liam jumped back into the hole and meticulously removed the soil. Feeling something plastic, he carefully brushed away the soil to reveal a black garbage bag and glanced up at Rebecca. Noticing his look straight away, she began to cry.

Liam climbed out and held her. "Are you okay?"

"Don't worry, they're tears of happiness because we found them," she said with a smile as they rolled down her cheeks. "Can I call the sheriff?"

"I wouldn't want it any other way."

At ten o'clock, they greeted the sheriff outside at the front of the mansion."

"What's so urgent?" he asked noticing Rebecca's red eyes and Liam's dirty clothes.

"We need to talk first," said Rebecca managing a smile and walking him inside. She brought the sheriff up to date, then played the audio of James.

"Rebecca, like he said, he's a crazy old man talking about witches, magic spells, and portions. Without physical evidence we don't—"

"You mean bodies?" she inquired.

"Yeah," he replied.

"This may be difficult for you to believe, and you don't have to it's your choice, but I would like you to keep an open mind?"

"All right, I will, tell me," he said honestly.

Rebecca told him about their vision, witnessing the murders, and James burying the bodies, leaving out the black mist, the Demon, and Liam leading her blindfolded from the car to the patio."

"So, you're telling me, you know where he buried the bodies based on your visions?"

"We thought you might be skeptical," she revealed, then took him out the front door down the driveway to her car and proceeded to tell him about being blindfolded and Liam leading her to the burial site.

Liam turned on a flashlight as they walked to the tent, went inside, and switched on a light. The sheriff followed them to the edge of the hole, and looked down as Liam's flashlight illuminated the black garbage bag below.

"That's Hetty, if we dig next to her in the middle, we will find Mandy, and next to her, Jason," concluded Rebecca.

The sheriff glanced up at them in shock. "I'll get a warrant and a team in her straight away," he said starting to leave.

"We have only one request?" asked Rebecca with a sad smile.

"Name it."

"We want you to dig up the other two bodies the same way, but leave them in there, like Hetty's and give us a few minutes with them before you remove them."

"You got it!" said the sheriff, not needing to know the reason and leaving.

Rebecca looked over at Liam and touched his face gently. "I should go and get Jason's grimoire…you have a spell to cast."

"I do," he whispered.

Rebecca kissed him tenderly and left.

When they had reached the final body, the sheriff asked Rebecca and Liam to enter, and requested everyone leave to give them a few minutes alone. Inside, they went to the edge of the site, where Rebecca removed the grimoire from her bag, opened it up to the spell, and held it.

Liam took a deep breath and read it quietly:

"Those in Darkness follow my White Witch's light,
Then reach for my outstretched hand and hold it tight,
With my heart, soul, and mind, I will pull ye free,
And break the Dark spell that has held onto thee."

As he read his body glowed, and when he had finished, he leaned down and reached out his hand. Immediately, he felt a small girl's hand grasp it, and pulled her up.

"Hetty," whispered Rebecca happily helping her out.

"Rebecca," she replied excitedly and hugged her.

They watched Liam as he pulled up Mandy, she hugged him, then embraced the two girls. Once Jason was safely out of the Darkness, Liam's light quickly faded.

"Liam, Rebecca," said Jason cheerfully putting his arms around them, while Mandy cuddled into Liam, and Hetty held on to Rebecca. "Thank you," he whispered.

"I'm just glad we found you in time," said Liam relieved then crouched. "Hi, Mandy, pleasure to meet you."

Mandy threw her arms around him and cried, making Liam and the rest cry with her.

"You're free," sighed Rebecca wiping her eyes then softly playing with Hetty's hair and giving her a delighted smile.

Jason suddenly noticed the tent's flap moving, swiftly grabbed Rebecca and Liam's hands, then put them together.

"Rebecca?" questioned Sheriff Lee walking in and looking at the couple holding hands and wiping tears away. "Are you two alone, I thought I heard you talking to someone?" he asked dumfounded.

Rebecca and Liam quickly looked around, but Jason and the girls had disappeared.

"I was just telling Rebecca, that I'm just glad we found them."

"And I was saying to Liam they're free now, and I, we, got a little emotionally."

"It's understandable," he replied. "Are you done in here?"

"We are," she replied picking up her bag, strolling towards him, and following him outside.

"Can we have a minute with you two in the house?" he asked.

They went inside, poured coffee, and sat in the solarium.

"I wanted to let you know that we still have to verify the bodies, which means they will go to the coroner, who will check their dental records, and in the case of the two girls, the cause of death. I'm going to ask him to examine one of the young girls first because their dental records are readily available. As soon as we get a match, I will issue a warrant for the arrest of James Childwall for at least one murder, which will probably increase to three charges."

"How long will the first examination take?" asked Liam.

"I'll tell them to make it a priority, so I'm guessing a couple of hours tomorrow morning, then a few hours to get the arrest warrant. We're looking at arresting him around lunchtime tomorrow."

"Can you keep us posted?" asked Rebecca.

"As soon as I find out anything, I will let you know."

"Thank you, I would appreciate that."

"In the meantime, I would suggest you get some rest, once the media finds out about this it's going to be a frenzy."

"Will we need to make a statement to the media," wondered Rebecca. "I'd prefer we were kept out of it, and I'm sure Liam feels the same way?"

"I do," confirmed Liam.

"No, you won't have to, but we will have to tell the press that you were researching the history of the Childwall family for the town's exhibit, which led you to the suicide of Jason Campbell, which revealed it may have been a murder. We'll also have to tell them about the signature in the book, the audio confession, James digging a garden prior to the first murder and then turning it into a patio after the last, how you dug up his garden then called me. I'm thinking out loud, but my main point is that we need to keep your visions out of the news," he explained. "We will ask the press to respect your privacy, not hound you for interviews, and reemphasize that we have provided all the information to them that you had provided to us."

"I think we are both good with that," said Rebecca glancing over at Liam nodding his approval. "What about the witches and spells?"

"Unfortunately, we can't keep that out because it's in the audio. Besides, it will show him as being very unstable, senile, perhaps feeling guilty."

Rebecca laughed. "Guilty, I don't think so."

"I understand, Rebecca, I really do, but we also need to remember what his family has done for our town and what they have given to this community over the centuries. And we need to at least try to ensure the Childwall name is remembered for the good things they did and not overshadowed by his heinous crimes."

"Sheriff, the only reason James Childwall confessed to Liam and me, was to ensure his legacy was left behind and nothing else. Unfortunately, because he did, we just can't ignore it and sweep it under the rug, nor should we try; that would be disrespectful to all his victims, and those families who have suffered because of his despicable acts," she said pausing briefly. "But I also hear what you are saying about his family. They were wonderful people, and innocent to his actions, and shouldn't be painted with the same brush as him. So, how do we accomplish that?" she asked rhetorically and contemplated momentarily. "What we need to do, is display him openly as the coldblooded murderer he really is. Always refer to him as James Childwall and be very public about his atrocious acts here in Amare, with Maggie O'Brien in Worcester, and Eleanor Peabody in Boston. While at the same time, distancing him from the Childwall family name by promoting their core beliefs and values, and reiterating all the wonderful things they have done for the town of Amare and the local community. Hence, ensuring the integrity of the Childwall family name by separating his legacy from theirs," explained Rebecca, who didn't realize she was crying. "That's my thought."

Liam smiled proudly at her then looked over at the sheriff.

"What do you think, Sheriff?" asked Rebecca.

"I believe that is the approach that I, and the town, will officially take and fully support," he replied decisively, then studied her. "You're quite a remarkable young lady, Rebecca, I'm very proud of you."

"Thank you," she whispered wiping her eyes.

The back door opened, and a deputy informed the sheriff they were almost done.

"Thanks, Ted, I'll be there in a minute," he said turning to him then back at Rebecca and Liam. "Do you need a hand tomorrow filling the hole and replacing the patio stones?"

"No," replied Liam, "we've got it."

"All right, then I'll say good night," he said standing and heading for the back door before turning. "You two did a fantastic job, thank you."

"Thanks, Sheriff," replied Rebecca looking over at Liam and smiling.

He walked over and held her. "You were magnificent," he whispered.

"I don't know what came over me. I didn't want to be rude to Lee, but I wanted to let him know that James's victims won't be truly free unless the truth comes out. Especially Jason, who was convicted of crimes he didn't commit."

"You spoke with your heart, mind, and soul, and everything you said was right," he said reassuring her.

"I must admit, after saying what I did, I do feel a whole lot better."

"Maybe that's a sign that you know you were right," suggested Liam.

"I believe so," she said glancing up and kissing him.

"What should we do now?"

"Well, Stinky Boy, I think you need a shower?"

"Hey, I'm a little dirty, but I'm not too sure about the stinky bit," he acknowledged looking at himself then sniffing his shirt.

"You are stinky, and dirty, but very cute."

"Before we go upstairs, how about we go grab a couple bottles of wines?" he asked then realized what he'd said. "I'm sorry, are you okay with that?"

"Fuck ya! He gave them to you, plus, he can't drink them when he's in jail!"

"True."

They picked two bottles of red, grabbed glasses, went upstairs, then onto the front terrace. Liam excused himself and jumped into the shower, moments later Rebecca joined him.

Chapter Thirty-Nine

"The sheriff just confirmed it is Hetty, they're going to arrest James around one o'clock," said Rebecca joining Liam on the terrace. "That's less than two hours."

"It would have been nice to see his reaction."

"Yeah, I would've loved to have seen that," she confessed taking the coffees and toasted bagels off the tray and placing them on the table.

"It's a beautiful morning."

"That it is, what are we going to do today?"

"I was thinking we should put the patio back together," suggested Liam.

"I can ask my mom and see if those guys from the vineyard want to do it, or I can ask Freddie?"

"Why don't we get the same guys to fill it in, then they can pick up their tools and take the tent?"

"And ask Freddie to do the patio?"

"Yeah, what do you think?"

"Okay, I'll call them," she said taking a bite of her bagel. "How about after we take down the tent, we go for a walk to the beach?"

"All right."

They had just finished folding the tent, and were about to leave, when Rebecca got a call.

"It's the sheriff," she said answering it and listening. "What?" she shouted. "Okay, we'll be right there?" She hung up and looked at Liam. "James Childwall did a runner, he left this morning."

"A runner? He can't even walk."

"Come on, the sheriff wants us to go over there and look at something."

The sheriff greeted them at the entrance, and they followed him into the security room.

"It seems James Childwall has taken off," stated the sheriff.

"How's that possible, he's in a wheelchair?" asked Liam.

"His maid showed up at nine, she let a guest in at nine thirty, was told to leave and come back at twelve. When she did, he was gone."

"I'm guessing were in here because they have security footage?" queried Liam.

"They do, but it's weird," replied the sheriff. "Roll it, Jack."

They looked over Jack's shoulder and watched the surveillance video.

"Here's the maid letting herself in, fast forward…here's the guest wearing a baseball cap and being let in, fast forward…that's him leaving at ten fifteen holding an envelope, fast forward…and here's another guest leaving at eleven…then at twelve, the maid returns, ten minutes later she comes out asking the front desk if they've seen James."

"Can we rewind to the guest arriving?" asked Liam waiting till Jack did. "Okay, can we zoom in?"

"His baseball cap and the angle of the camera hide his face," said Rebecca. "There must be other cameras that got him coming in the front door or walking down the hallway?"

They reviewed them.

"His face is hidden in all of them," said Liam.

"Let's go to the other guest, and review all those angles," said Rebecca.

"It's the same, his Panama hat is covering his face," stated Sheriff Lee.

"And how did James get out? Did he jump out the window?" questioned Liam frustrated.

"Did the maid say what the first guest looked like, what the man's name was?" asked Rebecca.

"White, attractive, regular build, in his late forties maybe fifty, and he said his name was Henry. Do either of you recognize him?"

"No," they both said in unison.

"Do you have them exiting the building?"

"I do," said Jack. "Here's Henry…and let me fast forward, here's guest two."

Liam and Rebecca looked on as guest two, with his hand covering his face, tips his hat to the camera, then jumps and clicks his feet in the air before strutting out of frame."

"I don't believe it!" shouted Liam. "That's him! That's James Childwall!

"No, it can't be?" said Sheriff Lee. "Go back and stop it when he looks up at the camera." The sheriff reviewed it closely. "Now, go forward." He glanced up at Liam. "James Childwall was wheelchair bound, this guy's kicking his feet in the air and strutting away, it can't be him."

"Jack, go back and pause it when he tilts his hat?" asked Liam.

Jack did.

"Rebecca, come here," he requested. "Have a good close look. Is that James or not?"

Rebecca looked at Liam oddly, how could it be, she thought. She looked at the man's partial face, he looked much younger than James, and was just about to turn to him and say no, until she saw his hand. "Oh my God! It is him!"

"What?" said the sheriff looking at the monitor.

"The gold signet ring on his finger," she revealed. "Jack, zoom in on the ring…Look, it has diamonds on either corner, and the letter 'J' engraved in the middle. That's his. That's him!"

"But how could he…?" wondered Sheriff Lee, then he realized something. "Jack, can you give us a minute?" he asked then waited till he left. "Let me guess, witchcraft, a spell?"

"Sheriff, there's only two explanations. The first, he was faking his condition, and intentionally aged himself. The second, the man who visited him lifted the spell."

"Or three, when you lifted the spell last night it gave him his strength back," added Rebecca.

"Sorry, make that three," stated Liam.

"This can't be witches, spells?" asked Sheriff Lee unconvinced.

"Okay, there's a fourth, James scaled down the wall in his wheelchair and rolled away unseen."

Rebecca laughed out loud.

"Okay, very funny guys," said the sheriff. "Don't mock me."

"I'm sorry, Sheriff, I couldn't resist, and it's the first time we've laughed in a couple of day."

"It is," agreed Rebecca.

Sheriff Lee smiled at them, scratched his head, and thought. "I'll check the surveillance cameras in the area and see if we can spot him."

There was a knock on the door and Jack came in. "There's a lawyer looking for you two," he said pointing to Rebecca and Liam

"Bring him in, then take a lunch break, Jack," suggested Sheriff Lee.

They watched as Mr. MacDonald walked in.

"Where's James Childwall?" asked Rebecca confronting him.

"I don't know," he replied unsure. "He told me to come here at one thirty and give you these envelopes."

"When did he give you the envelopes?"

"I was over here yesterday. I brought the documents, he signed them, then told me once I dropped them off my services were no longer required and handed me a very generous cheque."

"Did he say where he was going?" asked Liam.

"I didn't even know he was gone?"

"Sheriff, you know me?"

"I do, David," confirmed Sheriff Lee. "What were your dealings with Mr. Childwall?"

"I can't discuss them in detail, but I can say I was responsible for dealing with people, like Mr. Wilson, and Ms. Anderson, and their contracts. I only worked with him for several weeks, and all my interactions were with the locals in Amare, Ms. Mia Romano is another example."

"During that conversation regarding Mia's contract, James mentioned moving down to Florida to live out the rest of his days?" probed Jason.

"Like you, that was the one and only time I heard him say it," he replied honestly. "After I met with you, I was going to drop by and say goodbye to him before I left."

"How did you know we would be here at one thirty?" asked Rebecca.

"He told me you would be, I just assumed he had asked you to come here."

"Did he say anything else?"

"No, but he said give you this first," said Mr. MacDonald passing them a small envelope.

Rebecca opened it and read the note. "I wondered if you would have caught me, if I had said, you had forty-four hours?"

"What does that mean?" asked the sheriff.

"He told us we had forty-eight hours to find Jason, we did it in forty-six, and you were her at one. If we had done it in forty-four hours you would have been here at eleven and arrested him," answered Rebecca, then glanced at Liam. "He was timing us on catching him."

"We'll take the envelopes," said Liam reaching out his hand.

"First, you need to review and sign them," said Mr. MacDonald. "Is there anywhere we can go that's private?"

"Right here is private enough," replied Sheriff Lee.

"Unfortunately, Sheriff, I need to meet with these two alone."

"All right, I'll grab a coffee."

Mr. MacDonald waited till the sheriff left then passed them both an envelope. "Mr. Wilson," he said looking at Liam, "please remove the document, review, and sign. Before signing, you do have the option of having your own lawyer go over them first, but I assure you they are very standard." He then looked at Rebecca. "The same applies to you Ms. Anderson."

Liam opened his first and reviewed the document. "He gave me the wine in his cellar and the book collection in his library," he revealed glancing over at Rebecca then the lawyer. "Do I have to accept them?"

"I suggest you do," he replied and noticed Liam's reluctance. "Once you have, you are free to do with them as you please - donate them, sell them, pour them down the sink, or burn them - whatever you wish."

"Or you can get drunk reading?" joked Rebecca.

"True," he said smiling at her. "Where do I sign?"

"Here by the yellow sticker, and also the date," said Mr. MacDonald pointing. "Please sign both copies, one is for me, and the other is yours." He took his copy then turned to Rebecca. "Ms. Anderson, please."

Rebecca removed hers and read it. "He left me all the items that are in the secret room in the Mansion's basement," she said looking up at him curiously. "Are these for me or the museum?"

"They are yours," he replied, then watched Rebecca sign it, before giving her a small envelope with the words 'Keypad Code' written on it. "You will find the code inside."

"Okay," she replied taking it from him.

Mr. MacDonald gave Liam another envelope and instructed him to open it. Inside, was a generous bonus check for his work on the exhibit.

"You just have to sign and date the attached documents indicating you have received the check, and again, one copy for me and one for you," explained the lawyer, and waited till he had done so, before giving Rebecca hers.

Rebecca opened the envelope and removed three bonus checks. One was for Mia, the other for Brittany, and one was for her. She showed the amounts to Liam, then signed them.

Mr. MacDonald quickly put the documents in his briefcase, stood up, said goodbye, and left.

Rebecca turned to Liam. "Were you thinking about refusing them and not signing?"

"At first, I was," confirmed Liam. "But he's right, I can always sell the items, then give the money to charity."

"That's my thought too," she said standing with him.

They met the sheriff in the hallway and walked with him outside.

"What will happen next?" asked Rebecca.

"We'll send out an APB to the local areas and airports, contact the state police, then, if need be, other states. He has a few hours head start, which means he could be on a private plane out of the country as we speak," explained Sheriff Lee. "But don't worry, we'll find him."

"All right," she replied. "Is there anything else you need from us?"

"No, we everything," he said stopping and turning to them. "I just want to thank both of you again for all you've done, not only on behalf of myself and Amare, but for Jason and the girls' families."

"When will he be exonerated of any wrongdoing?" asked Liam.

"We will notify his family once the autopsies are completed, so with the next day or two, then shortly after, inform the public at our press conference."

"What about the Hetty and Mandy's families?"

"I'll meet with them tomorrow, separately, and let them know what we've uncovered," he confirmed. "At least they'll will have the bodies to bury now and have some closure."

"How sure that will mean a lot to them," acknowledged Rebecca.

The sheriff quietly nodded his head, glanced up at the cloudless sky, then at them. "What are you up to this afternoon?"

"We were going to go the beach before you called, so we'll probably drop by my place, make a picnic, and head there," she answered. "We could do with some R&R."

Chapter Forty

"You've been quiet since we left the sheriff, is everything okay?" she asked sitting on her towel and putting on suntan lotion.

"Yeah, just deep in thought," he replied.

"You know he fooled us again, with that 'forty-eight hours.'"

"I know."

"Do you think he went to Florida to hide out or fled the country?"

"No."

"Me neither," she concurred lying down. "He still has that last sacrifice to perform somewhere in Massachusetts, right?"

"He does," replied Liam looking up at the sky, "at the Epicenter of Darkness."

"He strutted out of there like he was ten or fifteen years younger. How did he do that?"

"I'm not sure," replied Liam, "I don't think he was faking being elderly or wheelchair bound, I believe he really was. That spell he had on Jason was physically and mentally taking a toll on him and draining his life, and as we became stronger, he started looking older and becoming weaker."

"Maybe when you lifted the spell last night it gave him his youth strength back," suggested Rebecca thinking back momentarily. "But the maid had seen him the following morning, old and in his wheelchair, so that couldn't have been it. Which means it has to be something else."

"But what?" he asked.

"The only other person to see him before his transformation was the man who visited him," recalled Rebecca. "Could he have something to do with it?"

"Perhaps…although the guest who left had an envelope just like ours, which would imply he was probably there to receive something from James…but like you said, he was the last person to see him," admitted

Liam wondering. "Let's say he did have had something to do with James's transformation, the question is, who is this man that visited him, Henry?"

"He said he had a son."

"What?"

"James said he had son," clarified Rebecca. "Who went to college, had a wonderful career, was happily married, had three children, and lived in a town that was not far from Amare…And he would be the right age."

"And?" asked Liam wanting her to continue her train of thought.

"James told us these last seven months his son was a vessel for the Dark Spirit, and doesn't know James is his father, and that this Dark Spirit lives within him because Darkness hides and only comes out when James says it needs to. So, without him even knowing, his son becomes Darkness' Host, and once Darkness is finished doing what it does, it goes back into hiding."

"You're saying his son unknowingly visits his father, let's assume for a business meeting because he was given an envelope, during which time James calls Darkness out to make him look younger and become stronger then sends him back into hiding."

"Exactly!" confirmed Rebecca happily. "Henry leaves none the wiser, and shortly after, a younger, stronger version of James appears and leaves."

"That's very intuitive," complimented Liam turning on his side and smiling at her. "I think you got something there."

"Does this mean we'll have to find out who Henry is and where James is hiding?" she asked hesitantly.

"No, that sounds like a job for the Gray Witches," recommended Liam, "but we will pass on what we know to them through your mom."

"All right," she said relieved, then moved close and kissed him.

"Well, look who it is Vanessa!" cried Crystal. "Don't they look like cozy lovebirds?"

"Oh boy!" sighed Rebecca laying on her back and covering her face. "Here we go!"

Chapter Forty-One

"The guys from the vineyard have been and gone," noted Liam as they walked through the mansion's backyard. "That was quick."

"My mom said they would be here sometime this afternoon," explained Rebecca looking around. "They did a good job."

"They sure did," agreed Liam before strolling with her to the back door.

"I'm glad my friends know about us," said Rebecca walking inside, "even though they teased me all afternoon."

"You loved it!" ribbed Liam placing the pizza on the counter.

Rebecca chuckled. "You're right, I did."

He grabbed two beers from the fridge and handed them to her. "Pizza and beer!"

"You're such a romantic," she said playfully, then kissed him before following him upstairs to the terrace.

As they ate, they leaned on the railing and watched the sunset.

"It's gorgeous," she cooed.

"It doesn't get much better than this," he said putting his arm around her.

"No," replied Rebecca, cozying in, and glancing up at him. The sun's soft rays illuminating his face reminded her of last night. "I've been meaning to ask, what did it fell like when you were glowing?"

Liam thought briefly. "It felt…tingly."

"Tingly? That's it?"

"It made me feel calm, tranquil."

"Calm, tranquil," she whispered then stared at the setting sun deep in thought. "You know I have to go to Worcester."

"I know," he replied kissing the top of her head.

"I was thinking we should go tomorrow morning after breakfast at my mom's."

"All right," he confirmed. "I was wondering when you were going to bring it up."

"To be honest with you, the reason I haven't is because I'm scared."

"You needn't be," said a voice from behind making them turn around.

"Jason?" asked Liam.

"Hetty, Mandy!" cried Rebecca happily. "Come her girls!"

They ran over, hugged her, then Liam before letting go.

"It's a pretty sunset," said Hetty looking over the railing. "Don't you think, Mandy?"

"It's beautiful!" she sighed, joining her.

"Jason, where have you been?" asked Rebecca.

"We've been waiting for the police, and the men in the backyard to leave, before showing ourselves to you" he revealed. "We will be here to the funeral, then move on."

"Rebecca," said Hetty nervously glancing over at Mandy who motioned her to ask.

"Yes, what is it, dear?" she asked sensing her hesitation.

"I want to see my parents before I leave," she revealed sadly before holding her.

"Me too," said Mandy moving towards Liam and embracing.

Rebecca and Liam looked over at Jason.

"Girls, why don't you go play in the bedroom while I talk with Rebecca and Jason," said Jason. "We'll be in shortly."

"Okay," they replied as they happily ran inside.

"I feel so bad for them," said Rebecca sitting. "Is there anything we can do?"

"Actually, there is," answered Jason sitting next to her and waiting for Liam to join them. "In my grimoire there's a spell that you can cast that allows family members to see and converse with spirits."

"For how long as?" asked Liam.

"For as long as the time specified by the Witch casting it," he verified.

"That's wonderful, can Liam do it?" asked Rebecca.

"You both can," he confirmed, then hesitated momentarily. "Rebecca, Liam, what you need to be very careful of is that some family members may want to see them, while others may prefer not to."

"How will we know who would and wouldn't?" asked Rebecca.

"There's only one way to find out, and that is by asking them, and I would limit it to just their parents," explained Jason. "If they agree, they will see them as a spirit, similar to what you see today."

"Okay, we can do that, we can talk to them" acknowledged Rebecca glancing over at Liam who was nodding his approval.

"Rebecca, I would strongly consider someone else," suggested Jason. "A person close to the family who they would trust, who is close to you, and a White Witch."

"You referring to my mother," stated Rebecca.

"I am, but that is something you, Liam, and your mother can discuss at a later date," he said. "First, I would like to speak to you, Rebecca, about Maggie. It's imperative that you leave tomorrow and bring her back here, with us, where she is safe."

"Safe?" asked Liam.

"Darkness has left this place, and although I feel it has other pressing priorities, I prefer not to take any chances and lose her."

Rebecca looked at Liam then Jason. "I'm really scared."

"You have no reason to be," said Jason gently holding her hand. "I listened to you talking with the sheriff yesterday, it was very moving and spoken like a true White Witch, and I believe Liam said it best when he said, 'you spoke with your heart, mind, and soul.'"

Rebecca recalled something and smiled at him. "Liam's mother told us that we both have to truly believe in our hearts, minds, and souls, that we are White Witches, then, and only then will we be able to set them free."

"She's right, and you are ready," he confirmed, "because you are a White Witch."

"I can do this," whispered Rebecca feeling empowered. "Is there anything I need to do?"

"Just be yourself, and let Maggie find out for herself the person you really are, that's the key."

"I will."

"I know you will," he said confidently then turned to Liam. "I would like mine and the girl's caskets containing our remains to be placed in the parlor the night before our funeral, and that Maggie's be brought here, too. Please, ensure that make sure she has a new one."

"Of course, it would be my honor," promised Liam.

"We would like a full Catholic funeral, and to be buried next to one another in the cemetery."

"Hasn't Maggie's been buried already?" he questioned.

"She was buried in unconsecrated ground in hopes that one day her spirit would be freed, and we could be buried together."

"I understand," replied Liam. "What happens if the girls' families refuse?"

"Once the girls' parents see their spirits, and the girls tell them that is also what they want, I don't believe you will have any problems."

"All right, is there anything else?"

"Not at the moment," he replied standing, "you have enough to deal with for the time being."

"Jason?" asked Liam.

"Do you remember everything in your life?"

"I remember every memory vividly."

"Up to when?"

Jason sat back down. "Up to the point where James put a cloth soaked in a magic potion over my mouth and I went unconscious. Then groggily waking up and seeing him wearing a balaclava and looking into Darkness' black demonic eyes before feeling the knife cut through my body," he recalled. "Then being in a pit of Darkness with the girls."

"How did you know it was James that was responsible?"

"I didn't at first, and it wasn't close to the end that I figured it out," he confessed. "One night I had a premonition of me lying on my kitchen table, someone writing a suicide note, and then a figure with black demonic eyes slicing me open like Maggie. Afterwards, I had a feeling that this someone knew me and Maggie, was now close to me, and was setting me up. After eliminating all the possible suspects, I was left with just one, James. And if my instincts were right, this meant he must have murdered the girls, probably buried them in his garden, and would bury me there, too, and put a spell on it."

"So, you knew if you gave him the patio book, he was going to build one over his garden?"

Jason chuckled. "His arrogance and narcissism built that patio."

"Isn't that the truth," stated Rebecca nodding her head.

"Always be careful of Darkness," he cautioned, "it will always deceive, lie, manipulate, and hide until it gets what it wants…life on Earth, then to open the Gates of Darkness."

"I believe we've experienced some of that firsthand," admitted Liam.

"You have, but that was just James," warned Jason. "Darkness is much more cunning, and you need to be vigilant going forward."

"We will," said Liam glancing over at Rebecca who looked anxious.

"What did the girls' remember at the end?" she asked.

"Well, I guess James had some humanity in him towards them," he revealed. "He strangled them when they were unconscious, so they only remember falling asleep then being in the pit with me."

"That's good," said Rebecca relieved.

"I need to let you get your rest," he said standing. "If you need me just call my name, otherwise, I will talk with you soon."

They followed him into the bedroom where the girls were playing on the floor.

"All right, girls, we need to go, and let Rebecca and Liam get some sleep."

Chapter Forty-Two

The following morning, Rebecca and Liam went to her mother's, where Liam put Jason's grimoire back and Rebecca removed Maggie's. Afterwards they went downstairs, and as they ate breakfast, Rebecca told her mom what Jason and the girls had requested.

"Don't worry, I know their parents well, and how to word it with them," she confirmed. "And then I will talk to the church, funeral parlor, and cemetery."

"Thanks, Mom," said Rebecca.

"The sheriff called and told me that the coroner will be releasing their bodies tomorrow. So, we will bring the caskets to the mansion on Monday, and bury them Tuesday," she explained. "I guess he told you he was doing a press conference at the town hall today?"

"He did," replied Rebecca nervously,

"Don't fret, dear, he told me about your conversation with him, and he will do what you advised because it's the right thing to do," she said reassuringly. "He knows he has our support, and once I speak with Hetty and Mandy's parents, theirs too."

"Okay," said Rebecca somewhat relieved.

"Do you have everything you need?"

"We do."

"When you arrive at the house, Anna and Alicia will be waiting for you, and Anna will instruct you from there," she explained looking at her daughter and squeezing her hand. "You will do fine."

Five hours later they arrived at Maggie's house, Rebecca grabbed her bag, then walked to the front door with Liam where they were greeted by his mom and Alicia.

"Hello, Liam," said his mom giving him a kiss and hug.

"Hi, Mom, Hello, Aunty Ally," said Liam letting go and embracing his aunt, while his mom hugged Rebecca. "Aunty Ally this is Rebecca, Rebecca, Alicia."

"Nice to meet you," said Rebecca.

"You too," replied Alicia. "I've heard so much about you from Anna."

"All good, I hope?" she probed anxiously.

"Of course, my dear, of course," she reassured her opening the door.

"I know you're nervous, but don't be," comforted Anna putting her arm in hers and leading her inside. "Now, we are all going to go into the living room, sit, and wait."

"Wait for what?" asked Rebecca.

"To see if she calls for you," she answered.

They strolled into the living room and before Rebecca could sit, the black pentacle on her necklace lifted up, pulling her towards Maggie's bedroom. She slowly walked through the open bedroom door into the middle of the room when suddenly Maggie appeared in front of her holding it in her hand as the door closed behind.

"Maggie," said Rebecca dropping her bag.

"You can see my spirit?" she asked looking at her.

"Yes, and hear you."

"How did you come by this?" she asked motioning to the necklace.

"It was given to me."

"By whom?"

"Jason."

"Why would he give you this?"

Rebecca told her about being pulled into the chest with Liam.

"Anna's son?"

"Yes, he's here with Anna and Alicia in the living room."

"Where is Jason?"

Rebecca told her about him, the girls, James, and Darkness.

"Did you free them?"

"No, Liam did, Jason chose him."

"Are you a White Witch, too?"

"I am."

"When was the last time you seen Jason?" she asked cautiously.

"Last night," she replied. "He wants your spirit to join him at the mansion and to be buried beside him."

Maggie smiled for the first time, then studied Rebecca. "You've had several trying weeks."

"I have," she replied tearing up.

"I also see that you care for them greatly."

"I do."

Rebecca slowly removed the necklace and placed it gently around Maggie's neck. "I thought this was for me, but now I realize Jason wanted me to give this back to you."

Maggie picked up the pentacle and admired it, then stared at Rebecca. "Will you keep me safe?"

"With all my heart, soul, and mind."

Maggie suddenly realized who Rebecca was. "You are not a Dark Spirit trying to trick me," said Maggie crying tears of joy, "you have come set me free me…you are my White Witch."

"I am, and I am here to take you to Jason," replied Rebecca holding her as tears rolled down her face.

"You can feel me," she said squeezing her tightly before letting go. "But Rebecca you need my…" She stopped and watched Rebecca crouch down to her bag and remove its contents. "My grimoire," she said admiring it. "Do you know which spell?"

"I do," she replied and was about to flip to the page.

"Wait," said Maggie.

Rebecca watched her remove an elegant gold posy ring from her right middle finger.

"Look inside, here at the inscription, what do you see?"

"A black pentacle, and next to it the words 'My Heart, Soul, and Mind.'"

"This ring came from my ancestors. The pentacle has always been there, but when I got engaged, I added those words," she explained. "I was planning on giving it to my daughter and telling her I loved her with all my heart, soul, and mind, but now I am giving it to you, the daughter I never had," she said placing it on Rebecca's middle finger.

"Thank you, it's beautiful," said Rebecca admiring it. She suddenly realized she had been chosen and looked up at Maggie. "I will treasure this forever."

"I know you will," she whispered.

Rebecca happily opened the book to the spell. "Ready?"

"I am," she said excitedly before calming herself down.

Rebecca took a deep breath, exhaled, then quietly read the spell:

"Those trapped by Darkness see my White Witch's light,
Then reach for my outstretched hand and hold it tight,
With my heart, soul, and mind, I will pull you to me,
And break the Dark spell that has held onto thee."

As Rebecca read her body glowed, and when she was finished, she reached out her hand and Maggie held on to it tightly as Rebecca pulled her from the Darkness into the Light.

Maggie stood in front of her and looked down at her pure form then glanced up at Rebecca. "You did it," she whispered tenderly stroking her face. In the living room she could hear people talking. "Now, let me talk with my friends before we leave."

"How do I do that?"

Maggie told her what to say and do, then watched her put the grimoire into her bag, before following her to the living room. Rebecca put her bag on the floor, strolled over to Anna and Alicia, and placed a hand on each of their shoulders and said:

"Those who cannot see,
Open your heart, soul, and mind, to me,
For someone you lost, stands in front of ye,
And for thirty minutes, will spend time with thee."

Maggie!" screamed Anna and Alicia in unison.

"My dear friends," she replied hugging them.

Rebecca slowly walked over to Liam beaming.

"You did it," he whispered.

"I did," she said excitedly as her put his arm around her.

Thirty minutes later, the friends said their tearful goodbyes, and Maggie approached Liam and embraced him. "I knew when you were a little boy, that one day you would play a role in saving me, as did your mother," she said looking over at Anna then back at Aidan. "Thank you."

"You're welcome," he replied. "You were so sad. It's good to see you smiling and happy."

"I have been sad for too long, and thanks to my White Witch, Rebecca, I am free," she said squeezing her hand. "Now, Rebecca, take me to my fiancé."

Rebecca glanced over at Liam, then Maggie.

"Oh, forgive me," she said realizing Rebecca didn't know what to do. She grabbed her grimoire from the bag, returned, and found the spell. "Hold it and read this."

Rebecca read the spell:

"I am your vessel, enter me.

Once we arrive, I will set thee free."

Maggie disappeared.

"Where did she go?" asked Liam.

"She's inside me?" whispered Rebecca.

"Can you talk to her?" asked Anna.

"No, she's dormant."

After lunch, they drove home, and arrived at the mansion at ten. When they walked in Jason, Hetty, and Mandy were waiting for them in the foyer.

"How did it go?" asked Jason anxiously.

Rebecca read the spell:

"I am your vessel, arrived have we,

I will say thy name, and set thee free..."

Rebecca closed her eyes and said, "Maggie O'Brien."

Maggie appeared, and upon seeing Jason, ran into his arms.

"Hetty, Mandy, come with me," said Rebecca grabbing their hands and following Liam upstairs.

Chapter Forty-Three

"That was my mother," said Rebecca yawning, "the parents don't believe her about seeing Hetty and Mandy, they want a guarantee."

"I don't blame them, three weeks ago I wouldn't have believed any of this either."

"What should we do?" she asked getting out of bed.

"I don't know," he said sitting up. "I'm guessing you only have to convince one of their parents, either their mother or father."

Rebecca thought for a moment. "Their mothers," she said looking around the bedroom. "How do we find the girls?"

Liam gave her a comical look. "Hetty, Mandy, where are you?"

"Here we are," said Hetty walking into the room with Mandy.

"Hetty," said Rebecca, "when your mom comes to see you, is there anything you want her to bring, that only she would know about?"

"My diary, everyone knows I have one, but only my mom knew that I hid the key under my mattress," she replied. "I would read what I wrote with them every night."

"Okay, Mandy, how about you?"

"Honey, he's my favorite teddy, and he's golden. My mom got it for me when I broke my wrist playing soccer and had to go to the hospital."

"All right, that's all girls," she said watching them leave.

"How are you doing?"

"Fine, just sad," said Rebecca sitting on the edge of the bed. "I'm starting to believe they're real and I know they're not, and come Tuesday they will be gone, and I'm going to miss them that's all."

"They're going to miss you, too," he said caressing her back.

"I know," she said managing a smile. "It's going to be a difficult day."

Chapter Forty-Four

On Monday morning, the caskets were placed in the parlor, and throughout the afternoon family and close friends came to pay their respects. At six, the viewing was closed, and Rebecca and Liam waited patiently for Hetty and Mandy's parents to return. At seven, there was a knock at the door, and the four seniors walked in.

"You are the two who found are little girls?" asked Hetty's dad, the

"Yes, we are," replied Liam.

"I hope you don't find us rude for not approaching you earlier on today, but we didn't want to talk about this in front of everyone," he explained.

"We understand," said Rebecca reassuringly.

"Thank you for what you have done for us," he said motioning to the group. "Tomorrow we can finally put our daughters to rest and allow them to begin their journey to Heaven."

"You're welcome," said Rebecca sincerely, "and I'm so glad that you agreed to have the visitation here."

"When your mother told us that we could say goodbye to Hetty and Mandy here, in this mansion, we didn't believe her at first. In fact, we were quite skeptical and terribly upset with her for suggesting such an impossible thing. But after she spoke with us yesterday and said that Hetty had told you she wanted me to bring her diary and where the key was hidden—"

"And that Mandy wanted Golden," added Mrs. Peterson holding the bear tightly, "and how I had bought it for her after she had broken her wrist and had to go to hospital. We knew they must have spoken to you because there was no way you would have never known those stories."

"We said that if Hetty and Mandy had spoken to you and wanted to leave from here, they must have their reasons, and that we should honor their final wishes," said Mrs. Downs.

"I think they will be very happy that you did," confirmed Rebecca. "This house is where their spirits were freed, which is why they remain here, and tomorrow afternoon when their caskets are carried out of here, they will leave with them, and as you said, begin their final journey."

"We believe you have seen and spoken to them, we really do," said Mrs. Peterson, coming forward, "but how do you know we will see them?"

"Because they want to see you," revealed Liam.

"I'll be honest with you, we are scared," said Mrs. Peterson.

"So were we," confessed Rebecca walking towards her and Mrs. Down and holding their hands. "Would you like to see your girls?"

"Yes," they said in unison then smiled at one another.

They led the couples upstairs. Liam took the Petersons to see Mandy in the front room, while Rebecca took the Downs to the back room. They walked into the room with their couple, placed a hand on their backs, and whispered the spell to themselves. When their daughters appeared, they left the room closing the door behind them, and met at the stairwell and proceeded to the kitchen.

"Do you think we're doing the right thing? They may think we are freaks and tell everyone what happened here."

"I was thinking that too," confirmed Liam.

"You two shouldn't worry so much," said Maggie appearing. "They're getting to say goodbye to their daughters, and I think their reaction will surprise you."

"I know this is all a little weird," said Jason, "but it won't get to this magnitude again. Going forward, events like this will happen much quicker, like with releasing Maggie."

"Are you saying that it doesn't end here?" asked Rebecca.

"Unfortunately, no. This is just the beginning, and it will only end when Darkness is defeated," stated Jason. "You both have an exceptional, powerful gift, and you will be called upon to use it again, and again."

Maggie walked over to Rebecca. "I see it in your eyes, your love for them. When you mourn their loss, seek comfort in what they have given you, and what you have given them."

"I will," said Rebecca. "Hearing you say it like that makes me feel better."

Two hours later, they met the couples at the bottom of the stairs, and Rebecca noticed they had been crying. The Petersons approached them first.

"Thank you, you have made us both very happy," said Mr. Peterson. "We feel like a great weight has been lifted off our shoulders."

"She was exactly as I remember her," said Mrs. Peterson. "Thank you, both."

"Hetty, too," said Mrs. Downs joining them. "She read to us both from her diary, like she used to."

"She sat on my knee while she did," added Mr. Downs.

"None of us ever thought we would ever get the chance to hold our daughter one last time and say goodbye, but we did," said Mrs. Peterson starting to cry and being comforted by her husband. "Don't worry they're tears of joy."

The couples headed to the door, stopped, and talked amongst themselves then turned around.

"Hetty and Mandy told us the reason that they wanted to leave from here was because they said they have been very happy staying here these last few days, and that they wanted families to stay here, and be happy too," said Mrs. Downs walking up to Rebecca and Liam. "We were going to ask your mother to turn this place into an inn to honor their last wish. What do you think?"

"I think that's a wonderful idea, and you should ask her," said Rebecca happily. "I believe she will be very receptive to your request."

Mrs. Peterson joined Mrs. Downs and glanced cautiously back and forth at the couple. "You must also understand that we will want to tell people what we witnessed here tonight."

Rebecca walked towards her. "What? No, you—"

"So, we have agreed," said Mrs. Peterson with a smile, "to tell them that upon our request, you let us in to visit the place where our daughters were found. Then went on a two-hour walk to give us some privacy, during which time, we believed we saw visions of our daughters. We will tell them that we spoke with their spirits and about the things we talked about with them. Some of our friends may believe us, others may think we are old and senile, either way we will know the truth," explained Mrs.

Peterson. "Upon your return, we asked if you had seen anything unusual in this house, to which you replied no, and looked at us like we were all crazy. So we decided it was best not to tell you what we had saw, thanked you, and quietly left."

"In other words, your secret is safe with us," said Mrs. Downs.

"The girls told us what you did for them, fighting off the Dark Spirit, and freeing them," said Mr. Peterson joining his wife.

"Why would you do that for us?" asked Rebecca.

"We can't imagine what you two went through, and we never will, all we know is that you found and freed our daughters, and we can finally bury them," said Mr. Downs holding his wife's hand. "There may be more individuals out there like our daughter who will need your help and we don't want to mess that up for you or them."

"Thank you, this means so much to us, we were so worried about how this was going to play out with you, the media," said Rebecca gratefully. "You have lifted such a great burden off of our shoulders."

They said goodbye to the couples, closed the door, and walked wearily upstairs to the bedroom. They quickly and quietly got ready for bed and within minutes were sound asleep.

Chapter Forty-Five

The following morning Rebecca and Liam met Jason, Maggie, Hetty, and Mandy in the living room for the last time.

"I'll never forget you," said Rebecca holding Hetty and Mandy as tears rolled down her cheeks. "You will always be in my heart and my thoughts."

"We'll miss you, Rebecca," they said giving her a kiss.

"I'll miss you too," she said standing and watching them go to Liam.

"We'll miss you, Liam," they said squeezing him tightly.

"I'll miss you," he replied unable to hold back his tears any longer.

"Don't be sad," said Mandy wiping them away, "you set us free."

"And we got to see our parents," added Hetty. "Now we can go to Heaven."

"Be happy, for us?" asked Mandy.

"I will," he said smiling and caressing their faces.

"Girls?" whispered Maggie. "Can you wait for us in the parlor, we'll be there in a minute?"

Liam and Rebecca hugged them one last time then watched them leave before turning to Jason and Maggie.

"I have something to give you," said Jason walking to Liam.

"Me, too," said Maggie approaching Rebecca.

"We're going to give you our Black Witch powers," revealed Jason.

"But we're White Witches?" questioned Liam.

"I know, which why we are giving them to you because it's the safest place for them," confirmed Jason. "Typically, if we had children, we would have passed them on to them."

"Our powers will lie dormant inside you," explained Maggie, "similar to when Rebecca transported me here."

"Can we use your powers?" asked Rebecca.

"Yes, and if the need arises, they will come to your aid," confirmed Maggie.

"At some point, you will each have to make a decision as to whether you want to become a Black Witch and pass on your White Witch powers or remain a White Witch and pass on our Black Witch powers," cautioned Jason."

"How will we know when to make that decision?" asked Liam.

"When the time comes you will know when to do one or the other," he replied.

"Ambiguity seems to run amok around here," joked Rebecca, making them laugh.

"Unfortunately, it's not easy to pinpoint these events," admitted Maggie sympathetically.

"I know," agreed Rebecca recalling what she and Liam have had to deal with these last few weeks.

"Can we use your grimoires?" asked Liam.

"Of course, they're yours," replied Jason.

"The majority of spell are written in black and are Black Witch's spells but those that are written in white, are White Witch's spells, and were given to us by Anna upon our request," revealed Maggie.

"How did you know you would need them and to put them in?" asked Rebecca.

"Because Black Witches are constantly battling Darkness, there is a chance that we may inadvertently fall under one of its spells, like Jason," said Maggie. "And since the only way we can be freed is by a White Witch reading from our grimoire it's a good place to have them."

"Call it our backup plan," summarized Jason.

"Do all Black Witches' grimoires have White Witch spells in them?"

"If they don't, they should," replied Jason.

"All right," said Liam looking over at Rebecca.

"Do you have any more questions?"

They both shook their heads no.

Maggie placed her hand on Rebecca's heart, and Jason did likewise with Liam. They closed their eyes, slowly whispered their spell, then stopped and opened their eyes.

"Rebecca Anderson, congratulations, you now have the Black Witch powers of Margaret O'Brien."

"Liam Wilson, congratulations, you now have the Black Witch powers of Jason Campbell."

Then hugged them.

"Now, it's time for us to go," said Maggie pulling away.

"We won't see any of you again?" asked Rebecca.

"No," replied Maggie with a sad expression and moving Rebecca's hair from her eyes.

"Okay," she said reaching for her hand, squeezing it, then letting go.

Jason shook Liam's. "There are no words to express my gratitude for what you two have done," he said letting go and giving him one final hug before embracing Rebecca as Maggie held Liam.

They pulled away, said goodbye, smiled then strolled hand in hand out to the foyer towards the parlor.

"Hold me," said Rebecca moving close to him.

Chapter Forty-Six

Hetty's casket was carried out first, followed by her family, then Mandy's, Maggie's, and Liam's. The last two out, Rebecca and Liam, closed the doors behind them and when they turned around, were surprised to see the large crowd of townspeople paying their respects. Rebecca quickly grabbed Liam's hand and held it tightly as they walked down the steps and onto the road doubled lined with the cars of family and close friends. They ambled to the front of the procession and watched as the caskets were slowly placed inside their hearses then followed their parents into their limousines.

Sheriff Lee jumped into his cruiser, started to drive, and was immediately followed by Hetty's hearse, then Mandy's, Maggie's, and Jason's. Next, were the limousines of immediate family and close friends, trailed by the cars of family and friends. They slowly drove down crowded Victoria Street, took a right onto Park Street, and then a right onto Main where people had lined both sides of the streets all the way to the church.

When they arrived, they got out of their limousine, slowly climbed the steps, and were sprinkled with holy water by the priest before entering the building and being seated in the first pew. They watched as the priest led the four caskets to the front of the alter, turn around and wait for them to be laid down, before looking up at the full congregation and beginning.

After the mass, they were driven to the cemetery, and looked on as the priest performed the Rite of Committal. When the service ended, family and close friends left for a reception at the mansion, while Rebecca and Liam remained.

"Are you okay?" asked Liam putting his arm around her.

"I am," she said smiling and cuddling into him. "I just wanted us to walk around their graves for a few minutes in private."

Chapter Forty-Seven

The following morning Liam woke up early and noticed Rebecca wasn't next to him. He got up, walked over to the terrace doors, and spotted her sitting outside.

"There you are," he said joining her. "Have you been up long?"

"Ten minutes or so," she replied holding his hand. "I was just listening to birds, enjoying the fresh morning air, and thinking about yesterday."

"How are you holding up?"

"I'm good," she admitted honestly.

"It was a beautiful ceremony."

"It really was…the church, the cemetery, all of it was very perfect," she confessed. "I was so happy to see all those people out on the streets paying their respects, I wasn't expecting that."

"Me neither."

"I thought the reception was very special, and it was lovely to see all their families and friends here," she said cheerfully.

"It was," he said.

"Although, you have a mess to clean up today," she teased.

"I do, do I?" he asked with a smile.

"I was just too tired last night," she confessed and glanced at him. "You don't think our parents, the Petersons, the Downs, and Alicia were upset we left them and went to bed."

"Of course not, it was a long day, it was late, and besides they were enjoying each other's company," he said squeezing her hand. "Coffee?"

"I'd love one."

Liam left, and a minute later shouted from the bottom of the stairs. "Rebecca, come here for a minute."

"What is it?" she asked walking down the stairs and joining him.

"Look around."

"I don't believe it, it's spotless!" she said strolling into the parlor and noticing something on the table. "What are these?" she asked picking up one of two small, wrapped packages. "This one says, 'All our Love, the Downs and Petersons.'"

"Go on, open it up."

Rebecca ripped off the wrapping and removed a six by nine framed picture of Hetty and Mandy smiling arm in arm. Rebecca burst into tears. "It's beautiful," she said caressing their faces.

"Look how happy they are," said Liam looking on.

"They are, aren't they?"

"Open the other one," said Liam taking the photo from her.

"This one says, 'Heart, Soul, and Mind, Love Aunty Ally,'" said Rebecca before tearing away the wrapping to reveal a six by nine framed picture of Maggie and Jason cheek to cheek. "Look how much in love they were," she said glancing up at Liam. "Just like us."

"Definitely," said Liam putting his arm around her. "You should put them in your living room."

"I will, but let's put them in here for a while," she said placing them on the end table closest to the window. "The afternoon sun brightens up this table and will fall nicely on their pictures. What do you think?"

"Perfect," he replied reaching out his hand and admiring them with her. "Come on, let me make you that coffee."

"We going to have to thank them for the pictures and whoever tidied this place up," she said taking a seat.

"Sounds like an ideal job for you!" said Liam pointing at her before turning around and playfully whistling.

"Oh, it is, is it?" asked Rebecca getting up and approaching him. "And while I'm running my ass off trying to find out who it was, buying them thank you cards and chocolates, what will you be doing?"

"Hmm?" he asked pretending not to hear her.

"You heard me, what will you be doing?"

"I'll be missing you," he replied with an exaggerated wink.

"What am I going to do with you?" she asked holding him.

"I can think of a few things."

"I bet you can," she said giggling. "You know, I'm glad I have you in my life."

"Well, you're stuck with me."

"Forever?"

"And ever," he said kissing her.

"Okay, but you still have to buy the cards and chocolates with me," she insisted.

"I wouldn't have it any other way."

"I know," she sighed with a smile. "I love you."

"I love you," he replied.

"Now, where's my coffee?" she asked snapping her fingers and returning to her seat.

"Coming right up, Ma'am," he answered and turned around to make it. "What do you want to do today?"

"I really just want to hang out here, I'm not in the mood to go out," she replied. "I wish there was something we could do."

"What about that secret room?" he suggested looking over his shoulder at her. "You said you wanted to wait till after the funeral."

"I forgot about that," she said excitedly. "I'll go get the code."

When she returned Liam handed her a coffee and followed her to the basement.

Chapter Forty-Eight

She opened the small envelope, took out the note, and read the numbers. "This four-number code is a thief's worst nightmare," she said with a fretful look, then pressed zero four times, and looked over at Liam and broke out laughing.

The door clicked open, they went inside, and turned on the light.

"Oh my God! I don't believe it!" she gasped surveying the room. "There's got to be over hundred pieces in here, easily."

"Wow, this is amazing."

"There's family portraits, paintings, vases, crystal bowls and glasses," she said pointing animatedly and walking over to a table. "In these boxes are dinnerware sets, silverware—"

"What are these?" asked Liam lifting up a large rolled-up sheet of paper and spreading it out.

"Oh, my God! That's the original house plan for the mansion," said Rebecca quickly grabbing another one. "This is the guest house plan…and this is one of their whole property with the mansion and guest houses."

"What's this last one?" asked Liam passing it to her.

"I don't believe it! This is the original plan of the town," she said excitedly. "These are incredible!" Suddenly a small chest caught Rebecca's eye, she went towards it, and opened it. "Ahh!" she screamed, startling Liam.

"Are you okay?" he asked as he watched her flipping through a book. "What's that?"

"This, my dear, is just one of Victoria Childwall's journals. The diaries I have talk about her daily personal thoughts and feelings, but these books contain her chronological accounts of events," she said calmly before shrieking triumphantly. "Can we start cataloguing all this right now?"

"Of course," he said knowing this would be a good distraction for her.

"Who knows what else is in here?" she pondered excitedly looking around as they headed for the door. "I can also give my mom some of these items for the inn!"

For the next three days they meticulously catalogued and numbered the items, got them ready to transport to the museum, and on Friday morning, the last pieces were removed.

"All that's left in the room are the items I think my mom would love to have for the inn, and the ones she doesn't, I will gladly accept into the museum," clarified Rebecca before taking a bite of her sandwich.

"What time is she coming?"

"Around one," she said looking at her phone, "so, ten minutes."

As they finished lunch, there was a knock on the door, and Rebecca answered it and let her mom in. They went downstairs and Rebecca showed her all of the items.

"So, what do you think?"

"They're magnificent," replied Christine, "and they will fit in quite nicely with the inn's ambiance."

"I knew you would love them. Wait till you see what I sent over to the museum," she said, closing the door, going upstairs, and joining Liam in the library.

"So, what the verdict?" asked Liam looking up from his book.

"She is taking them all," said Rebecca cheerfully. "What are you reading?"

"Just a first-edition copy of *A Tale of Two Cities*."

"Are you fucking kidding me?"

"Rebecca!" cried her mother unimpressed.

"Sorry, Mom."

"Funny enough, it was right next to where I found the Elegant Garden Patios book."

"Really," she said strolling over to him, taking it out of his hands, and checking it out.

"It's in perfect condition."

"It is" she agreed. "We should catalogue these books today."

"Rebecca?" asked her mother. "Rebecca!"

"What Mom?" she asked looking over at her concerned look.

"The books will have to wait," she said. "I have a friend joining us shortly and she needs to speak to you two about something."

"When?"

Christine looked at her watch. "Any minute now?"

"What friend?" asked Rebecca.

There was a knock on the door.

"This friend," she said leaving them to let her in.

Rebecca and Liam followed her out, and watched as a woman in her late fifties walked in.

Chapter Forty-Nine

"Mary how are you doing?" she asked embracing her.

"Fine, Christine, you?"

"Going well, thanks," she replied turning around. "Mary Blunt, this is my daughter Rebecca, and Liam."

"I'm delighted to finally meet you both, I've heard so much about you from Christine," she said approaching them and shaking their hands.

"Nice to meet you," said Rebeca.

"Pleasure to meet you, Mrs. Blunt."

"Oh, please, call me Mary," she said with a kind smile.

"Why don't we go into the parlor," suggested Christine showing Mary the way.

Rebecca and Liam quickly glanced over at one another before following them and sitting on the couch. Christine sat in an armchair while Mary walked over and picked up the picture of Hetty and Mandy.

"Lovely girls," said Mary looking at Rebecca.

"Yes, they are," she replied.

Mary placed the photo down then picked up the next one. "Maggie O'Brien and Jason Campbell," she said admiring it, "what a lovely photograph."

"You knew them?" asked Liam.

"No, not personally, but my mother was good friends with Eleanor Peabody, and I met her and her daughter, Lenore, several times when we visited," she replied placing it down and filling the vacant armchair. "Lenore was such a lovely girl. Back then, she was at least ten years older than me, and I remember she would take me out for ice cream."

Rebecca wondered who this lady was, why she was there, and looked over at her mother for an explanation.

"Mary is the Gray Witch Queen of New York," stated her mother.

"Oh, really," responded Rebecca studying Mary.

"I was born and raised in Thornton on Skaneateles Lake," she revealed. "Do you know where it is?"

"Yes," they both replied.

"Have either of you ever visited there?"

They both shook their heads.

"Well, if you get the chance, you should," she suggested then continued telling them about herself. "My husband received an offer with a law firm in Syracuse, so we moved there, but kept our house in Thornton as our summer home. My daughter, Gwyneth, just moved into it a couple of months ago. She's around your age Rebecca."

"Is she a Gray Witch?"

"Yes, she is, and very talented, but fairly new to it all just like you two," she confessed and paused momentarily. "I have been in contact with your mother these last couple of weeks, and the reason I am here is because she believes, as do I, that you can help me out. So, she invited me here to discuss my problem with you."

"Discuss what problem?" asked Liam.

"Almost eight weeks ago, June 6 to be exact, an eighteen-year-old girl was abducted around nine o'clock after finishing her night shift. The following morning her body was found by a couple of hikers. She had been murdered."

"Isn't that a job for the police?" asked Liam.

"Yes, and they are investigating it," she replied, "but the reason I am telling you is because she was the White Witch Queen of New York."

"At eighteen?" queried Rebecca.

"There is no age limit when it comes to being a White Witch, or Queen White Witch for that matter," answered her mother. "She'd only been Blessed eight months earlier and was under her mother's guidance."

"So young," said Rebecca sadly. "Are you asking us to investigate her murder?"

"If that was the case, the Gray Witches would take ownership, right?" questioned Liam.

"Typically, they would, and eventually they will once they've dealt with a more pressing matter in Massachusetts," divulged Mary. "In any case, they wouldn't be able to help me out with my request because it requires the powers possessed by White Witches. More specifically, two White Witches with exception powers…you two."

"I don't understand," stated Rebecca. "How can we possible help you?"

Mary leaned towards them. "The girl who was murdered, Beth Miller, was cut with a blade from her pubic mound up to the bottom of her chin, then sliced from ear to ear…and she needs your help."

"You got to be fucking kidding me!"

"Liam!" cried Rebecca and Christine.

About the Author

Edgar Waldgrave lives in

the small, quaint town of Skaneateles,

Onondaga County, New York.

You can contact him on his website:

www.edgarwaldgrave.com

Or on Facebook:

Edgar Waldgrave